Exile, Texas

Exile, Texas

Roxanne Longstreet Conrad

Five Star • Waterville, Maine

First Edition
First Printing: November 2003

Published in 2003 in conjunction with Tekno Books and Ed Gorman.

Set in 11 pt. Plantin by Minnie B. Raven.

Printed in the United States on permanent paper.

Library of Congress Cataloging-in-Publication Data

Conrad, Roxanne.
    Exile, Texas / Roxanne Longstreet Conrad.
—1st ed.
      p. cm.
    ISBN 1-59414-071-5 (hc : alk. paper)
    1. Women private investigators—Texas—Fiction.
2. Murder victims' families—Fiction.   3. Missing persons—Fiction.   4. Sheriffs—Fiction.   5. Texas—Fiction.   I. Title.
PS3603.O663E95 2003
813'.6—dc22   2003054457

Exile, Texas

Chapter One

I first saw the silver Lexus in my rear view mirror as I was writing up my ninth ticket of the day. Ticketing speeders on small state highways, like the ones I patrolled, was sort of a catch and release system: tourist conservation. Unless it was breaking the land speed record, I was inclined to let the Lexus go about its business. Too many tickets in a morning looked, well, overzealous.

Truth was, I sympathized with speeders. There isn't much else to do out in the middle of Nowhere, Texas; not many cars to bother you, not much to look at but orange-brown sand and spiky mesquite bush, and a whole lot of clear, clean, bowl-shaped sky. The Lexus would flash its brakes as soon as it saw me sitting in the shadow of the John Birch Society billboard. They all did.

I was still signing ticket number nine when the silver Lexus blasted past me like a mirage, shimmering, the exact color of the early winter sun. She hadn't hit the brakes, she'd hit the gas, and if it wasn't a land speed record it was certainly a contender. I handed over the ticket, waved the tan SUV on its way, and got back in the car.

The Lexus was still hauling ass.

All right, I thought, and flipped on the lights. If you want it this way . . .

I chased her for about three miles before I caught up. She—I was fairly sure the driver was a she—played hard to get, buzzing along for a good thirty seconds or so before she flared brake lights and pulled off to the shoulder in a orange swirl of dust. I parked behind her, left the lights flashing, and reached for the radio.

"Dispatch, this is Nine," I said. It still felt odd. In Houston, where I'd come up as a patrolman and until recently worked as a detective, radio cars had, well, bigger numbers. And nine was deceptive anyway. There were only four cars in the whole department. There'd probably only been a total of nine since the invention of the internal combustion engine. "Dispatch, come on back."

"Go, Nine," Farlene said, out of breath. Probably back from one of her fifteen visits to the coffeepot a day. She was one of those addicts who claimed drinking coffee made them sleep like a baby. To my mind, it was about the same as a drunk claiming he drove better that way.

"I got a routine speeder stop, silver Lexus, Texas license DLX-079, about a thousand yards past the town limits sign." I watched the Lexus. It wasn't moving. The shadow of the driver inside wasn't moving, either. A lot of people started fumbling around for license and insurance, but not this one. Stone cold quiet.

"Uh, roger that, Dan. Ya'll want me to run the check?" Farlene loved running plates, and while I didn't expect to find anything on the Lexus, it would be good manners to let her. I watched the Lexus idle, meek and sleek. No premonitions about it, just the vague ever-present hope that I wouldn't get shot when I walked up to it.

"Yeah, Farlene, better do that," I said. "Thanks. Nine, out."

I settled my still-new hat more comfortably and stepped out of the patrol car into the mild winter day. I took my time strolling up to the driver. Nice top-of-the-line Lexus, blurred with a good coat of road dust. Hard to say how far it had come, but the dealer's decal on the back said Dallas.

Unusual. We didn't get many from Dallas out this way; they kept to the interstate, where the drive was no less boring but the McDonald's and 7-Eleven stops were more frequent.

People from big cities complain about the demise of small towns and those charming mom-and-pop operations, and avoid them every chance they get.

The window rolled down on the Lexus as I stepped up to the driver's side window, and I got my first look at the driver. She was in her thirties, with dark, smooth, straight hair that fell like silk around her face and eyes the blue of a blowtorch flame. Her skin was as pale and perfect as milk, Snow White skin. No rose red lips, though; hers were tinted a delicate shade of lilac that matched her eye shadow.

The strength of will in her eyes was a shot of liquid nitrogen down my spine. I had to take a deep breath to get my heart going again. Those blue eyes could look innocent, at first glance; when I blinked, they were flat, cynical, and suspicious.

"Going pretty fast, Miss," I said. It was a come-on line number one, police-wise, and I winced when I realized I'd said it. She tilted her head slightly, looking at me; I had a strange feeling she was trying to place me, as if we'd met before. "Turn the engine off, please."

She complied. The purr of the Lexus died away, leaving only the whisper of the wind and the dry, steady click of the lights flashing on my cruiser. I smelled perfume, something expensive, applied lightly.

It hit me, like a late sucker punch, that she was maybe the most beautiful woman I'd ever seen in the flesh.

"License and insurance, please," I asked. She handed them over so quickly she must have had them ready. I was beginning to be glad I'd had Farlene check on this one.

There was such a thing as being too composed, and she was the poster child for it. I looked at the picture—a good one, for a wonder, and most definitely her—and the name. "Megan Leary?"

"Sorry, I don't give autographs." She had a smoke-and-bourbon voice, like a forties movie star, and the attitude to match. It was like she was daring me to write her up. While I was thinking about it, the radio beeped for attention. I went back to it, leaned in, and answered.

"Nine, go."

"Dan!" Something had gotten Farlene all excited, too excited to use codes that were mostly posturing anyway in a town that just barely qualified as a wide spot in the road. "Dan, you stay right there, and don't you let that woman go. Deputy Peyser's coming out to meet you. You keep her there."

Now, that was gravely unusual. Deputy Peyser was the sort of guy who patrolled donut shops and liquor stores, who every once in a while smacked the town drunk around to make himself feel like a cop. If Peyser was interested in my ice maiden, I felt sorry for her already.

"Driver's license says Megan Leary," I said. "That check out?"

Farlene let a three- or four-second delay go by before she said, "That's her. Peyser'll take care of this, Dan. You just let him, hear?"

She sounded nervous. I was starting to sweat, too, and I didn't even know why. I studied Megan Leary's license, but it didn't tell me anything besides her height—5'7"—and the color of her eyes, which was authentically blue. No hidden messages. What the hell was going on?

It would take Peyser about five minutes to make it from the other side of town. I should, I decided, at least go back and make small talk. The fact that she was about as gorgeous as Venus had nothing whatsoever to do with that decision, of course.

She was still sitting there, window down, looking as sharp and cold as a new diamond.

"Problem?" she asked. I handed her back her insurance card but held on to her driver's license.

"No, ma'am. You heading into Exile?"

The look she gave me was a letter-perfect mix of contempt and sophistication. "I might be. Why? Need a date for the prom?"

Ouch. I felt a surge of anger and tamped it down hard. When someone works this hard to be disliked, there had to be a reason for it, and the reasons were almost always interesting. "No ma'am, just trying to be welcoming. Exile's a nice little town. You ought to take a look if you have some time. Nice historical sites."

She had a hell of a smile, but it had a scary serrated edge. "Jail and courthouse. I've toured."

Okay, there was definitely something going on here, sharks swimming in deep currents. Get out of the water, Danny-boy, before you get something bit off that don't grow back.

Her eyes flicked down to my name tag, as if she was still trying to remember me. "Deputy¾Fox?"

"Dan Fox," I said, and managed not to blurt out something stupid like pleased to meet you. My imagination kept wandering into a Penthouse Letters zip code I knew I was never going to visit.

"Well, you're new around here." She sounded absolutely sure about it. "How long?"

"Three months," I said. Her smile turned acidic.

"Wow, you must be the first man to actually move into

this dump in twenty years. You honestly don't know who I am."

"No, ma'am."

"They're slipping. They should have at least mentioned my name by now."

"They who?"

She looked in the rear view mirror at the same time another cruiser was pulling over the horizon from town, its lights flashing hot pursuit to an empty road. As I looked back at her, I saw something in her face I didn't expect. Maybe sadness. Maybe a touch of fear. It was gone so quick I couldn't really put a name to it.

"I guess we're about to see," she said, and waited while the second cruiser pulled to a halt behind mine, spewing more dust, and the driver's side door slapped open.

I should probably say something at this point about Deputy Lewis Peyser. Take the ugliest English bulldog you've ever seen, stretch him out man-length, give him a half a good brain and a nasty sense of humor, and you will not have Lew Peyser, because Lew Peyser is not half so smart nor half that pretty. The reason he was a Deputy Sheriff—and we were equal in rank—was that he had been a hometown football hero. Small towns tended to like that in law enforcement officers.

I watched him get out of the car and felt a little shiver right through me. This is it, I thought. This is the day Peyser and me have to do the I-don't-like-you tango. It had been coming ever since I'd walked in the door of the Exile County Sheriff's Office, but the music had never cued just right. Today, they were definitely playing our song.

He gave me a sour glance, hitched up his pants, and did his usual John Wayne strut toward the victim.

"I got this one." He flung it over his shoulder at me like

a dirty towel. "You head on back to the station. Tell Jimmy Sparkman I'm taking care of his little problem."

Now, I had a choice. I could do the wise thing, get back in my cruiser, forget the name of Megan Leary, and coast along in my new home of Exile, Texas . . . or I could follow my gut. My gut was very unhappy.

I stepped back from the car and said, "All the same to you, Lew, I'll stick around. In case you need me."

Before we could get into it with me any deeper, Megan Leary did something that she must have known was stupid.

She got out of the car.

It became immediately apparent to me that if she was five-foot-seven, five-foot-three of that had to be legs. Her skirt—all four or five inches of it—rode the edge of decency; hell, in Exile they still put drapes around table legs. After the pleasant shock wore off, it was the cold, ruthlessly controlled look in her eyes that unsettled me. I'd thought Peyser's attitude was dangerous, but this woman's could shave steel. She shut the driver's side door, leaned back against it, and crossed her arms. Cocked her head at Peyser as he finally made his stand, about as late and unlucky as Custer.

"Buford," she said. She had a low, throaty, musical voice, maroon velvet and sandalwood. That didn't make her tone any friendlier. "I should have known you'd be driving the welcome wagon."

"You took the wrong turn back there, Meg, so you'd best get in your fancy car and drive right back the way you came." Peyser's blowtorch intimidation—usually enough to melt glass—bounced off. "And in case you forgot, my middle name's Bruford. Call me Buford again and some-body's going to be pickin' up teeth."

Meg gave him a strange little half-smile. "Call your den-tist, Buford."

He took a step at her, and I tensed. Meg raised her chin, practically daring him to punch it. Oh, man, I thought. Here it comes.

Instead of punching he reached out and grabbed her shoulder, spun her around to face the car, and kicked her feet apart. Hassling her over a traffic stop was a stretch, but it wasn't abusive. Quite.

"Assume it, Miss Leary," he said, and grinned. "Not like you ain't got experience at this kind of thing."

If she spread her feet any further apart, that skirt was going to violate state decency laws. Peyser starting patting her down.

Megan Leary turned her head and met my eyes. It felt like being plugged into a two-twenty outlet. It was like she was looking into my soul, and I had never felt so naked—so unprepared—in my entire life.

Peyser's hands slid down her waist, over the smooth curve of her hips. Oh, Jesus. This couldn't be happening. Peyser wasn't patting her down for a weapon, he was feeling her up. Oh, man, don't do this to me. I don't want to be in the middle of this.

But I was. No question about it.

She was still watching me. Wind blew strands of dark hair across her ice-pale cheek, and her eyes were no longer cool and distracted. They were angry and focused and vulnerable, and they asked a question I really didn't want to face.

What the hell was I planning to do about this?

"Peyser," I said. He ignored me. "Peyser!"

Peyser shoved her harder against the car. It was unmistakable now, he was pressed up against her, and he had his hand up her skirt. This had gone way past boys-will-be-boys. We weren't just bending the law, we were shredding it. We. In ten years of law enforcement, I was never part of the we.

"Shut up and stand there," he snarled at me. "Get the point, Meg? Want to push this any more, or are you going to be a good little bitch and get out of my town?"

Her eyes locked on me and refused to let me go. And then—incredibly—she smiled.

"Fuck you, Buford," she said, and threw an elbow back into Peyser's grinning face. His head snapped back, and blood spurted; he howled and grabbed his nose, stumbling away.

There was a big Freightliner semi barreling down the highway, smashing the speed limit. Two more steps back, and Peyser was going to be a grille ornament.

Meg turned, grabbed him by the shirt front, and dragged him to a halt just as the semi flashed by, raising a stinging whirlwind of dust that blew Peyser's hat off. Meg let go of him, and moved back out of grabbing range.

She turned to me.

Dust swirled and settled, leaving the sky as bright and clean as a new-washed plate. Her eyes were just the opposite, opaque with anger, the cold blue steel of a Saturday Night Special. I thought she was going to slug me. At the last second she turned her back to me and put her hands together behind her.

Waiting for her handcuffs.

As I snapped them on her, she said, "You might want to take my gun, Deputy Fox."

There ought to be a law against a felon having a voice like that, a purr like velvet, a core of abrasive concrete. I reached inside her jacket and found a very nice Beretta that was warm from her heat. I pulled the magazine. Full and gleaming.

"I guess you'd have a permit for that," I said.

"Sure. Front jacket pocket."

Peyser was watching us with rabid eyes, holding a handkerchief to his nose. I fished out her leather wallet and flipped it open. She liked a little drama, because it was the kind of wallet that did flip, and she had a gold badge and a picture ID. The picture ID certified her as a Licensed Private Investigator in the State of Texas. The badge, which looked a lot like the one pinned to my uniform, said the same thing.

Behind the ID card was one certifying her permit to carry. I nodded and pocketed the wallet, too.

"You're under arrest," Peyser mumbled around the handkerchief. He looked, if anything, madder than before. "Read the bitch her goddamn rights."

"In a minute," I said. "Tell you what, Miss Leary, why don't you just have a seat in my car for a few minutes. I need to talk to the Deputy."

I saw her settled in the back seat of the cruiser and came around to where Peyser was mopping at his swollen nose. He was going to have two nasty shiners. I retrieved his hat from the spiky arms of a mesquite bush, then leaned against the bumper next to him and studied the view. In the distance, the purple shadow of Guadalupe Peak smudged the horizon.

"Resisting arrest," he muttered. "Broke my damn nose."

"Don't think you'd want to file on that." I studied the toes of my boots, the drifts of sand. Leary's footprints were sharp little triangles with pinpoint heels like exclamation points. "I can't back you up."

"You what?" He took the handkerchief away from his nose to almost shout it at me; his nose started flowing bright red down his chin. "Goddamn it!"

16

"Tip your head back," I said, and handed him a fresh hankie. "Look, the way I see it, you stick your hand in a woman's skirt, you got to figure you have an elbow or two coming."

I could feel menace coming off of him like heat from an oven. "You don't want to get in my face about this. You really don't."

"No, I don't," I said quietly. "But I will."

That hung there in the air like a black smear of diesel exhaust.

"Want to tell me what's going on?" I said.

"None of your goddamn business," he whispered. He sounded tired now, and in pain. "You just stay the hell out of it. You be a good boy and drive her up to that station, let me take care of those charges."

I walked back to where Megan Leary waited in the cruiser, those fabulous legs crossed. I helped her out again, turned her around, and unlocked the cuffs.

"Hey!" Peyser yelled. I dug her wallet and license out of my pocket and handed them back to her. "Fox, you asshole—"

"Sorry about the trouble, ma'am," I said. "You be careful on the road."

She considered it for a few long seconds, her eyes steady on mine; I didn't mind the wait. It gave me time to notice green flecks in those blue eyes, like fine Indian turquoise.

"You watch your back, Deputy Dan," she said, and turned away.

She got back in the Lexus, stroked the engine to a deep-throated purr, and pulled out onto the highway. Heading for town.

I looked across the cruiser's hood at Peyser, who dabbed one final time at his swollen nose and looked at me with piggy, mean, distrustful eyes.

"You got no idea what you've done," he said. "No idea."

Peyser was wrong about a lot of things, but he was absolutely right about that.

I followed the tail lights of Peyser's cruiser into town and up to the big looming building that was the Exile County Courthouse. Both an eyesore and the most important historical building in town, it had seen the birth of the Republic of Texas, celebrated statehood, survived fire and economic famine. The Sheriff's Office was two floors up, tucked into one of the turrets that jutted out from the faux-castle walls. State of the art plumbing for 1922. We were lucky the electrical worked well enough to power two computers, a fax machine, and a ten-cup coffee maker.

Peyser bulled his way ahead of me once we came through the swinging wooden doors and beelined for the Sheriff's Office. I heard him start yelling, "Your damn wet-behind-the-ears city boy—" just before he slammed the door behind him. I was left standing there and wondering who it was I should go complain to; the only person around was Farlene, the secretary/dispatcher, who was putting the finishing touches on what looked like a whole new filing system. Farlene had taken a computer class a few months back, and it had gone right to her head; she was now computerizing everything, whether it was useful or not.

Her head might have been down in the files, but Farlene didn't miss much. She glanced up at me, at the Sheriff's Office behind her, and asked, "Nice set of shiners on Pit Bull. Tell me it wasn't you, I was just starting to like you, darlin'."

"Not me," I said. I leaned on the railing that corralled her desk. "So what's the deal with Megan Leary?"

In Sheriff Sparkman's office, Peyser paced and waved his arms. I couldn't see the Sheriff, but I could hear the occasional word and phrase from Peyser. My name came up, not flatteringly.

Farlene leaned back in her chair and smiled at me. She still had a young face, though I'd heard a rumor she was pushing fifty. I'd been warned about Farlene, first thing, on the morning I'd shown up for the job in Exile. Don't go there, Jimmy had said. She's got a husband who's meaner than Genghis Khan, and she loves to tease. I hadn't gone there, but I'd been offered the road map often enough.

Farlene drummed inch-and-a-half polka-dot-painted fingernails on file folders. "I don't think you're going to want to get into this Meg Leary mess, Dan. Let us handle it."

"Us?"

"You know, those from around here. Like the Chief."

The Chief being Sheriff Jimmy Sparkman, the principal reason I was in Exile. He'd started off a deputy, worked his way to the top by virtue of being smarter and fairer than any potential rivals. We'd been best friends in college, a long time ago, before he'd gone back to his home town and I'd gone on to the bright lights of Houston. He had lines on his face now, not all of them smile lines, and the fair hair had receded like the Houston tide, but he'd hung on as sheriff. People liked him. People trusted him.

Which made the mystery of Megan Leary even deeper, because I didn't for one second believe Jimmy Sparkman would "handle" anything in the way Farlene was implying.

The Chief's door slammed open, and Peyser came out. The bruises were just starting to fill in, and I'd been right, he was going to have a sunset delight of a pair of shiners. He'd shoved cotton balls up his nose, which didn't strengthen his resemblance to Clark Gable.

What unsettled me was that he looked triumphant. I tried not to care.

"Dan. In here." Jimmy Sparkman stood in the doorway. He looked just as sober and thoughtful as ever, but there was something in his eyes that made the hair stand up on the back of my neck.

I pushed open the swinging gate and went in to talk to the Chief.

He moved a folder full of old newspaper clippings off to the side, leaned back, and put his feet up on the desk. Should have looked casual, but it didn't. There was a long silence. It got longer. I felt myself break out in a fresh coat of sweat, and wondered what I'd done in a previous life to deserve this. I'd only been in town for three months, and it wasn't the kind of place a guy like me made instant buddies. Sparkman had hired me after I'd crashed and burned in Houston, and that meant I owed him. I didn't like owing anybody, and I didn't like the fact that I might have cost myself not only a job but a friendship.

Sparkman's eyes drilled a hole in my skull. When I was well and truly worried, he finally said, "Lew said she punched him in the nose while resisting arrest. He said you let her go."

"He left out some stuff in the middle," I said. Sparkman nodded. He didn't ask what that might have been.

"I should have stopped him from going out there in the first place. Don't worry about it," he said. As simple as that. I sighed and nodded. My eyes roamed around his desk, looking for something to do, and I saw the newspaper clippings he'd tossed aside. The top one read SWEETLAND BOX FACTORY DESTROYED, and the date was 1983 or 1984, I couldn't tell from my angle. There were other articles, too. Lots of 'em. I wondered what termite nest Jimmy was digging into; he'd always been a curious guy.

He dragged me out of speculation with a direct question. "So. What did you think of her?"

He picked up a baseball off the corner of his desk. It had signatures all over it, but I'd never asked what team had signed it. He tossed it in the air, caught it, kept his eyes on the ball.

I said, "Cool. Collected. Hell of a mouth on her."

"Go on." I hadn't surprised him yet. I watched him toss the ball and timed my next comment.

"She's a licensed PI with a gun."

He didn't drop it, but he bobbled the catch. He looked at me with true alarm.

"Tell me you're kidding."

"I checked the carry permit. She's legal."

"Jesus. She say anything at all about what she was doing in town?" I shook my head. He tossed the baseball to me, and I caught it one-handed. "You want me to remind you again that you're a just a deputy here, Dan?"

"You don't need to."

"You're not a hot-shit Houston detective anymore, you do remember that?"

"I seem to recall."

"And when I tell you that the worst thing you could do for yourself right now is ignore my advice, you're going to pay attention, right?"

"Absolutely, Chief," I said. I tossed the baseball back. He caught it like a fielder, not even looking at it.

"Good," he said. "What've you got active right now?"

"Nothing much. The missing person thing on the Galvan kid, I wanted to go back to the school and re-interview this afternoon."

"No need," Jimmy shrugged and dismissed it. "Let it go. Aurelia's been itchy to get out of this town for years now, no surprise she finally managed to make it."

"Her mother's chewing nails, Jimmy."

"She'll settle down. Look, we get thirty runaways out of this town a year. This one reads just like that last one, and the one before that." He disposed of the matter by tossing the ball in the air and catching it. "Keep an eye on Meg. Report back to me about what she's doing here, and who she's doing it with. This is important, Dan. It might be damn important. Now, here's the advice. You listening? Don't get close to her. I know it's tempting, but just don't do it."

"You act like she's carrying the plague."

"Let's just say you don't want what she's got," he said. "But I need to know what she's doing, and I can't trust Peyser or any of the others not to go off on her. So it's up to you, if you'll do it."

"You going to tell me the big secret?" I asked.

He didn't answer me for a few long seconds, then said, "Every town's got a dirty past, Dan. She's ours. And we don't want her back."

Jimmy Sparkman wasn't the kind of man who stayed in the office with a star on his door like a prima donna waiting for curtain; he was a working sheriff, out in the streets, always ready to pitch in and do his share of the work. It struck me as strange that he wasn't risking contact with Leary, until I remembered one very important fact.

Sheriff was an elected office.

When all was said and done, no matter the possible consequences, though, I knew I was going to do what he asked. The risk was damn near as irresistible as she was.

"I'm your man," I said.

Chapter Two

Megan Leary's Lexus was parked right down the street from the courthouse, in front of Town Estates Realty—the only real estate office left in town, as a matter of fact. As I cruised slowly past the big plate glass window, I saw that Leary was sitting down with Leticia Maldonado. Leticia looked none too happy about the honor. I parked down the street at the Stop 'N Wash, where Earl, town psychotic and part-time drunk, mumbled to himself and watched clothes tumble in the dryers. Whatever transaction Leary was having in the realty office was over within another five minutes, and then she got back in her car again. I took out the cell phone I still carried—souvenir of towns big enough to warrant the investment, say Hallelujah to roaming charges—and dialed Town Estates.

"Leticia," I said. "Deputy Dan Fox. How are you?"

"Oh, I'm fine," she said brightly. "How's my favorite policeman?"

Every policeman was her favorite if he didn't own his own home. "I'm good, ma'am. Listen, I was wondering—"

"It's a good thing you called, I was going to call you today about the interest rates," she said. "They went down again. There's never been a better time to buy, and I have the most perfect little house on Oak Street—"

She had nearly every house on Oak Street. The town had started hemorrhaging population in the mid-seventies and was still bleeding to death. The crash of the oil boom had taken thousands, and the resulting fall of the local economy had taken thousands more. Exile had, at its 1980 peak, been home to almost 16,000; today, it was half a ghost town of less than 8,000. Despite Leticia's hard sell, I wasn't stupid enough to become a property owner in a town even Wal-Mart had deserted. "Not just now, Letty. I wanted to ask you about the woman who was just in to talk to you. Megan Leary?"

"Yes?" She dragged out the word, and her tone went guarded. "What do you want to know?"

I resisted the urge to say everything, the call was costing me money. "Just what she wanted in your office."

"I couldn't possibly—she's a client—isn't there a rule about talking about your clients?" Leticia's tone told me it was a pro forma sort of protest.

"Much as I respect realtors, Letty, you aren't a lawyer. Whatever she says to you isn't privileged."

"Oh." Now she sounded downright relieved. "She wanted to get the keys to her house."

"She has a house in town?"

"Well, her mother's house," she clarified. "It's not on the market, she just lets us look in on it from time to time, you know, keep the vandals out. She said she was going to stay there for a while."

Things were coming clear. Megan had family in town, and there was bad blood. Small towns, long memories. Not as much of a mystery as I'd thought. As for her and Peyser, well, maybe baggage from high school. Maybe she'd been the first girl to tell him he was butt ugly and twice as stupid. Damn sure not the last.

"Where's the house?" I asked.

"Out on Coldfield Road, past the Burger Town." There was no Burger Town. There was an empty field where a Burger Town had once been—everybody in town gave directions that way, using landmarks that were mostly decades out of date. Another reason I couldn't get used to small-town life. "It's number 212."

"Thanks, Leticia. Maybe I'll think some more about buying something for myself . . ."

"I have a beautiful little three bedroom—" she said.

". . . later," I finished, and hung up before she could sign me up for a first-time buyer application.

Leary's car turned left at the stoplight of Main and Thornton; she wasn't in much of a hurry now, cruising along at the posted speed of twenty-five miles an hour. She knew that I was following her, because there was just no way to hide a big white Ford cruiser on a street with no traffic. We were playing a little game, the two of us—and she upped the stakes by edging the accelerator, pushing her speed slowly up to thirty. She was giving me an excuse to pull her over, if I wanted to take it. I thought that was damn interesting. I decided to play the game a little longer, and dropped back further, staying at twenty-five. After all, if she was planning to stay in town, she didn't have much anywhere to go.

Like any good prodigal child coming home, she went to the cemetery. It was tucked away in what had once been the outskirts of town, before the town had grown up around it like a slow-rising lake. If you wanted the history of Exile, the cemetery was the best place to read it; some of the markers, rubbed almost clean by the wind and sand, dated as far back as the pioneer days. There was something eerie and otherworldly about that place—the marble angels looked troubled, as if they'd intended to be someplace else, and a few were caught looking up as if they were about to spring into the sky and escape. Whoever had carved those early tombstones had been an uneasy genius.

I parked outside the chain-link fence, facing a more pro-
saic sort of headstone, a marble log with a squirrel perched
on top, and watched as Leary picked her way through the
stone forest. She was moving slowly, not as if she was
looking for something but as if she was hoping like hell not
to find it, and she didn't seem to notice, or care, that I'd
pulled up behind her. I lost sight of her behind the bulking
overblown Greek temple that was the Patterson family
crypt. She never came out the other side.

I rolled down the car window and listened as I waited.
Outside the wind was brisk and cool and smelled of dust
and the distant tang of burning mesquite; it was very, very
quiet. I'd lain awake nights the first couple of weeks in town
listening to that quiet. I could adjust to the people, the cli-
mate, the lack of nightlife, or even a decent radio station,
but the lack of sound—it was a weight on my chest, cotton
in my ears. It was a silence that didn't need people at all.

She was out of sight for long enough that I started to feel
an itch at the back of my neck. I got out of the cruiser and
walked along the chain-link fence, sun-bleached grass
crunching under my feet. Somewhere far away a dog
barked, not as if he was really interested, and tree limbs
creaked like an old man's joints. The few thin sounds only
pointed out the silence in between.

I couldn't hear Megan Leary moving around at all. Each
step along the fence gave me a deeper angle around the
crypt, revealed more and more rows of weather-beaten
tombstones; they didn't fall in a line, and it led me to think
about all those dead folks lying in heaps, at odd angles, as if
the graveyard was a battleground and they lay where they'd
died. I took another step, angling for a better look.

And all of a sudden, there she was. Her face was composed and very pale, and her fine dark hair drifted like

26

strands of silk, and her eyes were blind indigo. I'd never seen a ghost, but this was as close as I ever wanted to come to it.

She was looking right at me.

Neither one of us said a word. She turned and made her way slowly through the ankle-high dry grass. She shopped tombstones for a while, then paused next to one in the corner and bent down to take a closer look. For a long time, she stayed there, head bowed—a private moment I had no business observing. I looked around the streets instead. No signs of life.

The dog had stopped barking, and the wind whispered in my ears as if it wanted to tell me a secret. No kids playing, no cars growling along, not even the distant blare of a stereo. The two of us alone in a place full of presence.

She stood up, made what looked like the sign of the cross, and walked right up to the fence where I stood. We watched each other in silence for a few long heartbeats. I couldn't think of a damn thing to say.

"Going to follow me all day?" she asked. "By the way, you were right. I do love the historical sights in this town."

She moved away before I could think of a snappy retort. I watched her get back in her car and drive off, and in her absence the silence got deep and dark and strange.

She had practically dared me to take a look, and I could never resist a challenge. Or a puzzle.

I followed her footsteps to the back corner and studied tombstones. She'd been looking—probably too obviously— at a gray weathered stone that sparkled cold in the sun. I read the inscription.

It read PETULA J. FARMER, B. 1884, D. 1949. In small script below the incised bouquet of roses, it said: A GOOD TIME WAS HAD BY ALL.

"Funny," I muttered to the wind. "What were you looking for?"

We were still playing a game, one I had no intention on losing. I retraced my steps back to where I'd first spotted her, standing in the chilled shadow of the Patterson's gothic crypt. Even in daylight it was a gently creepy spot, and the rustle of leaves and dry grass suggested I leave secrets undisturbed. The quiet of Exile seemed to pile especially deep here among the knee-high tombstones.

I checked the padlock on the crypt door. Not surprisingly, it was broken. I swung the door open, waking a scream of hinges like a scared cat; after nothing lurched out of that darkness at me, I pulled my heavy flashlight and focused the beam inside.

Drifts of leaves like faded confetti. The startled reflective eyes of a rat that skittered off into the marble shadows as fast as its little feet could take it. As big as the Patterson crypt was, it came as something of a surprise to see that there were only four spaces in it, like file drawers, all of them labeled P for Patterson. Three of them were capped with engraved marble stones. I focused my light into the fourth.

Open, and empty of everything except another red-eyed rat.

Outside, my search turned up a couple of empty beer bottles and the pale flutter of a condom caught on a spike of grass. Cemeteries were irresistible for a certain segment of the teenage population, just like slasher movies and black eye shadow, but I couldn't see anything that could have drawn Megan Leary to this particular spot. I looked at the tombstones, one after another, reading names.

I almost missed it. It was a small rose-colored stone, low to the ground and overshadowed by the gray granite monoliths around it—a new grave, from a more conservative modern age where grieving was considered bad taste. Nothing on the stone except the name DORIS LEARY and the date of her death. MARCH 12, 1984. None of the usual platitudes served up by the undertaker and family, no BELOVED MOTHER or CHERISHED DAUGHTER. The stone was awfully small, and I thought about a coffin in proportion to it. I wondered if Doris Leary had been a baby. I wondered if she'd been Megan Leary's baby and, if so, how exactly she'd come to lie in this cold bed in the ground.

I wondered if Megan Leary would tell me. I had the oddest feeling she would.

I got back in my cruiser and drove around aimlessly, criss-crossing the town until I found the Lexus again. She hadn't really tried to lose me; she was sitting in the parking lot of the Dairy Queen sucking on a cold drink. I pulled up next to her and rolled down the window. A cloud passed over the beaten-silver glare of the sun, throwing a moving shadow between us. Somewhere over by the high school, the marching band—all forty or so kids—were enthusiastically mutilating a Sousa march.

"Deputy," she said in her smoke and sandalwood voice. "Let me guess. I'm in violation of the open container law."

I cleared my throat and tried for an authoritarian tone. "Who's Doris Leary?"

She took another long sip, leaving pale lilac kisses on the straw, equal parts merciless tease and cold-eyed calculator. "My mother," she said. "Beloved wife of Marlon Leary. Saint Doris. Genuflect when you mention her name, Deputy."

Don't know why, but the bitterness surprised me. It was like seeing past the armor to the vulnerable skin beneath.

Something I couldn't afford to let past my guard, not at this stage of what was turning out to be a very unpredictable and hotly contested game of wits.

"So you don't light any candles to her," I said. Her eyes narrowed, drifted half-closed as though she was seeing something just on the other side of me. She didn't say anything at all.

I noticed we were drawing attention. Not hard to do—the Dairy Queen was the center of social life for at least half of town, and this time of day it was filled with high schoolers blowing off class, the lunch crowd from the local factory, and everybody who didn't have a job. A fair number of them were watching the Lexus. A fair number had probably never seen one before, except in a TV ad.

One or two, I thought, might have recognized the woman in the car.

Her straw sucked bottom with a loud, liquid noise, and she put the cup somewhere out of sight inside the car. Time out was over. We were going back out on the field of play.

A game I wasn't winning. "I'm supposed to find out what you're doing here," I said. Confusion, they said, was good for the enemy; besides, being subtle wasn't likely to be a huge success. A flash that might have been humor lit her eyes, turned them cool pewter. "Want to tell me all about it?"

"All you had to do was ask," she said, and put the Lexus in gear. "Follow me."

Exile was sliced down the middle by the scalpel of Highway 140. On the east side of the highway the upper middle class, such as had resisted the mass migration out of town, spread out in tract homes and large green lawns; past them, some of the richest hid in transplanted Southern

mansions behind elaborate wrought-iron gates. A nice, se-
date part of town where nothing much ever happened, and
nothing much ever came of what did. That side of town
held Sunday brunches and garden shows and Music Society
concerts featuring the two local piano players, neither of
whom was any good.

On the other side of the highway, the west side, was
what Peyser liked to refer to as Mextown. The houses were
small, square, and painted aqua blue and lavender and mint
green; the cars were all one valve job ahead of the scrap
yard. It reminded me of Houston, where people lived close
and loud and sometimes violently, but at least they lived.

I wasn't too surprised when our little two-car parade
turned west.

Meg knew her way around, only hesitating once or twice;
we turned down a street called Paloma and eased into the
curb at a house just like all its neighbors—square, practical,
painted happy even if it had been built dour. Chain-link
fence around a yard of weeds cut through with dog-run
trails. Two battered bikes and a tricycle in the front, and a
lively-eyed mutt who looked half-spaniel.

I knew the place. I knew immediately, and from there I
knew why she was in town.

All this fuss over nothing.

Meg got out of her car and looked over at me as I got out
to follow; she put her hand on the gate, to the joyful barking
of the dog, and I put my hand over hers to hold her back. I
felt a tremor run through her, or me, or both of us together.
Neither of us were insulated against the shock. She pulled
her hand away.

"Just a minute," I said. "Let's talk."

"About?" She crossed her arms. A skittish breeze blew
between us, combing cold fingers through our hair.

"You know this is a waste of time."

"Not for me," she said. "Rosa hired me. I'm here to find her daughter."

"Oh, come on. Have you heard anything about this case? The girl told everybody she was running away, and she ran. We just haven't caught up with her yet."

"So that's your official position. No wonder Rosa had to call me."

"Look, the girl's only been missing three days. We're checking her friends, sending wires out up and down the bus routes—"

"Mighty white of you," she said, and meant it. "Come on, Deputy, this girl went missing and nobody gave a shit. She's seventeen and she's Mexican, and this town was founded by and for Anglos. How many Mexicans live on the other side of the tracks?"

I wanted to raise my voice, so I pitched it softer, a trick I'd learned on the beat in Houston. "That might have been true once, but it isn't now. If we honestly thought something happened to her, we would have been out day and night until we found her. But this girl—"

"Aurelia," Meg said quietly.

"—Aurelia, she talked all the time about cutting out of here. Told her friends, her teachers, anybody who would listen. Hell, she actually made it to Midland once before the Sheriff found her and got her sent back. Why should we believe it's any different now?"

Meg's gaze stayed on me, steady and unblinking. I had a lot of time to think about what I'd just said, what it implied. I had time to wonder if I would have done things the same for a white girl from the east side.

Yeah. I would have done it exactly the same. I knew it even if she didn't.

"Maybe you're right," she said at last. "But I'm going to talk to my client before I cut and run, I owe her that much."

I nodded. I was busy thinking, you came back to town for a seventeen-year-old runaway? Had to be some powerful motives behind that, and I didn't think the small paycheck she'd collect for this job would be one of them. It wouldn't even cover gas expenses for the Lexus.

"Got anything else to say?" she asked. I shook my head. Meg opened the gate and eased in. The dog barked himself happy. I followed her up the cracked, uneven sidewalk to the front steps of the house.

Rosa Galvan had painted her house a muted salmon, with teal blue accents; coast colors, I'd thought the first time I'd seen them. Or maybe just the paints that had been on sale down at the Ace Hardware when she last needed to throw a coat on. The place was well on its way to decay; the storm door, rusted a brilliant streaked saffron, had a toothless hole where the screen had been. Sharp metal edges still bristled angrily like barbed wire. One of many burglary attempts, or successes.

Meg swung open the screen and thumped her fist on the faded salmon door. The wood boomed hollow, a cheap brand that wouldn't keep out a determined wind, much less an intruder. I heard a retreating army of small-sized running feet, and after a minute or so someone eased the door open a crack.

I'd been told by somebody reliable that Rosa Galvan had been the Prom Queen of Taylor High in 1985, but it was nearly impossible to see it in her now; that sleek pretty big-eyed girl was now exhausted, frustrated, and dangerously obese. She looked at me first, no welcome in her closed expression, and then moved her gaze over to Meg.

Rosa melted. Melted like butter, a Hollywood smile lighting up the dark eyes. Suddenly she was a whole different person than the one I'd spent three days, on and off, arguing with. The idea of her as prom queen wasn't so hard to believe.

"Meg," she said, and held out her arms. I couldn't have imagined Meg hugging anybody, but she stepped right into Rosa's embrace. They clung together for a few seconds before Meg pulled back to arm's length. Rosa looked her over critically. "Ay, you bitch, you could have put on twenty pounds to make me feel better."

"Then I couldn't outrun the locals," Meg said, just a hint of a smile lurking at the corners of her mouth. "Can I come in?"

"Of course," Rosa said, and stepped back to swing the door wide. I followed Meg in, taking advantage of the fact Mrs. Galvan might not slam it on my nose, and got a glare from her for my trouble. "I see the new puppy followed you home."

"Rosa," Meg said reprovingly. "He's not a puppy, he's a full grown dog."

They ignored me as they walked down the narrow wood-floored hall, its walls grimed by years of small hands and shoulders, decorated with dim school pictures of the Galvan family. I stopped to look at the picture of Aurelia again; it was a casual yearbook shot and it had caught her smiling like the Mona Lisa. A pretty girl, bright-eyed, with an insolent tilt to her head.

I have a theory that the world can be evenly divided into two kinds of people—people who take great senior photos, and people who don't. Mine had sucked. I was willing to bet Megan's was knock-down gorgeous.

It hadn't escaped my notice that Rosa Galvan was

treating Megan like an old friend, not like the town leper. I wondered if it was a racial difference, or just old alliances that hadn't broken. Meg settled into the living room couch, which I knew from experience she'd regret; it had springs sharp enough to leave a tattoo. I took the straight-backed chair Rosa passed up, and waited.

"I didn't think you'd come," Rosa said at last. Somewhere in the back of the house a child shrieked, delight, not fear. Running footsteps thudded through the thin walls. The place smelled of old cooking and diapers, with an undertone of smoke. Rosa's husband had smoked, before he'd coughed up cancer last year and died six months later. She still kept ashtrays on the tables, out of habit I supposed. A strange kind of memorial. "I hoped you would, though."

"I cashed the check," Meg said. "Tell me about what happened."

I listened with half an ear to Rosa Galvan's story, because I already knew the melody and was listening for the false notes. Aurelia had gone off to school as usual, carrying her backpack—she'd gone to her first two classes, then disappeared. Her friends all claimed they didn't know where she'd gone, though I had my doubts. She hadn't come home. Hadn't called. Hadn't been seen, anywhere, by anyone.

She'd also taken her mother's credit card—there hadn't been any cash in the purse to go with it. Credit card hadn't been used yet, so far as we could tell, though if it was from someplace with just a hand-held swipe machine, like most places in the county, it wouldn't show up for a few days yet.

I'd gone through her room with Rosa. Aurelia had taken almost nothing with her, but she'd taken what Rosa said she liked—favorite shirts, jewelry, a death's-head ring that screamed Hail Satan! to paranoid parents everywhere.

Aurelia had been a Marilyn Manson fan, though—like most kids—she probably couldn't have said why.

Megan stayed quiet during Rosa's recitation, prodding with a word here and there when it was needed, a question when Rosa got off track. She was good at it, which somehow didn't surprise me. Even granting that as an old friend she had more credit in the bank of Rosa than I did, she used it well, not coddling, not wallowing, just spinning the facts into a comprehensive story. But in the end, it wasn't really a different story than what I'd heard before. Aurelia Galvan was gone, but there wasn't a thing to suggest foul play. Seventeen and unhappy was a powerful combination.

"Aurelia's boyfriend," Megan prompted. Rosa shook her head.

"He doesn't know anything. I talked to him myself, the day after she left—he called here, to talk to her. He went driving around looking for her." Rosa flashed me a look. "More than they did."

I could think of a lot of reasons why Aurelia's boyfriend might have made that innocent-me phone call. I'd interviewed Javier Nieves, and I didn't like him. Slick as a piece of oiled glass.

"Do you have any news for us, Mrs. Galvan?" I asked her. She gave me a distrustful look and shook her head. "Something her friends said, a neighbor saw, anything at all?"

"If they tell me, I tell you. There's nothing." For just a second I saw a wet glitter of tears in Rosa's eyes, but she blinked it away. "I never saw her after she left for school. Somebody took her, Meg. Somebody—"

"I'll do everything I can," Meg said softly. "You know I will, Rosa."

And there it was. She was committed. Jimmy Sparkman was not going to be happy about this. And I already knew there was absolutely no reason for me to open my mouth and try to convince anybody in the room to do the sensible thing. A grieving mother, a woman with a chip on her shoulder the size of Montana . . . two women with something to prove.

Nope. I kept my mouth firmly shut all the way out the faded door, the dusty walk through the dusty yard with the dog nipping my heels. Rosa Galvan didn't say goodbye to me. I found I didn't really blame her.

"This is still a police case," I said finally, as Meg and I reached the rickety gate. It was hopeless, but I had a duty and I discharged it. "Chief Sparkman's worried you're going to get hurt, Miss Leary."

That put a glint in her eye. "Jimmy Sparkman? Well, well. He ought to know better. I can hold my own."

"I'll look into the Galvan case," I said. "You got my word. I won't let this go. Just—don't stay here. I don't know what's going on, but it ain't good. Next time you meet up with Peyser things won't end so pretty."

She stepped forward, right into my space, close enough to kiss. "The next time he sticks his hand in my panties, I'll put a bullet in him. You go, deputy. I'm sure you've got plenty of speeders to ticket out there. I'm going to spend some time with my old friend."

And then she was gone, heading back to the house with decisive clicks of her heels on the cracked sidewalk. The dog followed, tongue hanging out.

I got back in my car. An afternoon of sitting in a chilly car watching the Galvan house was unappealing, to say the least. The temptation to know more was just too strong, and I wasn't going to find out from her what was happening here—she was enjoying the drama too much. I needed a reliable information source.

I went where people go when they need information.

I went to the library.

Civic architecture in Exile tended to the gothic, or had around the turn of the century and into what were laughably referred to as the boom times. The library, like the county courthouse, was a castle, a miniature with only one turret and a thick wall of quarried stone. It looked more like a penitentiary than a center of knowledge, and it smelled of mold, old books, and the ever-present glow of Pammy Howard's White Shoulders perfume.

I had become a pretty voracious reader since moving to Exile—crime novels and biographies, mostly, but I had an appetite for the occasional science fiction, too. I depended on Pammy to steer me to the good stuff. Like most of the working class left in town, Miss Pammy was older, the young folks having moved off to greener pastures. Miss Pammy wore tie-dye shirts and broomstick skirts, colored her hair apricot blonde, and generally acted as little like a librarian as she possibly could get away with. She had also just buried her third husband, and according to general gossip was cruising for a fourth.

"Dep-uty, aren't you a sight for sore eyes. My goodness, it's been days. Nothing new in since you were in last, I'm afraid, unless you want to talk romance." She fluttered false eyelashes at me. "But as I'm a woman of the world, I'd guess you're not here for that."

"Sweet thing like you deserves better than me," I said, and gave her my best smile. "Listen, I need to find out some things from a few years ago."

"How far back?"

"Early eighties, I think. I'm looking for information about a girl named Meg Leary, or a woman named Doris Leary."

She gave me a look, not the flirtatious Miss Pammy look, an entirely librarian sort of a look, and for a second she looked every bit of her age, and I felt every bit of thirteen.

"Well, well," she said, and patted her apricot confection of a hairdo. "Sit down, deputy."

I did, feeling like junior high was back in session; the chair was hard and wooden and loosened by generations of wiggly bored backsides. I braced my elbows on my knees and leaned forward in a listening posture as Miss Pammy came out from behind the counter and pulled up a threadbare armchair in whispering distance.

"First of all, there's two things. There's the Doris Leary tragedy, and then there's the other thing, and I'm not sure which one might be worse in the end." She was enjoying this, I saw—not scared of the information, like Farlene, but practically bursting with the need to share. "Nobody's told you anything?"

I shook my head.

"You poor man, no wonder you're confused. Megan Leary killed her mother, of course. Murdered her in cold blood. Let me tell you all about it."

Chapter Three

Meg Leary took a hell of a yearbook picture. She was too thin, her stare too defiant, but for all that she eclipsed the other girls on the page. She had a flare of personality the camera loved.

Miss Pammy's lacquered nail pointed to her. "That's her. Taken just days before the killing." She closed the yearbook and put it aside in favor of a yellowed newspaper. *The Exile Times-Record*, which had been out of business for ten years at least. Even then, it had been an eight-page weekly, and padded heavily with newswire fluff.

This issue had a screaming bold headline that read: MOTHER MURDERED; TEENAGE DAUGHTER ARRESTED! There was a picture of a thin, hunched girl with a jacket over her head being hustled up the steps of the Exile courthouse.

"Drugs," Miss Pammy said distastefully. "Ruined a lot of kids in this town, still does. We're right on the drug highway, straight up from Mexico, gets worse all the time."

As if I didn't know. "Meg?"

"Well, I was saying! She was some kind of drug addict, went home all hopped up and had an argument with her mother. The father—Marlon Leary—he was off at the Wandora, where he was every day. Meg found his shotgun. Some say she didn't know it was loaded, but I think she did. She shot her mother at point-blank range, then tried to shoot poor old Mr. Eaves, the postman, when he walked up on the porch to deliver the mail. Crazy from the pills, I think. In my day, we smoked a little weed, had some nice LSD trips, nothing like what these kids get up to. But you'd know, deputy. You'd know all about that."

I set the newspaper aside to make a copy. "They got a conviction?"

She shook her head. "Heck of a trial, biggest spectacle this town ever saw. People came from as far away as Dallas and Austin to see it, and Meg Leary sat there, never shed a tear, never expressed any remorse at all. They were all set to fry that girl, I tell you that, but then her father came forward with a confession."

"I thought her father was at the Wandora."

"He was, with his drunken buddies. Then all of a sudden he says he left the bar, came home, got in a fight with his wife, killed her and went back to the bar. Well, the bartender remembered him being gone, couldn't say for how long. His buddies couldn't remember much of anything." Pammy sighed. Another newspaper came out of the stack. "They let her go. Reasonable doubt."

ACQUITTAL FOR ALLEGED MOTHER-SLAYER! No question about where *The Exile Times-Record* had planted its journalistic feet on the issue. There was a blurred, grainy photo of Meg, head down, being hustled down the courthouse steps again, this time without benefit of a jacket to protect her from the cameras. Quite a crowd. The picture was better than it deserved to be; it caught a sense of menace and violence from the looming faces and shaking fists that told me more than the hyperbole of the staff writer. A tall, lanky man was shoving a path through the crowd for her, his arm around her waist. Not her father, not according to the caption. Texas Rangers escort Megan Leary from the courthouse. No family members with her, no lawyers. Just one cop.

"What happened?" I asked. Miss Pammy raised her plucked eyebrows.

"Well, she left town! Couldn't stay here, could she? Everybody knew the truth, and believe me, in a town the size of Exile you don't get along with an evil past like that. It just doesn't do."

Well, Meg was back now, with a vengeance. I nodded and started to get up. Miss Pammy held up a finger just like my second grade teacher, freezing me in place.

"I'm not done," she said. "And neither was she. Vindictive little so-and-so, you could see that in her eyes. She wasn't satisfied with getting away with murder, oh no. She went off to the big city, and from there—from there—she claimed that she was molested while she was a prisoner in our jail."

I had a sudden visceral memory of Peyser's hands sliding up her skirt. Oh, Jesus, what had I gotten into?

"She ruined a lot of good men in that department—in your department, Deputy Fox. Innocent men, sure as God watches over us. Some big-city jury fined this town three million dollars. Three million dollars. That was more than we ever had." Miss Pammy's face had taken on a hard, vindictive set. I wondered if she'd been one of the people standing on the courthouse steps, howling for Meg's blood. "She took the heart right out of this town, Meg Leary. And if she ever shows her face again, she'll regret it."

"Mind if I copy these?" I asked. She gave me a sudden burst of a smile.

"Still ten cents a copy. Machine's right over there. Are you doing some kind of article, deputy? For a law magazine?"

"Something like that," I said. I was too much of a coward to tell her.

★ ★ ★ ★ ★

While I was choking down a lunch of Dairy Queen hot dogs, Jimmy Sparkman radioed to tell me what a piss-poor job I was doing of handling Meg Leary.

"Sorry," I said. "I was busy finding out what you didn't bother to tell me about her past. The murder."

A brief hiss of static. "Then you know why we need to get her the hell out of this town. The pot's already boiling, Dan. It ain't going to boil over on my watch."

I sighed. "Where is she?"

"The high school. She's demanding to talk to students about Aurelia Galvan. Tell me she's not involved in this waste of time."

"Rosa Galvan hired her."

"God—" He bit off the curse. "Just get over there. If she wants to talk to students, fine, but I want you to be there. Don't let things get out of hand. I'm counting on you."

As promised, Meg's Lexus was in the high school parking lot. It had acquired some new amateur pinstriping since I'd last seen it: long uneven scratches down the driver's side. Somebody had carefully piled broken glass just under the tires, too. I kicked the sharp edges out of the way, shook my head about the paint job, and walked up the steps to Walker J. Taylor Senior High, home of the Fightin' Indians. It was a sign of how small Exile was that nobody had moved to change the mascot to something more politically correct. As far as I knew, nobody had even thought of it.

Two out of four cars in the lot had some kind of rebel flag decoration—not because the kids felt any loyalty to the Old South, hell, they'd probably flunked Civil War history, but because they had some dim notion it might piss somebody off. The parking lot, like the town, was evenly divided into two sections. Not teacher and student, which might have at least been logical; not even rich and poor, though of course it tended to fall out that way.

The two out of four cars that didn't have rebel insignia were sporting the red, green, and white Mexico flag, or bumper stickers advertising Hispanic activist groups. The two sides at Walker J. Taylor were still fighting the battle of the Alamo.

Meg's car could have been keyed just because it was worth three times any other car in the lot, or because she was white, or because she was Meg. I'd probably never know. There were three or four likely suspects hanging around in parked cars, smoking and drinking out of paper bags. Normally, I would have made it my business, but not today. And, from the stares they gave me, they sensed it.

Those stares followed me up the steps into the broad double doors of the school.

When the smell of chalk and cafeteria chili hit me, I was seven years old again, a book bag dragging at my hand, my mother's kiss still sloppy on my cheek. The hallway was empty, the floor polished to a high shine; classroom doors on either side were the old fashioned kind, with wide, square windows. As I walked past, I heard snatches of science, pieces of Shakespeare, and a yelling exchange that could only have been a prelude to the principal's office.

As I came even with the long row of gunmetal-gray lockers, someone turned the corner up ahead. No matter how old you are, seeing an adult figure coming toward you down an empty school hallway still gives you a twinge of panic. No hall pass. I put on my best cop-face and kept walking, but when I angled to go around him, he changed course to intercept.

"Deputy Fox?" he asked, and held out his hand. "Arlen

Steinman, I'm the principal here. Don't think I've had the pleasure."

He genuinely did look pleased. I wondered why; he was about the first in town. But then he answered that question.

"The Sheriff said you'd be coming by about—" His voice dropped as he leaned closer over our handshake. He was shorter than I was, but solid; a weightlifter's blocky bulk. Football, I thought. This little man would have moved like a tank, not quickly, just unstoppably. A coach's answer to prayers. "—about Meg Leary."

His brown eyes were earnest and serious behind horn-rimmed glasses.

"Where is she?"

"In the counselor's office. She wanted to talk to some of the students—Sheriff Sparkman said it was all right, but that you had to be present too." Arlen blinked. "She's pretty forceful."

I could imagine she'd enjoyed kicking the stuffing out of Arlen.

"This way," he said. "Better hurry, the bell's due to ring any minute."

It did just as we were passing the trophy case, with all its dusty cups and forgotten plaques. As if it were an air raid siren, kids poured out into the halls, running, shoving, a confusion of Hilfiger fashions and baggy Nike sweats, short skirts, and tight sweaters. Try as I might, I couldn't remember high school being so colorful in my day. Nobody paid us any attention; the crowd swirled past, intent on snacks and talks and bathroom breaks, and I concentrated on following Arlen upstream toward the administrative office.

Meg sat in a grimly functional plastic chair in the waiting room, her legs crossed, looking cool and elegant and untouchable.

"You ditched me. You were supposed to be at Rosa Galvan's house," I said. She looked at me with the utter disinterest of a supermodel propositioned by a nerd.

"Sue me," she said. "Let me guess. Jimmy sent you with the leash."

Arlen winced, but he didn't have the benefit of a half day with Miss Leary. I smiled.

"I left it in the cruiser," I said. "Got some handcuffs somewhere, though, if you're interested."

"Better save them for later," she said. "So, you're here to supervise me? Make me bark on command?"

"You have a dog issue, don't you?" I shot Arlen a look; he was standing there fascinated. "Who'd she ask to talk to?"

"Javier Nieves and Anita Flores."

If I'd wanted to find out about Aurelia Galvan, they would have been my two choices, too. I nodded. Arlen went about the business of pulling students out of class, assuming they were in class and not out in the parking lot keying Meg's car. I sat down next to Meg, stared across the narrow linoleum-floored room to the pale green wall. It had pictures of teachers lined up like wanted posters; some of them were the worse for student decoration. Mr. Sykes, for example, had a black eye and a clever-looking goatee. Mrs. Antweiller boasted a very fine Hitlerian mustache.

"Find out anything useful while you were gone?" Meg asked. She was studying a magazine, something educational. I couldn't believe she was fascinated by the latest in audio-visual equipment.

"Not about Aurelia."

She glanced up at me, blue eyes clear and innocent. "Did you get the party line about me?"

"I don't think I know what the party line is."

And I wasn't going to then, because Javier Nieves slouched in the door, shepherded by Arlen Steinman. Javier looked vague and calm, but then he always did. There was an empty distance in his eyes that had always made me feel a little uneasy, and it took hold again as Javier dismissed me and focused on Meg.

Who smiled, stood up, and said, "Let's have a chat."

Arlen opened the door to the counselor's office.

There were only two chairs—counseling was apparently a deeply private thing—and Meg took the big cushy one. I grabbed wall space and folded my arms as Javier flopped the way only teenagers can flop in the hard wooden guest chair. The room was full of happy horseshit posters that said things like You're just starting out! and Aim high! Most of these kids, God help them, didn't need to be encouraged with the word "high." The counselor was clearly into Peanuts—Woodstock and Snoopy on the desk, cartoons on the walls—which might have worked in elementary school, but I had the feeling the Buffy the Vampire Slayer generation just found it sad.

Meg didn't say anything. She looked at Javier for a long time, trying the silent approach; I could have told her it wouldn't get anywhere. Except for a faint, distant, dreamy smile, Javier didn't react at all. He looked ready to doze off.

"Where's Aurelia?" she asked, just as his eyelids sank to half-mast. If she was hoping to surprise him into a confession, she was disappointed. His eyes opened again—a little—and he shrugged.

"Don't know," he said. His voice was soft and musical, flavored with a picante of Hispanic accent. "Bitch took off."

"Just like that."

His eyes flicked to me, opaque as a shark's. "Yeah, just like that. You got a badge?"

"You keep using that tone, you'll have to pull my badge out of your ass to look at it."

Javier smiled, all teeth. "No badge."

I showed him mine, just to get rid of the smile. Damn, he was an unnerving little bastard—none of the surface cool most kids failed at so badly. He genuinely did not care. He was the kind who'd draw a gun and pop a cap in you without blinking.

"Tell me about the day Aurelia disappeared," Meg said. "Play nice, Javier, or believe me, I'll start playing hard."

Whether he believed her or not, he settled himself at a more comfortable slouch in the chair, stretched out khaki-clad legs in front of him, and said, "Saw her at breakfast before school. She was mad at her mother about something."

"What?"

"No sè. She was always mad about something. She went on to class. Supposed to meet me at lunch but she didn't show. I asked around, but nobody saw her. Figured she was mad at me, too." Javier cocked his head and looked at Meg. "I always take her home, but she didn't show for that, either. So I went looking."

"But you think she ran off without a word to you. Doesn't say a lot for your—" Meg hesitated, smiled, and finished him off. "—personal charm."

Javier wasn't smiling anymore. She'd punched a hole through the ice, and there was lava underneath. Another kid his age would have called her names, mouthed off about how Aurelia had been his love slave. Not Javier. He sat there and stared.

"Nice ring," Meg said. I looked at Javier's fingers. He had tattoos around three of them at ring-level, but on his right ring finger he had a death's head silver grin. I felt that sensation, that lurch of instinct meeting opportunity. Javier looked down at the ring, back up at Meg.

"Wouldn't look good on you," he said. It was coolly done, but he was definitely a little off balance. She put the wedge in.

"Can I see it?"

He slowly shook his head and held up his hand. "On too tight. Can't get it off."

"Dan," Meg purred. "I think we need some Vaseline. Maybe a chainsaw."

Javier stood up.

"Sit down and give me the ring," I said. Javier's smoking-hot eyes landed on me, burning in. He could have walked out, and he probably knew it, but after what seemed like a year of silence he sat down in the chair again, twisted the ring off his finger, and dropped it into the baggie I held out.

"It's mine," he said. "I want it back."

"You'll get it."

I sealed the bag and marked it with date, time and details. Without looking up, I said, "Better get back to class, Javier."

He cut his eyes to Meg, then slid out of the chair again and left without another word. Meg waited until the door was shut, then turned to look at me and the baggie I was writing on.

"Hers?"

"Maybe," I said. "Maybe they got romantic and bought matching skull rings. Even if we find her name inside that won't mean anything much in court. But he wasn't wearing it two days ago when I talked to him."

"Suggestive," she said. Meg was an expert on suggestive.

"He'd have to be an idiot to be wearing it if he killed her."

"Jails aren't full of thinkers." Meg smiled at me, a slow, delighted, predatorial smile. "Next victim."

I couldn't help but smile back.

Anita Maria Yeleña Dominguez y Flores was also seventeen, but that and Hispanic bloodlines were all she shared with Javier Nieves. She was graceful, delicate, gentle, and shy; she also didn't appear on Javier's radar because she was fast approaching two hundred pounds in a school where one-twenty was cause for anorexic hysteria. And she didn't seem to care. She dressed well, studied hard, and was generally ignored as "the fat girl." Which, in my opinion, was a mistake, because Anita was ferociously intelligent and observant.

She'd also been one of Aurelia Galvan's best friends. That said something nice about Aurelia.

She hesitated in the doorway, her dark eyes darting from Meg to me and back to Meg. She was clutching a stack of books. The notebook on the bottom had doodlings on it in black, red, and green ink; I could make out a very competent caricature of Ms. Antweiller, complete with mole.

"Anita," I nodded. "Come on in. Have a seat."

She obeyed instantly, set the books carefully on her lap, and let her backpack slide to the floor. She wanted to look at me, but Meg's silent, mysterious presence pulled at her attention.

"Mr. Fox?" she said politely, and quite a bit nervously. "Am I in trouble?"

"Tell me about what happened the day before Aurelia Galvan disappeared," Meg said. She caught Anita by surprise.

"The day before?" Anita asked. Meg nodded. "Oh. Uh . . . Javier brought her to school, we sat outside and ate breakfast. We had first period together, then she had gym and I had band."

"Nothing happened out of the ordinary?" Meg asked.

Anita looked at her for a long time before she answered.

"Who are you?" And then, immediately, as if she was afraid she might have hurt Meg's feelings, "You don't seem like somebody who lives here. You seem like—FBI or something."

"Or something," Meg agreed. "I used to live here. I know Aurelia's mother."

"Oh," Anita said, sounding even more confused. Meg as family friend probably made a lot less sense than Meg as FBI. "Well, nothing happened."

Meg leaned forward and said, very kindly, "Anita, please don't lie to me. I know what happened. Aurelia broke up with Javier."

I controlled the impulse to say, "What?" and saw Meg's eyes cut toward me in clear warning.

"No," Anita said, but it lacked any heat. "No, that's not—"

"Anita." Meg's firm, gentle tone demanded the truth. And got it.

"Yes," the girl said, and hung her head. "I should have said so before. I'm sorry, Mr. Fox, I wanted to tell you but Aurelia said not to tell—she told me that morning that she was going to get out of town. She hated it here. She wanted to go to El Paso, or maybe to Dallas, someplace big. She wanted to get an acting job. She was really good at it, you know. And she was pretty, too."

She looked down at the books in her lap, exempting herself from the pretty category.

"So she told you she was leaving. And Javier had already broken up with her."

"She cried all that afternoon. She said he'd lied to her, that he didn't love her. She said he asked for her ring back."

I started to ask the question, but Meg flashed me a quick, unreadable look and said, "You said she was leaving. Was she packed?"

"She had a backpack. I gave her forty dollars." Anita looked down at her books again, this time to avoid my eyes. "I should have told you but I wanted to give her time to get away from here. She never wanted to come back to Exile, never. But she said she'd call, and she hasn't called!"

"Javier asked her to give the ring back," Meg said. Anita nodded. "Did she?"

"No," Anita said. "No, she said it was hers. She wouldn't give it back. She said she'd die first."

I dug the baggie out of my pocket, unfolded it, and handed it to Anita. The silver death's head glinted in the light.

"This ring?" I asked. It was a formality. I heard Anita draw in a quick, shaky breath just before she looked up, her eyes bright and scared.

"Yes," she said.

"Great," Meg said. She was staring at the fresh scratches on the door. I thought a few more had been added since I'd left it, but I couldn't be sure. "Somebody's going to pay for that."

"I don't think you want to collect."

"It's not your car, you don't get a fucking vote." She threw open the door and got in. Sunlight glimmered on the silver finish, on the dark glory of her hair, on shattered glass embedded in parking lot asphalt like diamonds in coal. From somewhere over by the practice field floated the thin sound of the Taylor High School Marching Band. They were staging a rematch with Sousa and still losing big. Near the single tennis court, three lanky delinquents in blue corduroy FFA jackets dipped snuff and admired each other's cowboy boots. A cluster of darker-skinned boys hung around in the shadow of the school building and stared at us with identical cold expressions. One of them was Javier Nieves.

"Meg," I said, and leaned in the window. She fired up the engine but didn't put it in gear. She slid on a pair of blue Oakley shades and stared off at the sun-bleached bricks of the main building. "I'm going to put this the nicest way I know how, so listen up. You're not running off to scare a confession out of anybody. You're on a leash now, and it's short."

"Who's holding the end?" she shot back. "You?"

She didn't think I could hang on. I let a smile out of its cage, saw her head tilt just a little to consider it. The Lexus shivered delicately as the engine purred, a warm vibration under the palms of my hands. The inside of her car smelled like flowers and smoke.

"I need to find her, Dan," she said. "That kid's the first priority now."

"Then let's work together instead of all this territorial bullshit. I'm supposed to watch you. Don't try to shake me off, and I won't try to yank that leash too hard. Deal?"

She didn't answer directly. She drummed her sharp fingernails on the steering wheel and kept staring straight ahead, then turned and looked directly into my eyes. I couldn't tell what her expression was behind the Oakleys, but I thought I saw a hint of a smile curl her lips.

"I have to take this ring back and voucher it to the DPS lab," I said. "You go on back to Rosa Galvan's house, I'll meet you there."

"Get a warrant for whatever rathole Javier crawls into at night while you're at it."

And just like that, she hit the gas. I had to jump back to save my feet from being flattened as the Lexus shot away, weaving through the maze of cars to the parking lot exit. She turned right, accelerated, and was gone like a mirage.

I was going to pay for this, I suspected.

I had no inkling that both of us were.

I was typing up my report and the evidence voucher, along with the lab request, when Farlene yelled my name and told me to pick up line two. I punched buttons and heard the hiss of a bad connection.

"Deputy Fox," I said. I expected Meg's smoky voice. What I got was female, young, and unsure, with a Hispanic accent.

"They say you're looking for me," she said. I stopped typing, swiveled my chair, and covered the speaker of the phone to stage-whisper Farlene's name. When I got her attention, I mouthed trace the call and started her moving in a flurry of panic, looking for typewritten instructions. Not a lot of use for call tracing in Exile under normal circumstances. Well, it had been a faint hope, anyway.

"Aurelia Galvan?" I asked. A slight hesitation on the other end.

"Yes. I'm okay."

"Uh huh. Why'd you take off, Aurelia?"

"M-my mother. She was always after me, you know, always nagging at me. I wanted to be an actress. She wanted me to finish school."

Which anyone who'd known Aurelia would have known. This hadn't been her first attempt at hitting the road.

"Did you call your mother?"

"No."

"Why not?"

"Because I don't want to talk to her."

"But you want to talk to me."

"I just want to tell you—to say not to look for me. I'm fine. Tell her I'm fine."

"What are you doing for money, Aurelia?"

"I have money."

"Where'd you get it?"

"I don't have to answer your questions! I'm fine, I'm not doing anything wrong!" Distress and distance made her harder to understand. "Just leave me alone. Leave me alone!"

"Aurelia, I'd like to do that, but I can't unless you call your mother and tell her you're okay. Where are you calling from?"

"Austin."

"What's in Austin?"

"Nothing, okay? Just—get off my back!"

She slammed the phone down. Farlene made a helpless gesture with both hands.

"Did you get anything at all?" I asked.

"It was a 512 area code."

Austin. The best lies are always part truth.

Jimmy Sparkman had come out of his office, and he was looking at me expectantly. I turned around to face him.

"So she's all right," he said.

"Jimmy, I don't think so. I think this girl's some friend Javier roped into making the call. Aurelia's not in Austin. She probably never got out of Exile."

I showed him the ring.

"Those rings are a dime a dozen, you know that."

"He was wearing it like a trophy. She swore she'd never give it to him."

Jimmy gave me a long, compassionate look and said, "And teenage girls never change their minds. Look, it's over. Aurelia's in Austin, she's safe, and that's the end of the story. Let it go."

"You thinking about the girl, or about getting Meg Leary out of town?" I asked.

"Both," he said. "Close the case, Dan. Don't make me make it an order."

I wasn't looking forward to having the conversation with Rosa Galvan, my heart wasn't in it. But maybe illusions would make her life easier, for now. Meg wasn't going to take things so easily at face value.

I knocked on the faded salmon-colored door and waited while the parade of running feet receded into the distance and Rosa Galvan cracked open the door. Her face didn't warm up to me.

"Aurelia called the station," I said. I felt dirty saying it, but I said it. "She says she's in Austin, and she's fine."

Rosa's face stayed still for a few seconds, then crumbled into tears. She swung the door open, came out on the porch, and grabbed me in a breath-stealing hug. She pressed her damp face against my chest, and I patted her back and tried not to think that I had just told the worst lie of my life. When it looked like the storm was passing, I asked her where Meg was.

"Not here," she said, surprised. She wiped the back of her hand across her swollen eyes. "She said she had something to do. I don't know what. Did—did Aurelia sound happy?"

"I asked her to call you," I said. Not a lie, just a cruel

misdirection. Aurelia—or whoever was using her name—wasn't going to call. "If she does—let me know."

She nodded and smiled at me. The first time she'd ever smiled at me. I dredged up one from somewhere in response, and turned away.

After driving around town for a while, I found Meg at the Wandora.

Picture a barn big as a warehouse, build it out of second-rate wood with no windows and no paint job; put in dim smoke-cluttered lights and a floor that probably came already beer- and blood-stained; furnish it with furniture no self-respecting second-hand store would carry; staff it with mutants and mouth-breathers. Oh, and throw in a juke box that only plays Conway Twitty. I didn't know personally, but Jimmy had told me the Wandora was over a hundred years old, a town fixture like the sewage system. Seeing the Lexus parked in front gave me a sick ache in my head. If there was anyplace Megan Leary wouldn't fit in . . .

But Megan wouldn't go to the Wandora to fit in. That was exactly the point. She was promenading herself in every place in town where tongues could get wagging. She wanted the whole town to know she'd arrived.

A gutsy strategy. Stupid, though.

I pulled my cruiser in at the back of the building and called in to the office. Farlene was already gone for the day, and I got old Deputy Harlan, who took my location down without comment. It was an unusual night when one of us didn't stop by the Wandora, just to keep the lid on the boiling pot; I saw no reason to mention Megan in connection with it. If the grapevine was doing its job, they'd know soon enough.

The bouncer hanging around the Wandora's entrance was Joe Wilkerson, who pretty much headed my top ten list of People I Don't Like In Exile . . . my mother, who had never been confused with Will Rogers, would have called him a complete waste of body fluids. Joe was a walking social disease. He was also Lew Peyser's second cousin, which proved genetics was an exact science.

His face split into a ragged grin at the sight of me, and he swiped greasy hair back out of his eyes to say, "If it ain't the city boy. Looking for a little small-town backroom pussy, deputy?"

"Shut up."

"Now, that's not real friendly," he said, and studied his fingernails. He polished them on the barbecue stain on his flannel shirt. "If you're looking for Eulene, she don't come out for duty until late, you know that. Now, if you want me to fix you up special with one of them young factory girls, they're cheap but eager—"

I shoved past him into the Wandora's smoky doorway.

It was too early for trouble to be brewing, just a few tottering drunks clinging to the bar, the bartender Jerry half hypnotized with boredom. Somebody had stuck a quarter in the Conway Twitty machine, and it was grinding out the immortal country classic "You're the Reason Our Kids Are Ugly."

Megan Leary was sitting in the back corner of the bar, by the pool tables. She wasn't far into her evening yet, but she'd killed a few soldiers; she didn't notice me coming until I kicked the chair across from her by way of saying hello.

Her eyes were a little slow in focusing on me. Tequila had the same general effect as a swift kick in the head, if you did it earnestly enough. She looked a little beat up, but still game to keep on fighting.

"Deputy Dan," she said. "Pull up a chair. Have a drink."

"No thanks."

"Must be your bedtime," she said, and took another shot. "Want to know my theory?"

I sat down and put both hands on the table. "Probably not."

"People who go to bed early die young."

"People who stay where they're not wanted die young, too," I said.

"You get the warrant for Javier's crib?"

"No," I said, and told her why. I didn't tell her my suspicions. I didn't have to.

"Ever heard of a runaway calling the police to tell them she's okay?" Meg asked. I shook my head. "Javier got worried."

"Maybe."

"Maybe?" She laughed and tipped back a tequila. "Bullshit, 'maybe.' We have the ring, we have Anita's statement that he and Aurelia fought and she swore she'd never give up the ring. All we've got to do is—"

"Meg," I interrupted. "Case is closed."

She froze. "What?"

"The case is closed. Look, I don't like it any better than you do, but—"

"He killed her, Dan! You know he did! There's a body out there somewhere, and for her mother's sake—"

"Her mother thinks she's alive and well and in Austin; are you going to take that away from her?"

"So we just lie and let it go. Wow, Dan. Your tenacity is amazing. I knew I could trust you to do the right thing, you son of a bitch."

Her bitterness would have scorched the finish off the table, if there'd been a finish on it to begin with. I reached out and grabbed her wrist, held it tight when she tried to pull it free.

"You know why they've closed the case?" I asked. "Because that's how bad they want you out of town. Because the life of some teenage Mexican runaway is a small price to pay to get rid of Megan Leary. Most of these people couldn't spell matricide, but they know what it is. They want you gone."

She was pale when I finished, her eyes dead glass. I let go of her wrist. She had red marks.

"Who told you?"

"I went to the library. I talked to Pammy Howard."

"Jesus, you need a drink. She used to scare a year off of me every time I had to check out *Wizard of Oz*." She was trying for humor, but it was too much of a reach. "Have a drink with me, Dan. Just to prove one man in town isn't trying to kill me."

I let my breath out slowly, reached out and took one of Meg's tequila shots. It scorched down my throat and lit a bonfire in my belly. She held out an anemic salt-coated slice of lime; I bit into it and winced as the sour rush bit back.

"I'm off duty," I said, as if she cared, and waved my hand at the bartender to cut her off. Couldn't tell if he noticed or not. "Meg, I don't want to kill you. I can't speak for anybody else in this town, though. For God's sake, be smart. Leave."

She didn't answer. She reached for the last shot left on the table.

"Are you listening to me?" I said.

"Every word. You know why Jimmy Sparkman's so worried? I could tell some stories about Jimmy. I could tell stories about almost everybody in this ass-end of a town." She was already too drunk to drive out of town under her own power. Drunk and stupid and vulnerable. Daring them to take their best shot. "This is my home. I have a right to be here. I have a right to stay in my mother's house."

"The house where she died?" I asked. This time, when she reached for the tequila, I didn't stop her.

"Oh, be fair, now, deputy, call a spade a spade. The house where I murdered her?" Meg sucked on a lime, keeping her eyes on me the whole time. "You bet. Right there in the front living room. Blew her in half with the shotgun. Then I took a pot shot at the postman, just for the hell of it."

I let that sink in between us, big and ugly, before I said, "You finished?"

She tossed the drained corpse of the lime wedge on the table.

"I heard the story," I said. "You were acquitted."

"Being acquitted doesn't mean I didn't do it." She took a perverse sort of pride in that.

"A jury didn't think you killed her." I paused. "I don't think you did it either."

"Based on what, exactly?" Her gaze slid slowly down my chest to a spot hidden by the table. Message sent and received, and I couldn't exactly deny there was some rising interest in that area.

I cleared my throat. "Experience. Nobody comes back into trouble like this unless they've got something to prove. Look, this isn't the way to do it. You're not going to accomplish anything here. Nobody's going to let you."

"Is that why you left Houston? Nobody let you accomplish anything?" I hadn't been the only one digging up dirt, it seemed. I tensed all over, tried to relax. She took a mere sip of her drink, going for the distance instead of the buzz.

"An ex-wife named René who had me chained to a rock and was eating my liver. We're not talking about me. Nobody's trying to stick my head on a pike."

"You were a homicide detective?"

"No, property crimes. Not as exciting, but then you don't have to see so many decomposing bodies. And you're ducking the question I keep asking. Are you going to leave town?"

The front door of the Wandora opened, and the first shift of regulars came in—I checked my watch and saw they were right on time. It took about two minutes to drive from the Delta Faucet plant to the Wandora, and it was two minutes after five. Some of them looked our way. I didn't like that. I didn't like it at all, and I had the feeling I'd like it less once they had three or six drinks under their belts.

I almost missed it when she said, very quietly, "I tripped."

"What?"

Her blue eyes came up to fix on mine. "I'd skipped school that day. I got high, I got drunk. I tripped over her in the dark. I fell on top of her. I didn't know she was dead until I put my hand in—in her. Jesus, I was fifteen years old and she was my mother."

Her expression hadn't changed but I could feel it coming out of her, hot and raw and wounded. Killers didn't hurt like that.

Her eyes glittered wet, then cleared. "Don't give up on Aurelia Galvan. Don't you dare."

"If I promise to keep digging, will you promise to leave town in the morning?"

"Maybe." She drew her finger through a pile of salt, licked the end of it clean. Over at the bar, a cluster of guys with big belt buckles were discussing something, and I had the feeling it wasn't the sports scores. The bigger ones had that pumped-up self-righteous look, and they were downing beer at an industrial rate.

"Meg," I said. "We need to get out of here before we end up in more trouble than two of us can handle. Where are you sleeping?"

Her eyes met mine for a second. I felt that look all over me like a second skin, could almost feel her. Her lips parted.

"My mother's house," she said, slowly and distinctly, as if it wasn't the answer she expected to hear herself say. She tried for a smile. "The Hilton was all booked up."

"Give me your keys."

"What?"

"The car keys." She tossed me a set on a silver ring; I caught them in mid-air to test my reflexes. "I always wanted to drive a Lexus. Probably my only chance."

"Knock yourself out," she said.

The Lexus drove just like the goddamn commercials. Next to me, Meg stayed quiet. She stared out the passenger window at darkened houses, flickering lights. Whatever she was thinking she kept to herself.

"It's not a bad town," I said, half to myself. "Quiet. Not much trouble except around the Wandora."

"Keep saying that. Maybe it'll come true." Meg turned her face toward me, a slice of pale blue in the moonlight. "It's a roach motel. Shine a little light around here and you'll be surprised how fast they all scurry for the shadows."

"That why you came back? To shine a little light?" I turned left at the corner, past a closed gas station and an ornate empty building that had once been a drug store, complete with soda fountain. Or so they said. The Masonic lodge was still lit up for bingo night; after the balls stopped dropping, they'd head over to the Wandora to finish out the night and redistribute their winnings. Small town econo-mies of scale.

She looked out the window. The graveyard unrolled on Meg's side of the car, and her gaze followed it until it dropped out of sight behind us. A big shiny red truck passed us, heading the opposite direction, probably another Wandora visitor on the prowl. She closed her eyes and rested her head against the window glass.

"Did your mother have enemies?" I asked.

"Some. She had a temper, she was demanding. You know the story. She had lots more friends dead than she ever did alive." She opened her eyes as I turned the next corner, where a Burger Town had once stood in days of yore. "It's up there."

"Do you think your father killed her?"

"No," she said. "My father worshipped her. She sup-ported him, she let him drink himself to death. Why would he kill her? In his own way, he loved her."

I pulled to a stop in front of the house. It was just a shadow in the greater darkness, a slope of dark roof like all its neighbors. Pale brick broken by blind windows. I cruised up to the curb and put on the brakes, noticing that some of the windows were busted out. "You shouldn't go in there alone," I said. "Looks like some vandalism."

"Fuck 'em," she said. She sounded tired. "If they want me, I'm here. They all know where to find me."

"Meg—"

She reached out and put her hand on my leg, a hot gentle pressure that drove whatever I'd been about to say right out of my mind. Oh, damn. Damn.

It occurred to me that I had no way to get back to the Wandora, cabs being in short supply. Of course, I could walk—wasn't that far, and the night air would probably help clear my head. I needed some serious goddamn clearing.

She reached over to the ignition and took the keys. She went to the trunk and took out a suitcase. I watched her walk up the steps onto the shadowed porch, where she fumbled with keys and then the door.

She didn't go in. The door swung open, but she didn't go in. After a couple of seconds she took a step back and put her bag down. I couldn't see her that well in the dark, but I didn't need to. I thought about coming back to this house after all those years, opening the door, walking into the room where you'd tripped over your dead mother. She wasn't going in. She couldn't go in. She'd wait a few minutes, then come back to the car, and I could take her to the motel, or to my apartment.

She proved me wrong. She picked up the suitcase and disappeared into the darkness, and slammed the door behind her.

"Jesus." Well, then. That settled it. Meg was determined to stay, and I wasn't invited. I got out of the car and locked the doors—my peace officer duty—and started figuring how long it would take me to make the walk back. Fifteen minutes, probably. Maybe less if I walked quick, which I probably would with all this night quiet pressing down on me, and all the white blur of stars blooming in the sky. There shouldn't be so many stars.

My attention was caught by a glitter of warmth toward the rear of the house. Flashlight? Maybe. Maybe the vandals weren't just kids rocking the local spook house. Maybe there was more to it. And maybe you're just looking for an excuse to go back and save the day, Dan the Conquering Hero. She'll only kick your ass, and you'll deserve it, too.

I kept walking. I was halfway up the street when I

glanced back and saw light flickering at the back of Meg's house. Not bright electric light, but orange light moving at the window.

The window broke. Flames curled out of the empty frame like hot tongues, licking at dry wood and shingles.

The house was on fire.

Chapter Four

When I was a patrolman in Houston, before I got my shield, I partnered with a guy named Jerry Vinzetti. Jerry was without a doubt the most complete bastard ever to carry a badge, but he was smart. He was also colder than lake water in January. We'd pulled up to the curb in front of a crackhouse we were planning to raid one night, a bag of chili cheese dogs to split between us, and we hadn't even unwrapped the first one before we spotted an orange flicker in one of the old windows.

I'd reached for the radio. Jerry had stopped me.

"Kid," he said, "places like this, fire is your friend as long as you do not fuck with it."

I hadn't known what he meant until the junkies and dealers had started running out screaming, grateful as hell to be alive, not even inclined to fight the cuffs. Some of them hadn't made it out. None of us had run in after them.

Do not fuck with fire.

Except, of course, I was doing it now.

Smoke coated my throat and clung, yellow and bitter, even before I made it through that dark doorway and into the living room that was Megan's personal hell. I couldn't see it, only dim shadows and a thick oily haze. As I stumbled forward, coughing, I imagined Megan stumbling in the dark, falling forward over her mother's bloody corpse—

I only stumbled into the sharp edge of what felt like a coffee table. I blinked smoke-tears out of my eyes and yelled her name. I could hear the fire now, like the whispering roar of a huge, still-distant crowd. I also smelled the cold, metallic tang of gasoline. I dropped to one knee and felt the carpet. It was soaked.

Firetrap.

"Meg, goddammit!" I screamed. I saw a shape moving in the smoke and turned my flashlight toward it. Whatever it was, it scuttled away quick. Rats or arsonists abandoning the ship.

The next room was a kitchen with two doors. One of them was shut but I could feel the heat behind it three feet away. I tried the second door and found it cool. The water still worked at the sink, and I soaked a dishtowel and held it over my nose and mouth.

The next room was a dining room. Dim family pictures hung crooked on the wall. A ghostly sheet-covered table squatted in the middle. Somebody had been ransacking the place—papers scattered and torn all over the floor, drawers on the mahogany sideboard pulled open and hanging out like tired tongues.

Gas fumes burned my eyes and sawed at my lungs. I sucked another breath through the wet dishtowel and made for the other room beyond the dining area. My mental map showed that I was about a third of the way into the house, and the noise of the fire had increased volume from a whisper to an excited, wordless buzz.

I turned the corner and stepped into the hallway to hell. At the end flames undulated along the ceiling like waves of liquid; sparks embroidered the carpet. The first bedroom— maybe five feet away from me—had an open door, and I caught a flicker of movement inside.

A spark ignited the dark wide streak of gasoline running down the center of the hall carpet, and blue-tipped flame caught with a sucking whoosh. It rushed down the hall to-ward me.

Two choices. Backward into the gas-soaked living room, or forward into what might be my final resting place: the bedroom.

I lunged for it, got in a breath ahead of the racing wall of fire, and slammed the door on a licking orange tongue. Somebody started hitting me. I almost hit back before I re-alized Meg was trying to put out a fire on my jacket. I shrugged it off and stamped it into smoke, then doubled over for another coughing fit.

We were in what must have been Meg's mother's bed-room. Vandals had been here, spray-painting and wrecking; there was little left of what must have originally been a nice enough place. Meg turned away from me and frantically pulled open drawers, dumped out papers, flipped through books.

"We've got to go!" I yelled. The fire was a Super Bowl roar now, eating the house alive. "Meg, damn it!"

Smoke poured under the door. The synthetic carpet melted in a poisonous goo where it touched. Meg coughed rackingly but she kept pulling drawers, dumping boxes. She swung open the closet door and started in on the con-tents.

We didn't have time for this. We didn't have time for anything except saving our lives. I reached in and grabbed her shoulder, and she turned a grimed face toward me with eyes as smoking hot as the fire outside the door.

"Go," she croaked.

"What the hell is so important?"

"Just go!"

She shoved me off. The door was turning to ash, the finish liquefying and running milk-pale into the molten carpet. As I watched, little tongues of flame erupted on the surface.

We were out of time.

I grabbed Meg's shoulder again, too firmly for her to throw me off, and dragged her to the window. It had been fastened shut with fresh ten penny nails. I picked up a small white wooden chair that sat in front of a long-destroyed makeup table and pitched it through the glass.

Wind breathed into the room, as if the house took a big gulp. Behind us, the door exploded into flame.

I picked Meg up and tossed her out the window, never mind the sharp biting shards of glass still in the frame. When I looked back, I saw the fire coming for me. It moved like something alive, wild and writhing and enraged; it was beautiful, and I had never been so scared in my life. Don't breathe. It wasn't a thought so much as a primitive instinct. The air was superheated, it would cook my lungs into leather.

I dived out the broken window into cool, clean night. A piece of glass caressed a long hot line on my arm, and then I hit damp grass and hard ground, and Megan was hitting me again. I couldn't tell this time if it was because I was on fire or because she was so monumentally angry.

I rolled over on my back, gasping, and looked at a fire so bright and hot it seemed like a piece of the sun. The whole house was going, and going quick . . . the window we'd jumped out of was part of a solid wall of flame. Sparks jumped like burning fleas to the grass—and onto me—and when I felt the sting I finally realized we'd better move back.

Meg looked up at me when I stumbled to my feet, her face a smoke-stained blur with red, weeping eyes.

"Bastards," she whispered hoarsely. I nodded wearily

and held out my hand to help her up, and we weaved our way around to the front of the house. Even the winter-blasted tree was on fire now, burning like the centerpiece of a KKK rally.

My shoes brushed dew from the grass. It occurred to me that it was damn wet out here—pools of standing water in the gutters, the ground soaking wet.

We were in the desert.

There hadn't been any rain.

"Stay here," I said, and went to the nearest house. It looked deserted, all the lights off. Its lawn was wet, too. When I craned my neck to look up, I saw that the house itself was damp, too, drops of water still clinging to the wood trim. The roof dripped.

Sparks that made it over from Meg's house drowned without incident.

It occurred to me that I hadn't heard any fire alarms. The glow had lit up the town like false sunrise, and I could see the fire station from where I stood—lights on, a few dark shapes moving inside—but nobody was rushing to the rescue.

Jesus Christ.

I heard my first siren right about then—a police cruiser, heading over from around the Wandora. One dog barks, they all do—another siren picked up, and I finally heard the distant whine from the fire station. I watched that first cop car make its way toward us and pull up to the curb behind Meg's Lexus, cherry lights still strobing.

Jimmy Sparkman got out and stood there watching the fire. His face looked old and tired, and when he focused on me coming toward him, he looked startled and sick too.

"Jesus, Dan, what're you doing here? Where's Meg? Did you get her out?" He had to shout to be heard over the roar.

"Hope or fear, Jimmy?" I coughed up black mucus and spit it at the damp lawn. "She's all right. She's over there."

Jimmy's eyes followed my gesture to where Meg stood. Even smoke-stained, even still half-drunk, she was beautiful. I saw that hit him hard.

"Was this barbecue your idea?" I asked, while he was still distracted. His eyes didn't flicker. "Then who the fuck's was it?"

He was still my boss—at least, that's what his look warned me. But he said, "Probably accidental."

"Somebody dumped about half the water supply around the house to make damn sure the fire didn't get the neighbors, and splashed gasoline all over the goddamn carpet. You want to rephrase, Jimmy?"

He didn't. We both watched the fire for a while. Another cop car pulled up. Peyser got out and leaned against the hood, arms folded, grinning like a loon. He was watching Meg the way molesters watch children.

"They're going to kill her," Jimmy said. The words were flat, but not the tone. "You understand that?"

They. Then Jimmy wasn't part of it, but neither was he exactly against it. I watched the fire department cruise their pumper truck up, lights flashing; they weren't in a hell of a hurry to get lines laid down, and when the water did start flowing they sprayed down the other houses and lawns, not the fire itself. The fire chief—Anderson—strolled over, spit tobacco, and said, "Gonna let it burn itself out. House is a total loss anyway."

"No sense in risking the boys," Peyser nodded. He'd come over to join us. For the first time I noticed he was out of uniform and wearing blue jeans and a t-shirt that read PECOS CHILI COOK-OFF . . . IF YOU CAN'T STAND THE HEAT, GET THE HELL OUT OF TEXAS. "House was a firetrap anyway. Glad you made it out, Dan. What the hell you doing out here, anyway?"

I probably would have told him to fuck himself, but I didn't get the chance, because Meg Leary turned and walked over, passing right in front of me, and launched herself from a flat-footed standing start at Lew-otherwise-known-as-Buford Peyser like she might just tear his heart out with her bare hands.

Jimmy Sparkman caught hold of her waist in mid-air and tackled her to the ground, evidence his football-hero days weren't that far behind him. She kicked and punched at him, trying to writhe her way free, but Jimmy was a competent cop and she wasn't going anywhere. He pinned her down and stared into her face and yelled, "Stop! Stop it, Meg! Goddammit, just settle down!"

She made a sound low in her throat. It started off primitive and brutal, and then turned fragile. No words. She relaxed, panting, the black smoke on her face cut through with shocking pale tear-tracks.

"Please," Jimmy said, very quietly. "Please, Meg. Don't get yourself hurt."

She stared at him, then slowly nodded. He let go of her wrists and levered himself up to his feet, leaving her prone on the damp grass. He spun around on Fire Chief Anderson and snapped, "What're you standing around here for? Put out the damn fire!"

Anderson's pale eyebrows rose. He spit another brown string of juice and looked at Sparkman, at Peyser, at me. Last of all, at Meg.

"Whatever you say, Chief," he said, and went to join his crew.

Peyser walked away, too. That left Sparkman and me staring at each other as Meg got to her feet.

"Peyser," she said. Her voice—already throaty—had become a Hepburn velvet growl. "You know it was Peyser."

"If it was, I'll see justice is done," Sparkman said. "I'm sorry."

She gave him a scorching glare, transferred it to me—as if I deserved it—and walked away to watch the firemen avoid the fire.

"What are you thinking?" I asked Sparkman. He let out a shaky breath.

"Christ, things I shouldn't be thinking," he said. "Stay with her. I got to check on some things at the station. Dan?"

"Yeah?"

The firelight caught half his face, left half in shadow. Neither half smiled.

"Watch your back."

Chapter Five

The local motel—the Best Inn Towne—had a total of twenty rooms, but hardly anybody bothered to stay overnight; it was the venue of choice for bored housewives doing lunch-hour nooners. I drove Meg over in her Lexus, Jimmy Sparkman trailing me like a ghost in his white cruiser, and neither of us said a word on the way. She stared out the window. I stared out the windshield. We were both of us simmering mad and too damn tired to even talk.

I pulled the car into a space on the cracked, weed-decorated parking lot and shut the engine off. Metal ticked quietly as it cooled. The night had that oppressive silence to it, broken only by the temporary sound of our breathing.

"How bad is this place these days?" Meg asked. The OPEN sign flickered dull orange in the office window, and glowed on a fly-specked card taped beside it that read, in hasty block letters, RING BELL.

"Don't drink the coffee. Otherwise, the sheets are clean and the TV works. I wouldn't drink the water, either, but it probably won't kill you."

The dingy aluminum blinds peeked inside the office, and stayed tented for a good long look.

The NO VACANCY light quavered on, pale blue.

I slammed my hand into the dashboard. "Jesus, even the Bates Motel doesn't want you! You are the goddamn force of chaos!" Meg said nothing. "What do you want to do?"

"Let's go in and beat him like a screeching circus

monkey," she said. "Like a rented mule. Like a red-headed—"

"You first. I'm tired."

She leaned her head back against the upholstery and closed her eyes. The whole car reeked of sweat and smoke, with a sweet metal tang of gasoline thrown in. If anybody lit a match anywhere in town, we'd go up like a Roman candle.

"You got a shower at your place?" she asked.

"I've even got a comfortable couch. And my coffee doesn't suck. Plus, my rates are extremely affordable."

"Sold."

I started the engine and gunned the Lexus out of the parking lot, peeling rubber just for the sheer hell of it—as far as I was concerned, nobody deserved a good night's sleep anyway—and saw Sparkman's cruiser fall in behind me again. Gonna follow me all night? I wondered. I wasn't sure if he had my back or was just spectating. I wasn't sure if he knew, either.

"You and Jimmy go back," Meg said. She'd seen me watching the rear view. "How far?"

"College. He got me through a lot of hell." So he had—drunken depression, bad grades, crazy girlfriends, the lot. Jimmy always seemed to be the one with his head on straight—until Kitty Walker, who'd damn near got him killed, and left him so miserable it made no difference. And who'd then come back to marry him, to make it all that much worse. "We got back in touch after I left Houston. Figured it might be a good change for me out here in the big nothing."

"From a big-city detective to a small-time deputy," she said. "Genius career move."

I didn't answer directly. This tired, talking to her was like playing with a sharp knife.

"Home sweet home," I said instead, and pulled up into the parking lot of Exile's one and only apartment complex. It was called Silver Bell, and it made a great cinder-block design statement. The biggest difference between it and the you-lock-it storage down the street was the peach-colored paint job.

I led Meg up the walk to Apartment 4, opened the door, and flipped on the lights. Cheap thin carpet didn't make much of an impression on the slab foundation; the room was cold and smelled damp, like a cave. I had the comfortable couch I'd promised, and a TV and a tabletop stereo; I had a bed in the bedroom and a library full of books still in boxes. Not a hell of a lot to show for thirty-odd years on the planet. I had a flash of memory, of walking into my old house in Houston on Governor Street, the jewel-green lawn, trimmed hedges, the big white colonial door with the custom brass knocker. Carpet thick enough to need mowing. René meeting me at the door, flushed and breathless from a long bath—

Which just went to prove what a pathetic bastard I was, that I still longed for it.

"Shower's through there," I said, and pointed to the bedroom. "Beer or water to drink?"

"You're kidding, right?" She headed right for it, already unbuttoning her shirt. "I have never needed a beer so badly in my life."

I saluted her with a Coors Lite and popped the cap, downed about half of it in one long pull. Good God, I was stupid. And crazy.

She'd dropped something. It was a piece of a newspaper article, smudged with smoke and damp with sweat. I picked it up off the carpet and turned it over. One side contained half an ad for pork sausage, on sale at 59 cents a pound.

The other side was an article about a kidnapping. No date showing, and only part of the story. It had been ripped out of an album. The sausage side of the paper showed traces of old glue at the corners.

Chelsea Parman, age six, disappeared from her St. Louis home six days ago, according to police sources . . .

There was no date, but it didn't look recent. I wondered why Meg had chosen to save that article, out of everything in the house.

If she'd planned to save it at all.

The shower started running. I sat down and turned on the TV, flicked through the two-and-a-half channels available in Exile without cable. Infomercial, a rerun of "Baywatch Nights" and something in Spanish that looked science fictional, or it might have been bad reception. I kicked my boots off and put my feet up on the coffee table.

The water ran on, and on. I tried not to think too much about damp skin.

When she came out, thirty minutes later, she was wrapped in one of my towels. It hid her from the slope of her breasts to just barely decent, and if I'd been a lesser man my heart might have stopped right then. As it was, I nearly choked on my Coors. Mr. Smooth, that's me. I got up, offered her the promised cold beer, and went in without a word to the steaming shower. My clothes needed to be burned—as gas-soaked as they were, that wouldn't be a challenge—and I needed a long cold shower to get my head back together.

I was about halfway through that process when I had a *Psycho* moment and knew she was standing in the bathroom, watching me through the frosted glass door. That might be good, if she was carrying another beer. That might be bad, if it was a butcher knife.

I opened the door and looked out. It was a beer, and she was dressed in one of my old shirts.

"Are we friends?" she asked.

I took the beer. "I expect we have to be, if we're having this conversation in my bathroom and one of us is naked."

She didn't smile. Her eyes were still red, still deeply haunted.

"Give me a minute," I said, and shut the door. I rinsed lather out of my hair and swigged beer and generally wondered what the hell it was I intended to do, then killed the shower and opened the door. "Hand me a towel."

She held one out. I dried off in the shower and tucked up decent, then stepped out, beer in hand.

She didn't move back.

"Meg," I began.

"You don't think I killed her," she said in a rush. "What if you're wrong about me? What if you're dead wrong?"

"I don't think I am."

"You know what I was looking for? When the house was burning down around us?"

"No."

"She collected news articles." Her red eyes filled up with metallic shine, too hard to be tears. "I remember she used to cut them out and paste them in a notebook, back around the time she died. I never knew why. I thought it might have been important. But all I could find was one thing, and it doesn't make any sense."

"I'm sorry," I said. "Meg—"

"Somebody took everything. Everything."

It seemed to be the right moment to touch her, and I wanted to touch her, I was obsessed with the idea of it. I reached out and put my hand on her shoulder, pulled her toward me and into my arms.

Full body contact. She must have felt my erection under the towel. I leaned back a little, trying to kiss her, but her head stayed down against my shoulder. After a moment she pushed away, not looking at me, and said, "Couch or bed?"

I didn't need a referee to tell me there had been a flag on the play. But it was something else, too. She had switched off like a light, all the sexy energy gone out of her.

"You take the bed," I said. "The sheets are clean."

She glanced up at me. A faint smile raced over her lips and was gone. "Anybody ever tell you you're a gentleman?"

"All the goddamn time," I sighed.

As you might imagine, I slept for shit. Too much going on in my head, and in other parts of my body. I kept thinking what if I go in there, what if I just lay down next to her, would she pretend to be asleep? When I touch her—

I kept disconnecting right there, because if I thought too much about it, it was going to happen, and I was far from sure that was a good thing. Meg was the wrong end of a loose wire—was, I figured, at the best of times. This wasn't it. And I had a life to look after. Not much of one, but a life.

I closed my eyes and tried to think about René, who she was with, what she was doing. That was guaranteed to throw cold water on whatever flames I had stoked up.

It worked, but it had nasty aftereffects. When I finally fell asleep, I dreamed of going back to Houston.

I was standing in front of the white house, the colonial, with its wide white door and shiny brass knocker. The door glided open for me, and I went in, carried on a gust of wind like a puffball, floating weightless. When I looked

*down my shoes didn't touch the floor. I had a briefcase in
my hand.*

*Inside, the hall was dim and cool and quiet, wood
gleaming in the light from the mullioned half-moon
window over the door. A chandelier like a frozen waterfall
dangled from the ceiling. The glass shivered a little as the
air conditioner clicked on, and I looked up at the musical
soft chime.*

*My briefcase dropped out of my hand and disappeared.
I glided down that long, quiet, cool hallway into the living
room with its oversized Erté prints and pale champagne
carpet and lush butter-soft leather couches. I was tired,
suddenly. Exhausted, as if the carpet was quicksand
sucking me down.*

*There was a gun on the side table next to the couch.
My gun. It had a strange, beautiful glitter like a steel
jewel. As I watched, it slowly faded out and disappeared.*

*René began to yell at me, but I couldn't find her,
couldn't seem to argue with her because she was never
there when I turned around. Just her voice, jabbing at me
like a hot iron, twisting me one way and another, and all
of a sudden I was in the hallway again, yelling something
to an empty wall, and behind me I heard René say, very
softly, did you put the gun—*

*And something popped, very loud, and when I looked
up at the ceiling it was dripping blood, dripping blood
down the winding chain of the light fixture, down over the
crystal dangles.*

*I should have felt horror, I guess. All I thought, in the
dream, was she's going to kill me about the damn carpet.*

*Somebody was behind me. I felt the skin tighten on the
back of my neck and thought: don't look don't look don't
look . . .*

And I woke up. Sweating. Shivering. Thirsty.

No sound from my bedroom, where Megan slept. I got up and went to the sink, drew myself a glass of the lime-stone-flavored town water and drank it down in three quick, convulsive gulps. Had another.

I wanted her to get up and come ask me what was wrong. That was stupid, it was even dangerous, but I wanted it as bad as I'd ever wanted anything in my life. All this time, I hadn't talked to Jimmy about what had happened; I for damn sure hadn't talked to that harpy wife of his, though Kitty would have killed for the gossip and she badgered me half the time. I hadn't talked to anybody about Houston at all.

And that was the way it should be.

Meg never got up, anyway. I finished my water and went back to the couch, pulled the sweat-soaked sheets back over me, and settled in for a siege of sleep.

In the morning, things looked bad. Cotton-mouthed, red-eyed, I fixed coffee that didn't suck and a breakfast that did; Meg had another shower, as if she hadn't worked the smoke away yet, and came out dressed in one of my ratty old bathrobes. I never throw them away, even when they're held together by fluff and static electricity. This particular one was blue, and had a torn hem.

"You look like hell," she said, and took a coffee cup off of the hooks over the sink. There were four hooks, three cups. Two more than I'd ever needed before. Turned out one of them was cracked right down the middle, so I was officially down to two.

"You too," I said. "You don't have any clothes, do you?"

"Some blue jeans and a t-shirt in the trunk of my car for

emergencies," she said. "How scandalous would it be for you to buy some?"

I stared at her. She shrugged. My robe threatened to slide off her left shoulder, and I wondered if I ought to jump in and rescue it.

"Pretty scandalous," I said.

"Okay. How scandalous would it be for me to walk out of here wearing your bathrobe?" she asked.

"I'll go get your jeans," I said.

She looked good in jeans. This was not a surprise, but it had an impact all the same. The t-shirt fit tightly, but it had definitely seen better days.

"First order of business," Meg said. "Shopping. Nobody's going to take me seriously in a ten-year-old Steppenwolf concert shirt."

And being taken seriously, I thought, was high on Meg's list of requirements.

"I thought your cash was gone."

"My ID, my cash, everything but my hideout credit cards," she said, and opened up a plastic baggie that she'd pulled out of the wheel well of the trunk. "American Express and Visa."

"Where are you going?"

She smiled briefly. "Where are you taking me, Deputy Dan?"

"You're out of luck, our local Macy's is closed today. Guess you're stuck with either Estelle's Fine Clothing or Madie's Fashion Barn."

Her smile lost a little luster. "That's my choice?"

"In a town without even a Wal-Mart, you're lucky you get a choice. Farlene shops at Estelle's, so if I were you I'd give Madie's a try. You never know."

"I'm not big on appliqués and cow prints."

"Suit yourself," I shrugged. "You can always take the Lexus and go shopping in Dallas."

We walked out together into metallic morning sunshine, the sky a flat silver, the sun watered gold. The significance of the police cruiser sitting in the parking lot didn't immediately dawn on me until I remembered we'd driven Meg's Lexus here, not my patrol car.

Jimmy Sparkman was asleep in the front seat. He looked exhausted, ragged from a night's growth of pale beard, still grimy behind the ears from the fire. I tapped on the window and he opened bloodshot eyes and focused slowly on my face.

He rolled down the glass. The interior smelled of old smoke and the ghost of last night's stale coffee.

"Go home," I said.

"What time is it?"

"Bedtime, Jimmy. Jesus, Kitty's going to skin you alive and make a pair of shoes out of you. You've been out here all night?"

"Yeah." He scrubbed a hand over his face, washing away weariness. "Guess so. Ain't like this place would burn very easily, but you can't be too careful. Morning, Meg."

"Jimmy," she said quietly. "I didn't get to thank you last night."

"It's my job."

"Maybe." She hesitated. "Been a long time."

"Yeah. A lifetime." He looked at her, then quickly away, as if she hurt his eyes. "You've been doing all right, looks like."

"You too."

The silence got long and awkward. Jimmy finally picked up a giant cup of coffee that had to be long since expired and took a sip. He dumped the rest of it out, politely avoiding my shoes.

"You're leaving this morning?" he asked Meg.

"I'll think about it."

"This isn't some schoolyard hassle, Meg. These people are serious. There's only so much we can do to keep you out of harm's way."

"I don't expect anybody to throw themselves on grenades," she said, and I had the feeling she was talking to me, though she never let her eyes leave Jimmy's face. "My problem, Jimmy. It's been my problem a long time, and leaving town doesn't solve it. I get letters, sometimes two a month. Judgment is coming, you'll burn in hell, that kind of thing. They've got a long reach."

"Mailing a letter's a far cry from being able to stick a knife into you. You're making it too damn easy."

"I'm tired of hiding. And I'm not leaving town until I find Aurelia Galvan."

There, said and witnessed. Jimmy looked pained, as if she'd slugged him in the gut, and shook his head. He looked at me. I didn't have anything much to add.

"Hope you like Dan, then," he said. "Dan's not leaving your side until this is over."

She still didn't look my way, but a shadow of a smile crossed her lips. "I like Dan just fine."

We watched him drive slowly out of the parking lot, a tired and burdened man.

"Why'd you leave Houston?" Meg asked me.

"Because he asked," I said. "Because he asked."

The only good thing about Madie's Fashion Barn was that it was next door to, and accessible through, Madie's Uptown Coffee Shop. This was Madie's version of

Starbucks, without the high quality coffee or the smiling service. She made up for it with overly cute country décor—ducks in calico hats a specialty—and inflated prices. I bought a cup of hazelnut coffee, no milk or sugar, and parked myself comfortably at a table. I'm no expert, but the dresses hanging in the front racks of the Fashion Barn didn't look like they would flatter my fat aunt Lena, much less Meg Leary. As Meg had predicted, there was a high percentage of cute appliqués and calico.

I moved the carved, wooden hat-wearing duck off of my table, leaned back in my chair, and sipped Madie's hazelnut coffee. It was barely passable. Madie herself, a sturdy smallish woman with a perpetual frown, left me to amuse myself and went off with Meg to tour the rag racks.

I got on the radio and asked for an update on the investigation of Meg's house fire.

"Arson," Farlene told me crisply. "Person or persons unknown. Now, Dan, you're not taking on any trouble, are you?"

"Nothing I can't handle," I said. "Pull the Aurelia Galvan file for me and copy it, will you? I want to take a copy with me today."

"Darlin', I'm going home. Me and mean ol' Lester are having ourselves a picnic out at Killing Rock. I'll leave it with Joetta."

"You enjoy yourself."

"Well, I would, but I said it's with mean ol' Lester," she said. Lester was her husband. He was indeed mean and said to be old. He was also rumored to be really, really rich, though he and Farlene lived in a heavily fenced house outside of town and their one and only car was at least twelve years old. "Y'all be careful."

"Y'all be good," I said. I clipped the radio back to my

shoulder tab and opened a copy of *USA Today*, the closest thing Exile had to a local paper these days.

Ten minutes later, while I was in the middle of learning about pirates in the Philippines, Meg said, "I'm done."

I looked up. She was still wearing the hip-hugging jeans and Steppenwolf t-shirt. And an expression that could have broken glass at fifty feet.

"I'm sorry," Madie said. She wasn't, obviously. Her tone was just barely short of insulting. "Credit card machine's broken."

"Imagine that," Meg almost purred. I had a mouthful of faux hazelnut coffee; I spit it back out and shoved the cup away.

"You find what you needed?" I asked. She nodded. "How much?"

"About three hundred for everything."

Which was more than Madie was likely to make in Exile in a week, and we all knew it. Madie's face had gone blotchy with stress. I stood up and walked over, looked down at her, and said, "So which is it, Madie, you don't want the money or you don't want to sell to Megan Leary?"

She shot a murderous glare at Meg. I took out my wallet and handed her my credit card.

"See if that machine's working now, Madie," I said. "I'll bet you it is."

"You're new here," Madie said. She clutched my credit card in both hands, her knuckles white. "You ought to know a little bit more before you decide I'm the bad one here."

"Honey, I'm just judging by your coffee," I said. "Ring it up or I'll call Jimmy Sparkman and we'll have to take a look at how you run your business around here."

We left with purchases. Meg used the restroom at Carl's

Fina Station to change—brave woman—and came out wearing an outfit I couldn't believe could have been hanging in Madie's store. Sleek black pants that hugged her like a lover; a silvery raw silk shirt buttoned close, wide-collared; a butter-soft black leather jacket. New shoes. Meg slid into the car, fastened her seatbelt, and caught me staring. She raised an eyebrow.

"Not bad," I said. "Not an appliqué in sight."

"Thanks," she said. "I owe you."

"So you do." I pulled out of the Fina station. "If we can't get a warrant for Javier's place, we need to find out something about his friends, his habits, where he hangs out. I've got Farlene making a copy of the case file for me, I just need to swing by the station and pick it up."

She nodded, shoved silky hair back from her face, and turned to look out the window.

"You look good," I said. I saw the reflection of her smile.

"Just drive."

It was one of those quiet drives, a mutual cease-fire that turned out to be comfortable. A couple of times it seemed she might say something, but she'd just sucked in a breath, let it out again, and turned to look out at the town. Thinking about Madie refusing her credit cards, maybe. Or the smoking ruins of her mother's house. Or the deep scratches in the paint of her Lexus.

They'll do worse, I thought. I didn't say it out loud, because I didn't want to believe it.

"Wait," I told her as I got out of the car. She turned to look at me, a quick snap of her head with a little too much force behind it. Her eyes had gone opaque again.

"Dan . . ."

I waited, hanging on the doorframe, looking at her. It was a nice fresh morning, cold tingling on my skin. She'd probably need a heavier coat if a storm moved in. I wondered if I'd stretched my card to its breaking point, or if I could squeeze one more extravagance out of it.

She said, in a very soft, precise tone, "Don't think this helpful rube act has me fooled. Sparkman wants you to keep me muffled. I get the program."

She wasn't wrong, but the tone was. I hadn't said anything, hadn't done anything, and she was already finding reasons not to trust me. Had to be some sort of Olympic record.

"Just wait," I said. "You can shoot me when I get back with the file."

She didn't smile. I shut the door and jogged up the old steps into the maroon brick castle, up the twisting turret stairs to the office.

Peyser was sitting at my desk. He had his feet up on my file folders, squeezing one of those bald-headed ugly dolls whose eyes pop from pressure. I was suddenly very glad I'd left Meg downstairs in the Lexus. If the sight of Peyser made me boil, it might have made her explode. I still remembered her flying at him, smoke-stained and tear-streaked, on the lawn of her burning house. Speaking of which, he looked well-rested, the asshole.

He grinned at me, showing straight but yellowed teeth. Peyser was a tobacco chewer. "Dan," he greeted me. "Get any sleep last night?"

I ignored him. The dispatcher—not Farlene, but a mousy young girl by the name of Joetta Grayson—gave us both a wide-eyed nervous look and bent over her magazine, studying it like there might be a test later. Joetta was hunting another job. I hoped she found one soon—eighteen was too young to be putting up with Pit Bull. I'd caught him hanging around her desk too much, and I hoped she'd have the sense to tell Jimmy if she got too nervous about it. Probably not, though. Not at eighteen. It would be too easy for Pit Bull to scare her into something, if he hadn't already, by the look on her face.

"It was a long one," I said. "Want to take your feet off my papers?"

He raised his eyebrows and didn't move. I felt my heart speed up. It was a good feeling, blood pumping, muscles getting warm. But this wasn't the time, and it damn sure wasn't the place. Let him have the goddamn desk. All I had in it was a pack of gum and a broken pair of Ray Bans.

But this wasn't about the desk, and we both knew it.

"Joetta, Farlene said she'd leave me a copy of the Galvan file," I said. Joetta nodded and dug through a stack of envelopes. She handed one over. "Thanks."

I hadn't told Meg, but I had another file I wanted to pull. I studied the file drawers, but as I read the tags I realized that this wasn't going to be as easy as I'd figured. Farlene was computerizing. Half the folders were out of the drawers, scattered in no particular order around the room. The other half probably weren't in any better shape. Still, I yanked open the drawer and started thumbing through 1982.

"Sure I can't help you, there, partner?" Peyser asked. He tossed his squeeze-doll up toward the ceiling, caught it on the way down and choked the breath out of it with a squeak. "Don't know about you, but Farlene's got the place so screwed up I can't find my dick unless it's been bar-coded. Tell me what you're looking for and I'll see what I can dig up."

I kept flipping. Domestic disputes . . . burglaries . . . assault with a deadly . . .

"Unless you're looking for the file on Megan Leary," he said.

I stopped flipping.

"That one's gone missing," he said. The doll went squeak-squeak-squeak as he pumped it. "I already looked. She looked sweet back then, you know. Legs like a goddamn Rockette, ass like a wet dream—she was humping half the football team at fifteen."

There was no reason for it to piss me off. I wasn't Meg Leary's keeper; I wasn't some Southern gentleman defending her questionable honor. If he wanted to jack off about Meg, let him. He would have been in the half of the football team she didn't hump.

Besides, I believed him. He hadn't found the file. If he had, he wouldn't have bothered to tell me it was missing, he just would have made some phony show of amazement and bumbled around like a clown. This was his way of finding out if I was the one who had it.

I opened the drawer marked 1983.

"So, she still as good as she was?" he asked. I heard Joetta give a little gasp, and glanced over to see her head sink even lower. Trying to be part of the furniture. The room was dead empty other than the three of us—probably a couple of deputies on patrol, but nobody else was due in today. Nice, quiet place.

No witnesses.

I flipped through the "L" section looking for Leary.

"She sucks like a Hoover now, so I'm told," Peyser continued. "Deep throats like a pro. She was just an amateur when she polished my knob for me."

I marked my place in the folders and turned to face him.

"You know, if you want to get your ass kicked, all you

have to do is ask," I said. "This schoolboy bullshit's making me tired."

He got up and came for me, boots knocking on wood, leather belt creaking and jingling. Joetta shrieked and put her magazine over her head.

Just before he got to me, I pointed over his head. Calculated risk—he might have ignored it and popped me one, anyway—but it worked; he looked to where I was pointing.

To where the surveillance camera recorded everything that happened in the main bullpen area.

"Smile pretty," I said. "You throw the first punch, you know which one of us is on the street. Especially with Joetta here to tell what she heard. Now, Buford, you want to keep going with this little show, or you want to call your mommy to come get you?"

He looked at me again, and I was surprised—and a little spooked—by the smoking depth of hate in his eyes. He wanted to kill me. My life was hanging on something as small as that camera in the corner of the room, and my reaction time, because we were both carrying guns.

The feeling sweeping through me turned black and red and knotted up with dark glee. Go ahead, I thought. Jesus, please, do it.

Peyser bared his teeth in what looked more like an attempt to bite my neck out than a smile, put his hand on my shoulder and squeezed hard enough to make bone pop. He and his squeeze doll had been having quite a workout.

"Be seeing you," he said.

I was sure of it. He walked out, past the still-cringing Joetta, slammed the door behind him.

She slowly took the magazine off and lifted her head, looking for all the world like a turtle testing the air.

"Wow," she said softly. "Mr. Fox? He was about to kick your—"

She blushed. I remembered being that age. I probably wouldn't have said it either to somebody twice as old with a badge.

"—hiney," she finished lamely. "I never saw anybody make Peyser walk away before."

"We're just rescheduling, darlin'. Butt-kicking will follow." Knowing Peyser, it would probably happen in a nice dark deserted place with a bunch of his drunken buddies for company. Fair fights were not his style. "Sorry you had to hear that."

"No—no problem." She licked pale lips and looked down at the file folders piled on the corners of her desk. "Um—Deputy?"

"Yeah?" Peyser had left his squeeze-doll on my desk. I drop-kicked it into his trash can, where it splashed into a shallow pool of tobacco juice.

"I think if you look in that envelope I gave you there are two files in there."

So there were. The Galvan file, and a file labeled DORIS LEARY. Joetta was nowhere near as silly as she appeared. She'd had it all the time, probably knew Peyser was looking for it through all those stacks and file drawers. I took it and met her eyes. Clear gray eyes, half-hidden by tortoiseshell glasses. When she got her braces off, a haircut, and a makeover, the girl was going to be a man-eater.

She blushed and looked away.

"Thank you," I said. "But you never saw it."

"You bet," she nodded. "Be—be careful."

I was feeling pretty damn smug right then, until it occurred to me that I'd left Meg in the car, and Peyser had gone downstairs. I couldn't have mixed a deadlier combination with fertilizer and gasoline.

By the time I slammed through the doors out onto the courthouse steps, the cracked parking lot was empty except for a cold, cold breeze blowing through it.

The Lexus was gone. Meg had gone with it.

Chapter Six

I walked back to the Wandora to find my cruiser still waiting patiently in the parking lot, a little the worse for a couple of beer bottles broken on it and, from the smell, a nice coating of urine from the drunks. Nothing a car wash couldn't fix. I'd had worse in Houston; hardly a day had gone by without some minor, malicious damage to the vehicle. Key scrapings were not even worth a yawn. Broken windows happened weekly. If in Exile the worst they could do was a couple of bottles and some piss, they really were bush league.

I wondered what had happened out in the courthouse parking lot. Meg had been sitting in the passenger side. She'd seen Peyser come down the steps—

¾and scooted to the driver's side, gunned it and run? Didn't sound like her. But if they'd gotten into it they'd have still been fighting when I came out. Peyser's cruiser was gone, too. Had he followed her?

I invested almost an hour in circling town, driving past Rosa Galvan's house, past the still-smoking ruins of Meg's childhood home, past every other place she might have been drawn to, including the cemetery and the Wandora. Nothing. Maybe she'd taken the three-hundred-dollar wardrobe and taken to the highway.

I absently stared into the distance, watching cars. No Lexus, but a shiny red truck that looked too good for Exile. A beat-up black car with bondo patches on the quarter panels. A pickup truck held together by faded green paint and rust.

Like hell Meg had left town. Meg didn't run.

I keyed the radio and got Joetta. "Peyser reported his twenty?"

"No sir," she said immediately. "I've been trying to raise him. Got a burglar alarm out on Maple Street. You want it?"

"Better give it to somebody else."

"Well . . ." She said it in that panicked way that let me know there wasn't anybody else. At least nobody answering.

I sighed. "Give me the address."

She read it to me, and I placed it as residential, out in the more expensive section of town. Unusual. People over there didn't get burglarized a lot, simply because it was too damn much trouble. Still, there was always the entrepreneur with a crowbar and a car.

Then again, Meg was in town, and I was willing to play the odds on her and trouble occupying the same time and space.

I pulled out my cell phone and dialed Jimmy Sparkman's house.

"Hello?" Kitty's smooth voice, honeyed with Southern hospitality.

"Kitty, I need to talk to Jimmy."

"Oh, it's you." The honey curdled into jellied poison. "He's sleeping."

"I know he is, but I need him. Please." Kitty and I went so far back we measured it in decades. In college, she'd been a conniving Home Economics major who could chug jocks under the table, and had a habit of deep-throating pickles to prove her homemaking abilities . . . and she'd zeroed in on Jimmy Sparkman like a heat-seeking missile.

That wasn't the trouble. The trouble between me and Kitty stemmed from two things: one, I'd never liked her, and two, I'd turned her down four months ago when she wanted to put me on her afternoon motel happy-hour schedule. I hadn't told Jimmy. She was still wondering when I would.

"You want to tell me where he was all night?" she asked sharply. I started my car, turned on the red flashers but not the siren.

"That's between you and him, Kitty. But if you're thinking about throwing around words like infidelity, you might want to think twice. Now, you going to let me talk to him?"

There was a loud click, and for a second I thought she'd hung up on me, but then Jimmy picked it up. "Dan?" His voice was blurred with sleep. "What's the trouble?"

"Who lives at 671 Maple?"

A second's pause before he said, "What's happening?"

"Burglar alarm, and I can't find Meg or Peyser. I just had a hunch it might be connected."

"It's Joe Hillyard's house. You don't know him, but he used to be—" Jimmy hesitated. His voice sharpened. "He used to be a big cheese around here. Was sheriff for a while."

"Back in the eighties?"

Silence. Silence was expensive on a cell phone. I started to remind him of it when he said, "Better get over there and see what's up."

"On my way," I said, and hung up.

It was a short jaunt across town to tree-lined streets, graciously declining houses. A fair number of them had leaning, sun-faded FOR SALE signs pounded into their browning grass. You could always pick out the yards with sprinkler systems; they looked odd and alien, surreally green even this late in the year. Rainbows glimmered on mist as I drove past one, and I thought about the eaves of Meg's neighbor's house, dripping rain from an empty sky.

It took a lot of time and energy to hate someone that much. And I still really didn't know who her faceless enemies were. Couldn't be everybody in town—people just weren't that self-motivated. No, there had to be ringleaders. People will do a lot of things in mobs they would never do alone, so maybe there were several ringleaders, lots of followers. Not the whole town, but even five or ten people would be enough to get the ball rolling.

Arson, harassment . . . no telling what was coming next.

I turned on Maple and cruised slowly, looking at numbers. I didn't really need to, because Peyser's cruiser was parked blocking the road, flashers on, and the house on the left side of the street had its door standing open. I braked and keyed the radio.

"Joetta?"

"Right here, Dan."

"Peyser still hasn't reported in?"

"Not a word," she said.

"He's at 671 Maple," I told her, and turned the wheel toward the curb. "I'm going in to take a look."

Farlene would have called another car to back me up, but I wasn't at all sure what Joetta would do. I unlocked the shotgun from the rack behind me. Nothing like a shotgun to put the fear of God in people—including Pit Bull, if he needed it. It made a truly horrifying sound when you pumped it.

The Hillyard house had a pre-fab ranch-style charm, with brick facing and neatly painted trim. The former sheriff was one of those sprinkler fanatics. The lawn was an emerald carpet just now starting to look winter-stripped. A monster big oak tree, at least a hundred years old, reared over the house. In the summer, it would have put the roof squarely in shade; now, the big bare branches rattled like bones in the wind.

There was nobody moving in the doorway. I walked up to it and came straight in, no hesitation; silhouetting myself in the doorway had been beaten out of me as a rookie. The entry hall was dim and muffled, at least ten degrees too hot for comfort. Nobody home.

I smelled a sharp, acidic odor of decay. Sweat broke out on my back, down my chest. I held the shotgun ready, walked to the end of the hall, and eased myself around the door into the kitchen.

Where Lew Peyser bent over a man lying dead on the parquet floor. He looked up at me as I came in, and I could see he was honestly surprised to see me. And a little grateful, maybe.

"He's dead," he blurted. I knew that. When there was that much blood and that little skull, it was self-evident. "No pulse."

"Who is it?" I stared down at the corpse—a soft-featured man in his fifties, with small clouded blue eyes. The eyes bothered me. The right pupil was huge, the left a pinpoint. Something to do with the gunshot wound to the head, I figured. He was wearing blue jeans, a plaid work shirt, and a belt with a buckle large enough to serve a roast. And scuffed work boots. He died with his boots on. I had to bite my tongue to keep from saying so.

"Joe Hillyard." Peyser's voice was none too steady. "Lord a mercy, there's gonna be a shitstorm over this. I can't believe he's dead."

From his expression, Joe Hillyard couldn't believe it, either. No weapon in his hands—they were upturned, the fingers loose and clean. No defense of any kind. Lot of times people tried to throw up a hand at the last minute if they saw it coming, but Hillyard had gone down meek. Which was odd, considering that on the other side of the pass-through bar, in the living room, he had half the National Guard Armory displayed on fancy pegs and shelves—assault rifles, shotguns, pistols, derringers. Made me wonder what he kept in the large camo-green gun safe. I carefully lifted his hand. The whole arm lifted as one, stiff with rigor. Blood had settled, too. The back of his hand was purplish from pooling.

"No Mrs. Hillyard?" I asked, but I already knew there wasn't. Women didn't have houses like this. If they had to put up with the gun collection, they'd strike back in little ways—brighter colored furniture, maybe, or flower arrangements, or plants. They'd make themselves felt, even the most timid of them, especially in the kitchen. Joe Hillyard's kitchen was strictly there to store his food.

"Sarah left town fifteen years back," Peyser said. "After—"

He shut up so quick I heard his teeth snap together. I waited, but he had realized his mistake and turned away. His shoulders were shaking. I realized with some amazement he was fighting off tears.

"Hillyard a friend?" I asked, a lot more gently. Peyser didn't turn around.

"That man was—" Peyser didn't have the vocabulary. "He took care of me after my daddy died."

"I'm sorry." I meant it, even though Peyser and I hadn't exactly built rapport. "Head wound like that, he probably went quick."

Even that was a bit of a lie, because there was too much blood. His heart had pumped a while, but he probably hadn't known it—hadn't known anything from the sun-bright muzzle flash on. Memory came over me like a thick, suffocating blanket, and I had to stand very still and close my eyes and wait for it to go away. Jesus, don't think. Don't think about that.

By the time I'd managed to breathe through it, bring myself back to Joe Hillyard's stifling place of death, Peyser was reaching for the phone.

"Fingerprints," I said quietly. He stopped in mid-gesture. "Use the radio in your cruiser."

He nodded and edged past me out down the hallway. I squatted down and looked closely at Joe Hillyard. Nothing to see—there was a powder burn around the wound, so the killer had been kissing-close. Took either guts or panic or utter emptiness to do that. I let my eyes unfocus and roam the room, and my attention caught and held on a rough patch in the dark wood paneling. I stepped around the corpse and went to look at it.

Somebody had dug something small out of the wall at just about chest-level. The edges were still raw with splinters. I straightened up again, looked at where Hillyard was lying, imagined the place he would have been standing up. The angle of the bullet.

It was clear what had been removed from the wall. The question was why.

I had started to think about questions to ask, places to start, when I realized that I wouldn't be working on the murder of Joe Hillyard. I wasn't a detective. I was a glorified night watchman waiting for cars to bust the speed limit out on Highway 140.

I looked down into Joe's eyes—one pupil tiny, one huge—and said, "I hope like hell you deserved it."

I went outside to wait for Jimmy Sparkman to tell us what to do.

★ ★ ★ ★ ★

It took a good four hours to secure the crime scene, take photographs and video, and remove the body to the local morgue, which was also the local mortuary—the Texas Rangers would be sending their area investigator over to have a look, according to Jimmy. The Rangers tended to get flustered when law enforcement—even ex-law enforcement—was gunned down. I watched the proceedings with interest, making suggestions here and there when it looked like small-town good manners might be getting in the way of proper police procedure; Peyser sat, shell-shocked, in the cruiser and made calls, letting all of his buddies know, I supposed. Maybe it was my personal prejudice against Pit Bull, but I didn't like the look on his face. Small-town justice had a mean and ugly reputation, and it had it for a reason. If Peyser suspected who'd done it, Hillyard wasn't likely to be the last casualty.

I definitely did not care for the fact that Meg was nowhere to be seen or, apparently, found.

Sparkman arrived to take charge of the scene, bleary-eyed and freshly showered and shaved. I was taking a statement from the sixth of Joe Hillyard's next-door neighbors, who hadn't seen anything, heard anything, or suspected anything. Or anyone. Everybody liked Joe. Hell, even Peyser liked Joe.

Which made me wonder, given small-town politics, why he was ex-Sheriff Hillyard while he was still of this world. He was the kind of man who was likely to die in the saddle.

"Dan." Jimmy tapped me on the shoulder and jerked his head. I followed him out to a quiet space on the sidewalk, just past the fluttering come-and-stare police tape. The wind had kicked up again, and it sighed through the lacework of branches overhead. Jimmy shoved his hands in his coat pockets and turned to look at me. The tan cowboy hat he was wearing threw his face into shadow, turned his eyes dark and secretive.

"Sorry, Chief. Peyser was bound to screw this up if I left him alone."

"No, you did right," Jimmy nodded.

"Mind if I ask a question about Joe Hillyard?" I asked. The morgue wagon had come and gone, but it seemed like every time I closed my eyes I could see Hillyard's uneven pupils staring back at me. Taken without a fight. That bothered me.

I had expected an automatic "yes," but Jimmy kept looking at me. Silent. His breath steamed a little in the cold breeze, and behind him the sky was that famous, cloudless Texas blue, and it went on forever. A cold turquoise sky, almost the color of Joe Hillyard's eyes.

"He was sheriff when Meg was arrested," he said. "You know about the lawsuit?"

"I heard."

"He was accused of cleaning it up. When it didn't clean up well enough, he was voted out of office. The town wanted it to go away. He—he wanted to see justice done, if there was any justice at all."

"I thought somebody confessed."

"Darrin Peyser," Jimmy nodded. He was looking away, but he knew I was following every word. "Lew's father. Darrin admitted he'd had sex with her, claimed it was consensual. Jury didn't believe any of it. Meg's suit won her nearly the entire net worth of this town."

Lew Peyser's father. That explained a few things.

"You think Peyser was the scapegoat?" I asked. Jimmy let his breath out in a long white cloud.

"How the hell would I know, Dan? He confessed. He did

some time—not much. Six months after he got out of jail, he blew his head off with a shotgun. That's what I know."

"Joe Hillyard have anything to do with it?"

"Ask Meg when you see her. And tell her he's dead."

"Why?"

"Because I want to know what she has to say about it."

I didn't find Meg, in the end. She found me.

My cell phone rang as I cruised past Hermann's House of Burgers, thinking briefly of lunch; it had been so long since I'd gotten even a wrong number that I'd forgotten what the warbling sound was for. I fumbled for the phone and switched it on.

"Dan the man," Meg said. "You're hard to find, for a guy in a car with flashing lights."

"Where the hell have you been?"

"Here and there. Talking to people. I found out something about Javier and his happy little friends. Meet me?"

"Sure." And when I got there, I was going to handcuff myself to her. "Lunch?"

She made a humming sound of agreement that was sexier than I'm sure she meant it to be.

"Meet me at the Dairy Queen," I said.

Chapter Seven

We ended up at a chipped red Formica table in the Dairy Queen, and I ordered pairs of Beltbusters and onion rings and cherry Cokes. Meg took the Oakleys off and laid them aside as I put the food down between us. Without the shades, her eyes were cold enough to freeze lava.

"Gee, Beaver," she said, "are you going to give me your letter jacket too?"

"Bite me, Leary."

"Tempting."

I wasn't quite sure what that meant. She reached for the onion rings and nibbled. I put down the envelope holding the two folders between us on the table. I slid the contents out and picked the one I wanted.

A plain manila folder, edges fuzzed with time and hard use, with the name LEARY, DORIS on it, followed by the file number.

Meg froze, then transferred her stare to me. "Not funny," she said.

"Not meant to be. Look, I know we're looking for Aurelia, but let's at least talk about this other thing, too. If you didn't do it, there's got to be some holes in the story. We just need to find them."

She nodded, but she wasn't looking at me, she was looking at that folder as if it was a black pit into the center of the earth. I took a bite of hamburger—the best food in town, real beef, crunchy lettuce, crisp juicy tomatoes—and flipped open the cover.

The succulent mouthful of burger turned to sawdust as I saw the photograph of what had been done to Doris Leary.

It was a color crime scene photo, overexposed. She lay on her back, her arms flung out to the sides, hands upturned and fingers curled as if she was holding something fragile. The dress she was wearing had once been pale blue, but from her neck to her waist it was rust-red, and the splatter continued up to her face. There were blood drops at the corners of her eyes, as if she'd cried them. Her eyes were open and pinpoint-blank, and they were dark brown, not the color of Meg's at all.

Her rib cage had been shattered by the force of the shotgun blast, shredded into meat and bone. I remembered Meg saying I didn't know she was dead until I put my hand in her. She'd tripped over this in the dark, come face to face with her mother's ghost-pale face crying bloody tears.

Meg made a sound. I looked up, startled and guilty.

It took me a couple of seconds to realize that grating sound was a laugh. As I watched, she reached for the bottle of ketchup and poured out a dollop for her onion rings. She trolled another one through the ketchup and held it out to me, moist and red, onion showing pale.

"Hungry?" she asked. I didn't say anything. She shrugged and ate it. "Suit yourself."

I sat, frozen, watching her. There was something ugly in her eyes, something cold and ferocious.

"Jesus, Dan," she said. "What do you want me to do? Break down? Cry my little eyes out? Don't you think they waved it in my face when I was fifteen years old so often that I could have drawn it from memory? Don't you think I wake up every morning—"

She stopped, stopped cold, and took a deliberately slow sip of her cherry Coke.

"I know what the fuck she looked like," she said. "Turn the fucking page."

I did. The next page was the official scene report. The murder had been called in at first as an attempted murder by the postman, Alvin Eaves, who claimed Meg had fired at him when he came to the door to deliver the day's circulars and bills. The deputy—Chris Brennan—had arrived to find Meg sitting next to her mother's body clutching the shotgun in bloody hands. She'd pulled the trigger on him, too, but the chambers were empty. He'd asked her what happened. Meg's reply had been completely unintelligible, and Brennan had taken her into custody. Her father was found later dead drunk at the Wandora, where alibi placed him for at least six hours, far outside of the possible time of death.

Then things had really gone wrong. Meg's alibi folded. She'd had a fight with her mother about skipping school and drug use. Blood tests showed Meg to be a walking pharmacy, higher than a kite. At least two friends gave statements that she'd smoked PCP-laced marijuana and dropped some uppers only an hour before the estimated time of her mother's death. In short, she was screwed.

I handed the page over.

"See anything wrong with it?" I asked. She read it carefully, shook her head and handed it back. "Nothing?"

"No, it's right."

I raised my eyebrows and turned it face down. The next thing was the autopsy report—nothing surprising there. Massive trauma from the gunshot wound, cause of death aspiration of fluid into the shredded lungs. She'd drowned in her own blood. The manner of death was, of course, homicide.

I didn't offer it to Meg. She didn't reach for it. I went on to the next piece, which turned out to be a thick sheaf of statements about Meg and her relationship with her mother. Not a pretty picture. Meg had not been mama's little angel, and though from all accounts her father was a drunk, he wasn't a violent one. Meg had never racked up the hospital history to support any kind of abuse charge against either her father or her mother. A broken arm when she was ten, but consistent with a fall from a bicycle onto a curb. Meg's character references painted her as wild, rebellious, angry, bright, and dangerous.

Nothing I could disagree with. Meg passed on those as well.

Powder tests conducted at the jail showed that Meg had fired the shotgun. No surprise; she'd admitted to taking aim at the postman. Her mother's blood was all over her. She had motive, means, and opportunity.

I looked up at Meg. She took a bite of her hamburger, but I didn't believe she tasted it any more than I did mine. The greasy smell of the frying meat clung to the back of my throat like a coat of plastic wrap.

"Well?" she asked.

"Shit, I can't believe they acquitted you."

"You're a lot of help."

"Seriously." I flipped pages, finding more and nothing that helped. "It was just your word against all this?"

"Not exactly." Meg reached over and flipped pages in the file, dragged one out for my review. "There's my father's confession."

My wife and I fought about money. She called me a worthless drunk and told me she was leaving me. I grabbed the shotgun and it went off. I dropped it and went out to drink more. I wanted to forget.

It went on and on, but the rest was just rambling. "He was alibied," I said.

"Yeah, a bunch of constant drunks and congenital liars. Truth is, they don't know what they remember." Meg's eyes had gone dark and focused. "He confessed during the sixteenth day of my trial—they tried me as an adult, you know. He didn't even try to put up a defense, he just pled guilty. They gave him twenty-five years."

"He told you it was a lie?"

"He didn't have to." Meg pulled the file closer and looked through the yellowing paper. "My father was a drunk, but he wasn't a killer. And he and my mother never fought. She loved him. She supported him. She would have done anything for him, and she'd never have left him. In a lot of ways, he was the kindest man I've ever known. And the saddest."

I noticed a signature on the report I was holding, and said, "Joe Hillyard's dead."

She went still, very still. Her eyes closed, then opened. Still shiny-bright. "Really."

"Bullet in the head," I said. "Close range. Probably sometime yesterday afternoon, judging by the rigor."

She didn't give me any comment. She didn't give me anything at all.

"I know he was sheriff at the time your mother died," I said. "I know he was in charge of the jail when you—were in there. How'd you feel about him?"

"How'd I feel?" she asked, amazed. Her face distorted, just for a second, as if something moved underneath. "Oh, I loved him, Dan. Wouldn't you?"

A picture slid out of the folder. I rescued it from a near-collision with Meg's ketchup and found myself holding a mug shot of a fifteen-year-old girl with deep haunted eyes and long straight hair, a girl who had been Megan Leary, all those years ago. Alone and scared and friendless in a town that still blamed her.

I couldn't shake the feeling that it was all excessive, somehow. Maybe she had, at fifteen, killed her mother. Forced her father to take the rap and die in prison. But small towns had tragedies, and scandals, and people forgot, by and large. Memories weren't that long.

But then she'd done the unforgivable. She'd taken away their illusions of superiority. And three million dollars of money in a town already going broke.

Across from us a table full of housewives out for a girls' lunch stared and whispered among themselves. She had been one of them, and they'd turned their backs on her so completely they'd let her house burn to the ground without a word, without a qualm.

"Jesus, Meg, what did you do to this town?" I said it out loud, still watching the women across the aisle. Meg shuffled papers back together into the file and slammed the cover shut.

"I killed it, too," she said. "Let's find Aurelia."

We left the Lexus in the DQ parking lot to collect a fresh set of tool marks and took the cruiser back to the west side of town.

"So what did you get on Javier?" I asked. Meg was reading through the Galvan case file.

"He's a mean little son of a bitch, put a previous girl-friend in the hospital, and is probably the point man for most of the serious drug dealing in town."

I blinked. "How the hell did you find that out?"

"I asked," she said smugly. "Some things in this town you have to grow up with, Deputy Dan. Pammy Howard's not the only loose-tongued gossip in the world."

"So who'd you talk to?"

"Father Guillermo, over at Lady of Peace—he's been here a long time, since before my time. And Dolores Sanchez."

Dolores Sanchez ran the Drive-N-Stop, a cut-rate convenience store that sold gas and cigarettes and tamales made the old-fashioned way, from meat skimmed from boiled pig heads. She carried Mexican soft drinks and sold molé sauce in burp-and-seal containers; she was seventy if she was a day, and she knew everything about everybody on the west side of town. She probably could have known about the east side, too, if she'd cared to, but Dolores was a specialist.

And I should have known to ask her.

"Anything else she can tell us about Javier?" I asked. Meg smiled.

"Sure. I didn't want to make you feel bad. Besides, I need a bathroom."

In five minutes, we were parking in the empty lot at the Drive-N-Stop.

"Hola, Danny!"

Dolores greeted me as the cheap bell chimed over my head and I stepped into the dim barely-clean store, with Megan Leary just a step behind. Dolores shuffled out from behind the chipped green counter. She always wore the same kind of traditional shapeless Mexican dress; this one was magenta, with yellow and blue birds embroidered around the neck and hem. She wore battered pink house shoes to match. "New pralines for you, fresh. Just wrapped today!"

She knew I had a weakness for sweet brown-sugar pralines, the kind that melted into granular richness on the tongue. I reached into the display piled on the counter and picked up two, passed her a dollar, and her bright eyes flicked past me to take in Megan Leary in her sleek black outfit and blue sunglasses.

"Ay," she said. "The company you keep. That one, she's nothing but trouble."

"Be nice, Mamá."

"I am being nice," Dolores said. "I just heard they burned your house last night. I'm sorry."

"De nada. That house died a long time ago." Meg saw me staring at her. "Mamá Dolores used to take care of me and Rosa Galvan when we cut school."

"Bad girls, the both of you," Dolores said, but not without affection. "Rosa, she got married, had her children—but not you, pequiña."

"I'm not the motherly type."

Dolores sighed and didn't dispute it. "So. You met our new gringo."

"He's definitely a gringo," Meg agreed. "What else can you tell me about him?"

Dolores' black eyes focused on me, wicked and full of laughter. "He's all right. He needs a woman."

"Does he?" Meg's smile was edgy enough to shave steel. "Well, I know what I need. I need your bathroom, Dolores."

"In the back."

As Meg disappeared down an aisle thick with pastries and potato chips, I said, "Meg tells me you know a few things about Javier Nieves."

Her face smoothed out, all of its laugh lines disappearing. She looked at me for a moment, then went back behind the counter and rang up my dollar purchase on her old register. I waited. I'd taken the opportunity to scan the store; nobody was shopping the beer cooler or the pork rinds. The aisles were deserted.

"What do you know about the gangs?" she asked.

"Is Javier in a gang?" Her silence told me he was. "La Muerte? Chollos?"

"El Ojos," she said, half a whisper. It wasn't a good thing to say too loud. If Javier was involved with El Ojos, it was deadly serious business, especially at his age. They'd started in the toughest of California prisons, battling for their lives, and they were ruthless in ways that other gangs wouldn't touch. While still in Houston I'd heard about a journalist who'd done an unflattering story about the gang; they'd killed him, beaten his wife to death, raped and murdered his two daughters, and shot his six-month-old baby boy to death in his crib. When they'd caught the two nineteen-year-old killers, they'd laughed about it. Laughed all the way to death row. Were still laughing, probably.

I was putting Dolores in danger just by asking her.

"How big a presence do they have?" I asked. I had to. Dolores shrugged.

"Ten, maybe fifteen. Young kids, ay, nine or ten years old, they teach them to be like animals. The older ones, there's only five or six."

"Do you know where they hang out?"

"Anywhere they want," Dolores said. "Too many empty houses here, too many old buildings. You won't find them. Not before they find you. Let it go, Danny. Not enough policia in this town to make any difference to them. They shoot you and go on with their business."

"Aurelia Galvan," I said. I had to talk fast, because a shiny black-and-silver Impala low-rider was pulling up in the parking lot next to my cruiser. "They may have her, Dolores. She may still be alive."

Dolores looked old, suddenly, and tired. She shook her head and made the sign of the cross, kissed her fingers, and turned away to stock cigarettes.

Meg came back from the bathroom, hugged Dolores, and bought a Coke to go. As she paid for it I watched the Impala idle. Its windows were tinted to an illegally dark shade, too dark to see who was in there watching us. Dolores shoved packs of Camels into slots.

"Thanks for the pralines," I said, and handed one to Meg. "Hasta luego."

"Bona suerte," Dolores said. "You know where the old grain elevator is?"

Of course I did. Everybody did. It was ten stories tall, echoing and empty, its walls dark with spilled graffiti. I waited while she sorted out red and white packs of Marlboros.

"I only say it because I wouldn't go there if I were you," she said. "Adios."

The bell chimed us out. The Impala, I noticed, was leaving, tires crunching rock; sunlight slid cold along its black shiny flanks. It turned sideways and started slowly rolling toward the parking lot exit.

"Down!" Meg yelled, and hit me hard from behind, slammed me down on my stomach, her weight crushing me into the sharp-edged gravel, then rolling away as my ears registered the loud shattering boom of a shotgun. Pellets rattled off of brick. Glass exploded in a white spray and cascaded out over me, and I took a tip from Meg and rolled left under the cruiser. Rocks bit hard at my elbows and knees, and I tasted panic and burnt oil.

From the back window of the Impala, a black tongue of shotgun tested the air. It didn't find a second shot. The car spun tires and spit gravel on its way out of the parking lot.

I had the license number. I fumbled for a pen and inked it on my wrist. Next to me Meg was cursing steadily like a sailor, unhurt except for a livid bleeding cut along one porcelain cheek; I wriggled out from under the cruiser and ran into the store.

Dolores crouched against the cinder block wall, glass decorating her graying hair like crown jewels. I got down next to her and felt for a pulse, but she blinked and looked up at me very seriously and said, "I told you so, you meddling gringo fool."

Not a mark on her. No thanks to me.

I was shaking, a fine fast vibration like plucked wire, and I should have been scared. I wasn't. All I wanted to do was find that black Impala and all of its chickenshit bastard riders and kick their guts out. Watching her cry cranked the rage up to dangerous levels. A shadow in the doorway made me spin but it was Meg, looking pale and hard as bone. She was wearing her sunglasses again. I couldn't see her eyes.

I stood up and keyed my shoulder mike. "Joetta." My voice was way too tight. "Get somebody over here to Dolores' store, somebody took a shot at us in the parking lot. Black Impala, tinted windows." I gave her the license number.

"Dan, my God, are you okay? Dan?" Joetta sounded close to tears. Shootings were rare, and here we were with two in one day. "Should I—what should I do?"

"Get Merle over here with the paramedic truck," I said. "I don't think Dolores is hurt, but he should probably take a look at her."

"But what about you? Are you—"

"Joetta, did you hear me? Black Impala. Run the goddamn plate right now."

This time she did start to cry. I didn't care. Meg went

115

past me to Dolores, crouched next to her on the floor, and smoothed glass out of her hair. Hard to believe she could be so gentle. Maybe she'd gotten shot at so much it was just another day for her.

Sure as hell wasn't for me. I clicked the button on my radio again. "Joetta, goddamn it, whose car is it?"

"It's—it's on the hot sheet, Dan. Somebody stole it from the high school parking lot this morning—"

I shouted it this time. "Whose car?"

"Javier Nieves," she yelped, gulping air between sobs. "Please don't yell at me."

Stolen. Like hell. I clicked off and looked at Meg. She looked up at me.

"We really shouldn't do this," Meg said. "You know that. It's dangerous."

"Get in the car if you're coming," I said. "Stay or go, I really don't give a shit."

Having guns go off near me makes me feel like I need to prove something, and it's easy to let that get out of hand, especially when dealing with kids who aren't scared of badges. Insults lead to wars. Wars lead to bloodbaths. I should have been worried about that, but I wasn't.

If they wanted a real war, they'd shot at the right guy.

"Dan," Meg said. I glanced over at her, at the winter sunlight bouncing off of blue shades. "Slow down."

I looked down and saw I was doing sixty in a thirty-five. I backed off the gas and took a deep breath, shook out the tension in my shoulders. Meg looked cool and completely untouched, except for the cut on her cheek and a bright red smear of blood, like war paint, along that delicate arch of bone.

"You shouldn't do this without backup," she said.

"Backup?" I bared my teeth in a sharp smile, minus the humor. "So who else do you trust to put at your back with a gun around here?"

She hesitated, then sighed. "Jimmy."

"Jimmy's got his own troubles. He's all alone. And he's got a family, if you can call Kitty family. Besides, he's from here. He's part of this, even if he doesn't want to be. You and me, we're—"

"Idiots?" she murmured.

"Free agents."

The grain elevator squatted at the edge of town, a giant gravestone marking the death of the local farming community. Before white men had put up fences, the land had been desolate, silent and stealthy, an area not even the local Indian tribes had wanted. The original leaseholders—rattlesnakes and black widow spiders—were reasserting their claims.

Didn't matter. I would have walked into a nest of rattlers the size of a football field if the black Impala were parked at the other end. There's something great and intensely satisfying about rage. Things get very simple. I was going to the grain elevator. I was going to find the Impala, was going to shove my foot up the ass of the kid—hopefully Javier Nieves—who thought shooting a gun was the answer to his problems.

I was aware that was demented. I didn't care.

"Dan—" Meg tried to be the voice of reason, not a role she was in danger of landing. "Dan, let's back off a minute. Pull over."

"Wait, let's not." In the holster on my belt, I had a gun. It was a good gun, clean and shiny. I hardly even thought about Houston anymore when I touched it, but I thought about it now, thought about the blood that had been spat-

117

tered on the walnut grip, how warm the barrel had felt when I'd picked it up from the carpet. René thought I was crazy to keep it, but a tool is just a tool, and if a tool works you don't throw it away, do you? The gun had killed. It knew its job.

So did I.

"Dan?" Meg's voice broke through the fog. Somewhere in that thought I had let go of the wheel, and I had drawn the gun. It was a cold, alien weight in my hand. She was steering the car left-handed, and the whip-crack of nerves in her voice brought me back completely. I hit the brake and pulled the cruiser to the shoulder in a crunch-snap of gravel, a spray of dust that drifted pale red on the wind. I shut the engine off and the silence took over, the damn heavy silence like a thick suffocating blanket never more than a breath away.

I was shaking. Meg's hand touched my fingers, trying to get me to let go of the gun. Neither one of us said anything. I couldn't have explained myself, had no idea how to start. Ahead, the silent gray bulk of the grain elevator rose high into the sky, a forlorn monument to WPA and the postwar boom.

I put the gun away, took a deep breath, and said, "I'm okay."

Meg said nothing. Behind her shades, she was unreadable. But I think she knew what a lie it was, and the fact that she let me get away with it was as great a gift as I have ever received.

"If you're going to do it, let's do it," she said.

I brought the cruiser back up to speed gradually, the engine purring, then growling, as we ate up road on the way to the gray concrete mountain at the edge of town.

The chain fence around it had been broken, the lock

snapped clean. The swinging gates stood open, one rusted leaf leaning at a drunken angle. This would be the place kids brought dates in the middle of the night to scare the bejeezus out of them, the place crackheads—we had a few in town—would come to light up and dream. I pulled the cruiser in, blocking the exit, and shut off the engine. Meg pulled her gun from her shoulder holster and looked at me.

"Stay here," I said.

"Fuck you," she said mildly. "I'll be behind you."

"Thanks for the backup."

"Don't thank me, I'm using you as a human shield."

The sun glimmered bright and chilly overhead, but in the five-story shadow of the grain elevator it was already winter night, the parking lot a lunar landscape of pock-marked asphalt. Nothing to tell me anybody was home here, except the prickling at the back of my neck. I glanced over at Meg on the other side of the police car, just to make sure she was still there, and started heading for the gaping rusted door of the elevator.

From the ground to a height of seven feet on the concrete structure was a tangle of graffiti, layered so thick it was impossible to pick out anything but the most recent gang sign. The quaint seventies sentiments like Road Dogs Rule! had been buried under angrier, more elegant curlicues, like script from another world. Layers of rage and alienation in neon-bright colors. The wind shifted, and I caught a heart-skipping smell of decay. Dead dog, probably. Rotten slops. God, I hoped so.

"Dan," Meg said. She took the Oakley shades off and put them in the pocket of her jacket. "Let's live through the day, okay?"

I nodded and led her into the darkness.

Chapter Eight

It was warmer inside, and it stank. If smells had color, this one was a bitter yellow-green mix of stale human waste and ashes. A thin oblong of daylight glittered on the concrete floor. A piece of broken glass scraped under my shoe, and the echoes flew up like bats to spiral off of the smooth dark walls. The prickles on the back of my neck became knife-points. I heard fast breathing and realized it was Meg's, she was close behind me.

"Ready?" I whispered. She touched my shoulder in acknowledgement.

I switched on the flashlight, holding it out and away from my body, and braced myself for whatever might come.

The bright flare of halogen lit up blank gray concrete, made broken beer bottles sparkle like Christmas tinsel. Something that looked like a body made me focus the light on it, but it was a stained and empty sleeping bag, yellowing fluff foaming from rips. An empty bottle of Jim Beam lay unbroken next to it, and some crumpled DQ paper bags. Crack vials.

A torn blue backpack with retro flower-child emblems stitched on it. I walked over to it, bent down, and eased the flap open with a pen.

A girl's clothing, crammed in as tightly as possible. A makeup bag. A small plastic baggie full of cheap costume jewelry.

"Dan," Meg whispered. "Left."

I swung the light that way and caught a flash of reflection, like giant glowing eyes. It resolved into the chrome bumper, the headlights, the black paint shimmering like oil on water.

We'd found the Impala.

"Get out!" I shouted. I advanced on it, holding the gun ready, landed a kick on the driver's side quarter panel. "OUT, you fuckers! Right now!"

Silent as the grave. The Impala's engine still radiated heat to the palm of my hand, and those damn tinted windows gave me back nothing at all. I sucked in my breath and reached for the driver's side door. It opened at the first yank.

Inside, the car was empty. Leather seats gleamed. The steering wheel was a tiny ring of chain, polished to high gloss. An air freshener in the shape of a naked woman nodded from the rear view mirror. The car smelled of chemical flowers. In the back seat lay a shotgun, and when I bent to sniff the barrel it reeked of gunpowder.

"They're long gone," Meg said. "What've you guys got for a forensic kit around here?"

"You know those Junior G-Man kits they used to sell?"

"Yep."

"We can't afford one." I was still breathing too fast, my heart racing. My eyes kept probing shadows, but the vast echoing emptiness did too good a job of hiding them, if anybody was there. Now that my eyes had adjusted I could make out a faint edge of light at the far end around huge double doors. They'd driven in that way, probably run out the same way. Shit. I wasn't sure whether to be enraged or relieved. "I'll call it in."

I reached up for the radio on my shoulder, and paused when I heard a soft, deliberate, definite scrape out there in the shadows. Meg was standing at the edge of the flashlight's glow, unmoving. Her head turned in the direction of the noise. So did her gun. The rest of her stayed utterly still.

I clicked off the flashlight. It made us an irresistible target. Without it, though, we stood a more than decent chance of shooting each other.

"Hey, pendejo," a voice said out of the velvet dark, echoing around the chamber. He wasn't close. That was all I could tell. "This time was just practice. Next time we blow you in half."

He wanted me to switch on the light again, light myself up. He wanted us to panic.

The silence was mercilessly thick, pressing like the weight of an ocean. Don't move, I begged Meg silently. If she moved, I wouldn't know where anything was.

I forced my breaths to come slow and even, though they burned in my chest.

Somewhere out there in the dark, ten steps away or a hundred, he laughed. "Puta," he said, and I heard his foot-steps moving away. The echoes were too confusing. There was no way to get a direction on him.

When I switched on the light, it showed me graffiti-thick walls and a couple of open, dark-mouthed doorways. If he'd been there at all, if I hadn't just dreamed him up, he was long gone.

We were alone.

I heard the breath Meg let out, a long trembling sigh. She altered her rigid stance and turned her head to me.

"Next time," she said, "shoot the motherfucker."

I couldn't help the laugh that spilled out of me, wound tight and high-pitched.

She stalked out of the grain elevator and left me with the car. All in all, I didn't really blame her. I was shaking all over, on the verge of laughter turning to something much scarier. I swallowed it like a black rubber ball and followed her out into the sunlight.

Two hours later, Jimmy Sparkman leaned against the side of my cruiser and stared at nothing in particular, and said, "Yesterday I would have known who was getting shot at. Today—when you decide to make enemies, Dan, you do a bang-up job of it."

"Thanks," I said modestly. "Didn't start out that way."

"Never does, does it?" He shook his head. "Everybody's so goddamn right all the time, you ever noticed it? You're right, Peyser's right, hell, even Meg's right, God help us. Court of law said she didn't do it. Her father paid his life to give her that chance. Why the hell would she throw it all away coming back here?"

I watched the forensic team—who'd already put in what they considered a full day's work from the Hillyard crime scene, and were none too happy about doing it twice—wander around the shiny black car and ask each other questions about procedure. One of them thought he was Sherlock Holmes. He was crawling around the car scooping up microscopic clues nobody in their right mind would ever pay to have analyzed on a small-town budget. He'd probably suggest a DNA analysis of the sweat on the seats next.

"Kitty's leaving me," Jimmy said.

"Kitty says that all the time."

"She's found somebody else."

I bit my lip on the urge to tell him she'd found plenty of somebodies over the years, and tried to stick her hand down my pants on five or six occasions. As sexual oblivion went, Kitty was a world-class explorer. That was something we'd never discussed, but until this moment I'd thought he'd had at least had some idea. Damn her.

"Don't know who he is," Jimmy continued softly. He wasn't looking at me, wasn't looking at anything in particular. "Probably not a local boy. Kitty's looking to find somebody to take her shopping in Dallas and Houston."

"Jimmy—" I let all my good intentions out with the sigh. "How long have I known you? Take it from me, every single day you've been with Kitty, you've been miserable, and Jesus Christ anyway, I'm the one who got shot at, why the hell we talking about your marital problems?"

He shook himself like a dog, pushed away from the car, and said, "I can tell you who it wasn't. It wasn't Peyser. He was covered the whole time." Jimmy suddenly turned and looked at me, straight into my eyes. "You think it was the kid. Javier."

"Yeah, I think it was Javier. And I think we're going to find Aurelia Galvan out here someplace, someday—a pile of dry bones, once the scavengers get done with her. I think she's been dead since the day she disappeared. Once we show that backpack to her mother, we'll know for sure."

"I haven't had a dead body in this town for two years. Meg Leary busts in, and I have one definite and one possible in forty-eight hours. And arson. And attempted murder. God Almighty, Dan, get her the hell out of my town!"

"She didn't do anything."

"We flunked college chemistry together," he said. "But I figure we both still remember what a catalyst can do. I don't want to be in charge of cleaning up the post-Meg explosion."

Meg had been talking to one of the forensic guys, an older gent with a grizzled mustache and dirt-stained Stetson. She looked up and saw me watching her and started our way. She had a self-conscious, almost swaggering walk. Always on display, always prepared. Maybe that lesson had been drilled home to her in those perpwalks to and from the courthouse, with flashbulbs popping and people holding up nooses and placards. Every second, she could still feel those eyes on her, I imagined.

I looked away. Seemed like the only decent thing to do.

When she joined us, she stripped off her sunglasses and squinted through the haze of sun and dust.

"Jimmy," she acknowledged. He nodded back. "I think they're about done screwing up the crime scene. Nothing much I can do here now."

A spark of hope blazed up in him, and burned to ashes in me. "Leaving so soon?" he asked, not as casually as he would have liked. She smiled.

"Not exactly. I'm going to borrow your deputy for a couple of hours, if you don't mind, maybe take a ride out to see old Sam Larkin. I understand he's retired from practice. Word is Javier Nieves has done some work for him in the past."

"Sam?" Jimmy's eyebrows climbed. "Yeah, he's out at his place. You know he bought the old Miller business on Route 40."

"Kev Miller finally cash it in?"

"In manner of speaking. Got his head bashed in by a piece of falling marble," Jimmy said. "In 1988. Larkin bought it for cash from Old Lady Miller. Been running it ever since."

Meg's expression was a study in bemusement. "That's— unusual."

"Uh huh."

I felt it was time to ask. "I never heard of Larkin . . . what's the old Miller business?"

Both Meg and Jimmy grinned at me. Combined, they were blinding.

"Wait and see," she said. Jimmy snorted with laughter.

Tombstones.

Actually, the sign said MILLER MARBLE AND MONUMENT, but I didn't see a single thing in that big overgrown field that wasn't some variety of graveyard marker. No call for marble in this town for any other reason.

"Weird," Meg said softly. I pulled the car into the packed-dirt lot with a bump as we left the pavement. She was looking off to the right. That direction held statues— angels, mostly—that had probably been carved seventy years ago, from the extravagance of them. The biggest was more than six feet tall, a full avenging angel with outspread wings and upraised sword. Unlike most angels, this one was male, and the face was stern enough to strike fear a hundred feet away.

"You know this Larkin?" I asked. She nodded slowly. "Shoot."

"He worked with my mother at the hospital. Nice guy, but a little—" She hesitated and made the loopy gesture around her temple. "He always liked her. I thought maybe he'd have something to say—not so much about Javier, probably, but maybe about my mother."

"You think he knows something about how she died?"

She shrugged. We looked out the window at the gleaming forest of petrified marble angels, and I thought, what the hell? It was better than getting shot at. Loony old doctors with marble shops—it was just another day in Exile, after all.

The office—if you could call it that—was a slapped-together construction of corrugated tin and wood, with a flapping sign out front too rusted to read. There was a brand-new screen door, a Sears special that hissed like a snake as Meg pulled it open. Beyond it was another door, ancient weathered wood. It squeaked open, too, at a shove from Meg's fingers.

Air blew out freezing cold, and I heard the dry-bone rattle of the swamp cooler—another new Sears model—as the compressor started up. My eyes adjusted to the dark quickly enough to pick out a vintage Smith-Corona typewriter, a rickety desk, endless ranks of filing cabinets, and an empty wooden chair.

Somewhere off to the right a toilet flushed. Meg and I exchanged a look, hers just barely holding off a smile, and a door flew open to admit a burly old man with white cotton-wool hair. He was dressed in a worn flannel work shirt and blue jeans, and his hands and face were burned a deep tan, weathered like a piece of jerky.

"Your fly's unzipped," Meg said coolly. The old man looked at us both blankly, frozen in the act of wiping his hands on his pants. He had huge blue eyes, vacant as a doll's until he smiled.

"Damn right," he said. "Get more girls that way. Impress 'em with my huge pecker. Don't know you, do I?"

He'd been talking to Meg, but slapped the question at me like a hockey puck. I touched an imaginary hat brim.

"Daniel Fox," I said. "Might want to tuck it in, I'm with the Sheriff's Office."

His eyes went back to Meg, and for just a second the vacancy was gone, and the intelligence behind that stare was impressive.

"That so?" he asked. "Didn't think I'd ever see you jumping on that train, young 'un."

"You know who I am?" she asked. She moved a pile of old newspapers out of a rusted folding chair and perched on the edge of it, hands on her thighs.

"I'm old," he said. "Not stupid. Not likely to forget you, Megan Leary. Pretty, smart, angry—have a scar right over your left hip, as I remember. Pulled a piece of broken glass out of there when you were no more than five years old. Pepsi bottle."

She smiled slowly. "I drink Coke now."

"In cans, I hope." Larkin zipped up his pants and sat down in the creaky wooden chair. "What in God's holy name brings you back to this snakepit, Meg?"

"You," she said, "among other things."

He leaned forward, put his elbows on the desk. "You're going to do it. You come back to find out about it."

Meg said nothing. Larkin nodded briskly, shot another look at me, and said, "Well, come on with me, then. Take a good look around."

I had no idea why a tour was necessary, but Meg didn't argue and I was just a ride-along on this one. I fell in behind them as Larkin led her out the front door into the wintry sunshine.

"I guess you heard about old Kev Miller," he said. "That there's the hand of God that did him in."

He pointed to the severed arm of an angel lying off to one side among flakes and chunks of broken marble. The back of the arm still had rusted brown stains streaked on it.

"Walking around in here one day and blam! Out of nowhere, this angel smites him down," Larkin finished, and grinned. He still had all his teeth, or a damn fine set of dentures. "Don't see a lot of that, now, do you?"

"Smiting? Not a lot." Meg followed him around a weeping angel with hands covering her marble face, dust heaped on her fingers. "Dr. Larkin—"

"Sam," he corrected. "Gave that crap up years ago." His voice echoed crazily off of marble, dropped off into the pooling silence too quickly. I walked faster to keep up.

"Sam—you saw my mother the day she died. Do you remember anything odd about it? Anything at all?"

He led her around two more angels, weaving through the field. The ground between them was uneven and sandy, and some of them leaned, I thought, dangerously far over. We passed a massive angry-faced statue missing an arm. The smiting spot of Kev Miller.

"Ah," Larkin said in satisfaction. "Here we are."

We were at the beginning of a new field of monuments. Tombstones. Some of them were old, some gleaming and discreet, the new fashion. The odd thing was that they had names on them.

Rejects? The old man had made a lot of mistakes, if so.

"Inventory," Larkin said proudly, and looked at us to see if we got it. I didn't. Neither, I could see from her expression, did Meg. "You got any idea how long it takes to carve a tombstone? To do it right, I mean? And I ain't a young man. Old Kev Miller was having trouble, too, that's why he came up with the inventory idea. I just carried it on."

I still didn't get it, until I spotted a name I recognized in the second row of headstones.

JAMES ALAN SPARKMAN. The sight of it drove breath out of my body and for a primitive second I thought, he's dead? But I just talked to him!

And then, as I caught sight of the stone next to his named KATHERINE ELIZABETH SPARKMAN, I realized what he'd meant. Inventory.

"None of these people are dead," I said out loud. Larkin beamed proudly, and I remembered the gesture Meg had made at her temple in the car.

"Not yet!" he crowed. "That's the point, boy. One of them keels over, the family comes here, all I got to do is haul the son of a bitch out of inventory, put on the date of death and load it on the truck. How's that for efficiency?"

Creepy, I thought. Weird. Crazy.

"Interesting," Meg said, which was one hell of a lot more polite than I expected from her. "Mind if I look around?"

"Don't mind a bit. Bet there's a few people you'd like to see with these marble hats, right? You go right ahead, girl. I'll just rest here with your young fella."

She sent me a glance that was on the verge of hysteria, and I tried to look like a young fella. Watching her walk away among those tombstones of the living gave me a chill that wiped away whatever humor I might have felt.

"Sad girl," Larkin sighed. He was burly, built like a wrestler, but he barely came up to my chin. His cotton-wool hair was thin enough to show baby-pink scalp beneath. "Her mother was a lovely woman."

"Meg doesn't seem to say much about her."

"Doubt she likes to remember." he said. "Saddest thing in the world, what happened to my girl, there. They hurt her so bad. So bad."

Meg had stopped somewhere in the fourth row, staring down at a name.

"Got one out there for Joe Hillyard?" I asked. Larkin's sky-blue lunatic eyes widened. "He's dead. This morning."

"Is he?" Larkin didn't seem surprised. "I'll pull him from the line, then. Always figured Joe would go one too far."

"With anyone in particular?"

"I thought you wanted to know about Doris Leary," he said, and leveled those clear cloudless eyes on me. "Joe,

Doris, the rest of us . . . one by one. Pretty soon there'll just be one."

I felt a weird prickle along my spine, intuition prodding me for attention. "Joe, Doris, you . . . who else?"

He didn't seem to see me, really. He said, softly, "Cal. He was the one who thought it up, you know. Me and Doris, it was just bad luck, bad roads . . . we shouldn't have even been there. Sin and punishment. That's what it was."

"Punishment for what?" I asked. My voice kept dropping, trying to be the voice coming from inside him. He blinked and focused on me with unnerving speed.

"Foolishness," he said. "Meg never did hate her mother. It wasn't hate that killed Doris Leary anyway."

"What did?"

His face twisted. "Greed."

I hadn't heard Meg's approach, but I felt her hand on my shoulder and had to bite my lip to keep from a yelp. Too many tombstones and angels for my peace of mind. When I looked back, Larkin looked back to normal, as if we hadn't been taking a trip into the Twilight Zone.

"Like your headstone?" Larkin asked her equitably. She nodded. "You're dependable, girl. Some of these women keep me hopping, what will all the divorces and remarriages. Pammy Howard, she's a pain in the ass. You're my kind of girl, Meg. Probably die a Leary."

"You have a nice one, too, Dan," she said.

"What?"

"Second row, sixth one over," Doc Larkin said. "Daniel David Fox, born November 1, 1964."

Meg turned to look where he pointed. I cleared my throat and said, "I'll be in the car."

I waited in the car for another thirty minutes while Meg

131

toured the living graveyard and coaxed details out of Larkin about her mother. Frankly, I wanted the hell out of there; I'd come within a few inches of needing Larkin's inventory today, and the less I thought about it, the better.

When Meg joined me, she got in silently, fastened her seatbelt, and stared straight ahead. I didn't say anything, either, just put the engine in reverse and backed us out with a gentle bump of tires onto the blacktop of the road.

It was only after a small hill hid Miller Marble and Monument from sight that Meg let out her breath and said, "You're quiet."

"Dead men get that way."

"Don't get freaky on me. I had a headstone, too. Miller carved it for me when I was fifteen; I guess he figured I might get the death penalty." She scrabbled in her purse for a cigarette, which she hadn't done for a while, and lit up. "Any word from the office?"

"About what?"

"Jesus, Dan, I don't know . . . my house burning down, somebody shooting at us, Hillyard's murder, Aurelia . . ."

"Nothing," I said somberly. "Not a peep. Listen, Larkin was rambling on about some stuff . . . was your mother friendly with Joe Hillyard?"

"Not enough to notice," she said. "Why?"

"How about Doc Larkin? Were they close?"

She jerked her head away to stare out the window.

"Meg, I'm sorry. I didn't mean—"

"Yes, they were having an affair. It was pretty much common knowledge," she said. "My father didn't care. He probably couldn't get it up anymore, anyway, with all the booze. But nobody ever thought Larkin could have killed her. He was at the hospital, anyway. Alibied seven ways from Sunday."

"I'm sorry," I said again. She shook her head.

"Nothing to be sorry about. I knew if I got into this there'd be things I didn't want to know, or remember." She laughed suddenly. "Nothing like taking a look at your tombstone to give you some perspective on things, though."

I was suddenly and uncomfortably aware of her, of how beautiful she was, how real, how warm. I had the urge to pull the car over to the side of the road and throw her in the back seat, and I knew that had something to do with the shotgun aimed at us earlier, and the tombstones with our names on them. I was vibrating like piano wire, too keyed up to keep my mind off of the peach-smooth curve of her breasts under that shirt.

She slowly turned her head back in my direction.

"I'm hungry," Meg said huskily.

"Really?" I tried to sound casual about it. "Me too. I guess Dairy Queen's out of the question. Kind of limits our formal choices."

She turned her head toward me, and her butane-blue eyes were clear and absolutely level.

"I think I'd like some home cooking, Dan," she said. "How are you in the kitchen?"

"Never had any complaints."

"Set off any fire alarms?"

"A few."

Her smile touched me like warm, intimate hands. "My kind of cook."

I stopped the car in a flurry of dust at the shoulder, put it in park, and reached for my seatbelt. Before I could get unhooked her hands were on my face, pulling me closer, and her lips were hot damp silk, unbelievably yielding, and she tasted of smoke and something a lot more delicious. Which led me to wonder what had happened to the cigarette, but just then I opened my eyes and saw her frantically tossing it out the window. The first button of her blouse had come undone, and I eased the fabric back to slide my fingers in along skin that felt like hot velvet, oh God, she tasted like heaven and touched like an angel, and she had the devil's own instinct for where to put her hands on me. I groaned into her mouth and wondered if there was room in the front seat. I figured we'd need a lot of room, the first time wasn't going to take long because I was halfway there just from the kiss, but there was going to be a second round, and a third, however many I could survive.

"Dan," she whispered, and the second button of her blouse came open, showing me a sheer mesh bra that reminded me to thank Madie at Fashion Barn later, because it was the sexiest damn thing I had ever seen, and I bent my head to suck those dark-rose nipples through the sheer fabric. She arched against me, panting, both hands on my head holding me close, and she tasted like rain and cinnamon, a taste that was driving me wild, and her nipples grew under my tongue, rising to meet me.

Just then, the cruiser's radio crackled and spat out my name.

We both froze as if it had dumped ice water on us, me with my mouth at her breast, her braced panting between the car door and her seat. Staring at each other. What I read in her eyes was blind anguish slowly wiped out by dawning embarrassment—and I knew she was seeing the same thing in mine.

I slowly sat up, took a deep breath, and picked up the cruiser's radio handset. Cleared my throat. Meg adjusted herself back into the seat and pulled her blouse back together; the wet spot on her bra where I'd sucked was just barely visible. She buttoned back up as I clicked the transmit button and said, "Fox here, Joetta. What's up?"

Me, for one. It was going to be tough to work around that for a while.

"Dan, sorry, but Jimmy says for you to get right back here. With her." Joetta sounded nervous and excited. "Right away."

"What's going on?"

Joetta was gone too long. I didn't like the delay because I knew it wasn't Joetta's doing. When she came back on, she sounded subdued. "I think you'd just better get back. Hurry."

I put the siren on.

The courthouse was busy—for Exile, anyway. The lot was choked with rust-colored pickups and faded station wagons, and one shiny red truck like a dealer's ad in the middle of a junkyard. People doing their daily business, nothing to do with me and Meg. I hoped.

But I didn't like it. It wasn't like Jimmy to just summon me in without a personal contact unless there was something going on below the surface. Peyser, I thought. Peyser making trouble. That wasn't unexpected, and it wasn't altogether unwelcome, either. If I couldn't take Meg back to my apartment for hours of hot sweaty Olympic-level sex, then I would gladly take on Peyser for a bare-knuckle fight. One way of working out my frustrations.

We went up the steps in silence, three flights. I wondered what Meg was thinking, because her face gave away nothing at all; the wet spot on her blouse had almost dried. It could have been a drop of rain, a tear, anything.

At the top of the steps, at the double doors, she reached out and took my hand, just for a second. Premonition, promise—it was too brief a contact to tell, and then she let

135

go and stiff-armed the door open and walked in with all the cocky brass-balled confidence I'd come to expect from her.

Except she faltered at the sight of the man Jimmy Sparkman was talking to. It wasn't much, but it was enough to make the skin tighten up on the back of my neck.

She covered it well. She kept walking as the man turned toward her and smiled, and it was an evil cold son-of-a-bitch smile that never reached his dark, cool eyes. He was older than either of us, probably in his mid-fifties, dark hair going iron-gray in streaks, face leathered and lined like a dry desert ravine. It could have been a kind face, but the eyes gave him away.

I'd seen him before, in a grainy newspaper picture, escorting her down the courthouse steps on her acquittal.

"Miss Leary," he said. "Ain't it a small world?"

Jimmy looked miserable, absolutely wretched. He met my eyes and said, "Deputy Dan Fox, this is Jonathan Gentry. He's with the Texas Rangers."

"Not the baseball club," Gentry said, and extended his hand. He also gave me a milder version of his satanic smile. "Pleased to meet you, deputy. I'm in town to look into the murder of Joe Hillyard."

He looked at Meg as he said it, weighing her reaction, his eyes as avid as if he was sucking the marrow out of her bones. Her expression had gone very still, her eyes opaque. I didn't like the pallor of her skin.

"Good luck with that," she said, and her voice was every bit as cool and controlled as it had been taunting Lew Peyser to take a swing at her on Highway 114. "Life's full of little ironies, detective. Weren't you the one who threatened to take him out behind the Wandora and—wait, let me get it right—kick his butt until he was breathing through his asshole?"

His smile never wavered. Neither did his eyes. "My personal likes or dislikes aside, Miss Leary, I'm still a Texas Ranger. I'll do my job. You know that about me."

"Oh, I know," she almost purred. "Anything I can do to help—"

"Stay in town," he said. The smile disappeared like a snuffed flame. "I want to know where to find you. All the time."

"That's kind of difficult, considering somebody just burned down my house. Maybe you should put me in a cell," she shot back.

"Volunteering?" His thin eyebrows arched up. One of them had a scar through it. That, and the nose, made me think he'd done some boxing once upon a time. "Wouldn't have thought you'd be eager to go there, Meg. All things considered."

She said nothing. The look smoked, though, and he seemed to like the heat just fine. He smiled again, like she'd said something funny, and turned back to Jimmy Sparkman.

"The coroner's recovered a .38 caliber slug from Hillyard. I want you to courier the evidence up to the lab in Austin. I'm going to give you a note, you tell the courier to give it to Angela Barr up there. She'll walk everything through and make sure we stay at the top of the list. I want to talk to the neighbors, the neighbors' neighbors, the bums, the milkmen, the postmen, and every kid with a paper route in two square miles of his house. And Deputy Dan, you keep your eyes on Miss Leary, now. All the time. I don't want her wandering around town unattended." His smile suddenly showed teeth. "Pretty lady like that, accidents happen."

"You're a specialist in that, aren't you?" she shot back.

Gentry let the smile slip away and kept holding her gaze.

"You and me," he said, as softly as if it was just the two of them standing there. "We got to talk, Meg. You know that."

"No," she said, flat and simple, and turned around and walked out. I stood there, flat-footed, looking at Gentry and Jimmy Sparkman. At her desk, Joetta looked mesmerized by the floor show, and the phone rang, and rang, until with a jolt she grabbed it and muttered a greeting.

"Go after her," Jimmy finally said wearily.

"Jimmy—"

"Just do it."

At least she couldn't take off on me this time. I had the keys to the cruiser, and the Lexus was still cooling its tires back at the DQ parking lot. Still, she wasn't anywhere in sight when I came down the courthouse steps, chilled by the gothic shadow of the castle turrets.

She was sitting on the side of the courthouse, on a set of little-used back steps, staring out at the bones of a rose garden that was maintained—barely—by the Ladies' Police Auxiliary. In the blast of the winter wind, it was just a tangle of leafless sticks and thorns.

"Gentry was the investigating detective on your mother's murder," I said. "I remember his name from the reports."

I took a seat next to her on the chilly concrete. In the distance, a primer-gray Chevelle started up with a noise like a wood chipper, coughed black smoke, and cruised out of the parking lot. The driver was a pimple-faced kid with his hands in the ten-and-two position, and in the passenger seat next to him rode an ancient patriarch of a West Texas ranching family, burned leather by the sun, wearing his battered straw hat in the car because it was too much part of his head to ever take it off. Some kind of taxes had brought them here, I guessed. The old man didn't look happy about it.

"Gentry's a cold bastard," Meg said. "It would give him a hard-on to be able to put me in prison for Joe Hillyard's murder. And please, don't tell me that if I'm innocent I have nothing to worry about, I'm going to vomit if I hear that again."

"Meg, we need to be careful now. We're up against—"

"We?" she asked. Her eyes turned hard. "We're not up against anything. When they take me off in handcuffs you get to go home, take a shower, and beat off thinking about me. Women in chains get you hard, Dan? Got a little jail fantasy going on?"

"Whoa!" I interrupted her, holding up both hands. She was scaring me, the look in her eyes, the tone of her voice; if words were knives, she was slashing wildly at me with the ginsu edge. "Calm down. Look, I'm sorry about—about what happened in the cruiser, but I can't say I didn't enjoy it. I did. I hope you did too, but if you didn't, Jesus, all you have to do is say so. I hope you know that."

She looked away.

"Meg, I'm going to take silence for refusal. Ten seconds, and I'm going to assume you want me to leave you the hell alone. How's that?"

Seconds ticked by. I counted eight before she said, without turning back toward me, "That's not what I meant. It's just—Gentry. Peyser. The jail. It's all—and Jesus, Dan, you're a fucking deputy!"

She said it with a kind of despair.

"I have been from the beginning," I said. "I haven't changed."

She managed a smile, sort of.

"Maybe I have," she said. "Let's find Aurelia. That's

about the only thing I can think of to hold me together right now."

It had, I thought, been a full enough day already.

"Tomorrow," I said.

Chapter Nine

The flag of sexual truce was still flying. I had a dreamless night of sleep on the couch, too tired to torture myself with speculation, and for all I know Meg slept like a baby too. She certainly never came slinking out of the bedroom for hot sweaty sex in the middle of the night.

In the morning, over coffee, we talked about Aurelia Galvan.

"She had money," Meg said contemplatively.

"Forty dollars isn't money in this day and age. Aurelia had her mother's credit card, but she was savvy enough to know she couldn't use that without getting caught early."

"She never showed up at the bus station?"

"Not that we can find—which doesn't mean she didn't, but I don't feel like she ever made it that far."

"How else would a teenage girl plan to get out of town?"

It was a good question, and one I hadn't thought out all ways. "Fed-Ex truck pulls in every morning, leaves in fifteen minutes. UPS comes, too. Mail trucks. We got all kinds of delivery trucks on regular schedules, maybe one of the drivers picked her up or had planned to. It'll take a long time to check. Plus, we get long haul drivers coming through. She could have stuck out a thumb."

"So that won't get us anywhere—not without a lot of leg-work," Meg nodded. "Back to the money. There used to be some cousins around, when we were kids. Two brothers—"

"Hector and Gesualdo. Gesualdo works on a road construction crew, Ward Construction, I think he's out on a job near Amarillo. He's been gone for two months. Hector works out at Mayor Worthen's car place. Mechanic."

"And if you're looking for money, once you tap your friends—"

"You tap your family," I finished. "Okay, let's go have a talk with Hector. Maybe I can test drive one of those Infinitis."

Meg tipped the rest of the coffee back in a quick slug, made a face, and pulled her jacket off the back of the chair. The black leather jacket was the same, but the shirt today was a silky, shiny, tight-fitting thing with three-quarter length sleeves. Tight wine-colored pants. Damn, she looked good. My three hundred dollars had done its work well.

I looked down at my blue jeans and plaid work shirt. When I looked back up she was smiling.

"No dress code at Cal Worthen's," she said. "Let's make a deal."

There was a manila envelope sitting on the seat of my cruiser, with a hastily written note in rounded schoolgirl lettering.

Dan. Joetta's writing. *Farlene said to give this to you. It's from the Chief.*

I opened up the envelope and found another file folder, this one marked LEARY, MEGAN. Another criminal complaint, and this time Meg was the victim.

She had just slammed the door on the passenger side of the cruiser, and was looking at my envelope with considerable interest.

"What is it?" she asked. I made a split-second gut-level decision, and crammed the folder back in the envelope.

"Court cases," I said. "Speeding tickets, mostly. I have appearances coming up."

I slid it behind my seat and started the engine.

"Cal's doesn't open for at least another hour," I said. "Breakfast? How do you feel about Chico's Tacos?"

Her face lit up with a brilliant smile.

Chico's Tacos sat on the highway, just about half a mile from where I'd originally pulled her over in the Lexus; it was a love-it-or-hate-it kind of place. They made rolled tacos, beef only, liberally drenched in melted cheese and soaked in homemade salsa. They served them in flimsy paper cartons and offered Coke, Dr Pepper, and a variety of Mexican soft drinks. You'd think it was an unusual choice for breakfast, but the parking lot was full from open to close. There were no time limits on Chico's Tacos.

Meg speared half a rolled taco with a plastic fork and lifted it to her lips, dripping with salsa and grease. Her eyes closed in ecstasy as she chewed. I took a bite of mine, savoring the hot-sweet bite of the pepper sauce, the thick chewy corn tortilla, the oily meat. Hot and delicious and bad for your heart, a description that applied equally to the woman sitting across from me. We were eating in the cruiser, both to save time and to avoid any unnecessary problems, though from the look of the folks inside Chico's there wouldn't be any trouble. Nobody cared about us. About half of the diners were tourists looking confused at the lack of selection in the menu.

"Damn," Meg breathed. She rested her head against the seat. "I can't believe I forgot about Chico's."

"Makes life worth living," I said. "Jalapeño pepper? Fresh roasted, they grow 'em in the back."

She fished one out and bit in with gusto. I passed her a drink when she waved for it, wheezing.

"Strong," she coughed. Her eyes were watering. I took another bite of mine and shrugged. "Jerk."

We ate in companionable silence, finishing off four tacos apiece and at least a couple more peppers, disposed of the grease-soaked trash, and headed out to cruise the car lot. I was uncomfortably aware of the folder behind my seat, and I wanted a chance to at least have a cursory read, but something told me it wouldn't be a good idea with Meg in the car. I'd just have to wait for it.

Cal Worthen's car lot was gaudy and profitable, a fading circus of flapping flags and blinking lights. The centerpiece of it was a giant twenty-foot caricature of a West Texas hayseed, complete with battered straw Stetson and cowboy boots, made out of fiberglass and latex, that periodically boomed out "Worthen is worth it!" Combined with the crackling announcements paging one salesman or another, it made the place frantic. The only thing missing was hurdy-gurdy music.

We'd no sooner pulled the cruiser up than a middle-aged salesman was at my car door, bending down and grinning.

"Always glad to see law officers, yes sir!" he said. "And the little—"

If he was about to say lady, it had a heart attack and died on his tongue as Meg opened the door and got out. She couldn't have been more alien to the housewives of Diller if she'd come with a ray gun and a spaceship. She took one sweeping look around and put on her Oakley sunglasses.

"Your name?" I asked him. He was still shaking my hand.

"Jerry. Jerry Higgins." He produced a card—like the handshake, it was an automatic gesture, no thought behind it. "Ah—you look like a Ford Taurus man—"

"I'm looking for Hector Galvan," I said. Jerry looked blank. "He's a mechanic."

"Oh. He'd be around back in the shop, then." Distress

had taken over from the blankness. "Damn. Listen, take my card—"

"Thanks, Jerry, maybe later." I slapped him on the back and joined Meg at the back of the cruiser. We walked down the row of glittering new cars, heading for the shop. Two more salesmen tried to intercept us, but Meg handled them with a look and two words: "Get lost." Not my approach, but then she didn't have to run into them at the Sav-A-Lot picking up groceries next week.

When we turned the corner, the new cars were gone, and we were in a whole other world. This one was greasy, dark, and unpleasant, and the cars parked back here were junkers and skeletons being raped for parts. The booming scratchy "Worthen is worth it!" was drowned out by loud Tejano music and the sawing scream of an air wrench, and loud wordless shouts being tossed back and forth over the hood of a 1988 Chrysler.

From the quality of the wolf whistles, they spotted Meg first. The air wrench cut off, leaving me feeling deaf, and a medium-height guy dressed in a faded oily uniform stood up on the left side of the car. On the right, two other men came to attention.

The wolf whistles faded into an uncomfortable silence, because Meg wasn't having any.

"Hector," she said, steel-hard and windshield-clear. "Hector Galvan."

The one who'd been abusing the air wrench came around to the hood of the car, wiping his hands on a greasy rag. He was small and lean, like a miniature greyhound. Small, dark, unreadable eyes, and a scar on his chin that looked freshly scabbed over.

"I'm Hector," he said. "You?"

"Megan Leary," she said, and offered her hand. He

145

glanced down at his own, speckled and smeared with oil, and made a vague, apologetic gesture. She accepted it with a nod. "You're Aurelia Galvan's cousin."

"Yeah, second cousin," he said. "So, you find her yet? Rosa's been calling night and day, half out of her mind."

"You don't know where she is?" Meg asked.

"No sè," he said, shaking his head. "Odessa by now, probably. Maybe already in Dallas."

He kept swiping nervously at his hands with the cloth, though they were as clean as they were going to be. I kept my eye on that, and on the way he shifted his weight gradually, one foot to the other. A slow, almost imperceptible rocking.

"You think so?" Meg purred. She came a step closer and lowered her voice confidentially. "I don't think so, Hector. I think she never left town."

He flinched back from her as if she'd slapped him. "But—"

"Her friends say she was leaving town, all right, but that she was coming here first to borrow some money," Meg continued. It was a lie, but smoothly told, and I could see Hector buying every syllable. "Coming to her cousin for help. So what happened then?"

"She—she never got here. Maybe she changed her mind." Hector's eyes darted around, looking at his other mechanic buddies. They'd taken a step back and were working hard to pretend they were someplace else. "They were here, too. They'll tell you. Aurelia, she never come here."

I looked at the other two, who might have been brothers—same height, same burnished-copper skin tone, same dark eyes, only one sparked with mischief and the other looked vaguely confused.

"Just that one time," the confused one said. All eyes went to him. "She come here once looking for Hector. She had a backpack with her."

It was news to Hector, clearly. He looked pale and shaky.

"When?" I asked. Mr. Confused looked, if possible, more confused.

"Maybe—last week? Week before? It was before payday, though."

"Couple days ago," interpreted the mischievous one.

"You saw her, too?"

"No, not me."

I turned back to Mr. Confusion and took out my notebook. "Your name?"

"Roberto Cruz," he said. "This is my brother Manny."

"Deputy Dan Fox," I said. "Roberto, you know this girl is missing now, right?"

Roberto slowly nodded. His brother, next to him, looked tense and no longer amused.

"But you saw her, here, with a backpack? Do you remember what time it was, maybe?"

He thought. He thought a long time before he said, "Maybe eleven o'clock. Before lunch. I was working on an Escort, eh, Manny, you remember, the one with the bad tranny—"

Thank God. Even if he didn't remember dates, he remembered car repairs, which was almost as good. We could pull the service records and narrow it down.

"What did she do?" Meg asked. Roberto thought some more.

"I saw her come around the corner, there, and look in the shop." He pointed a grimy finger, tracking an invisible girl as she walked closer. "She didn't say nothing. She went

147

on over that way." He pointed to the other side of the garage.

"She didn't say anything to you at all?" Meg pressed. He shook his head. "And you, Hector, you never saw her?"

"I—I must've been on a break or something," he mumbled. "I didn't know—"

"Did you see her again, Roberto?" I asked. "Maybe coming back?"

He slowly shook his head again and said, "I never seen her again."

The hot swell of interest in my chest had turned into real pressure. We were onto something, we both knew it. Meg leaned forward, a hunting dog catching the scent, and there was something pure and powerful in her blue eyes.

She was opening her mouth to ask another question when the back door of the garage banged open and a West Texas comic-opera voice boomed, "What in the blue hell's going on here, anyway? I don't pay you fellers to sit around, now do I?"

Striding around the oil smudges and tools came Cal Worthen, whose twenty-foot idol out in the parking lot continued to boom that he was worth it—whatever it was. Over six feet tall, not counting the bright white Stetson, Cal wore Wrangler blue jeans, cowboy cut, a plaid western shirt with pearl snap buttons, and ostrich pointy-toed boots, the kind my grandmother had always called roach stompers. He dressed like the Marlboro Man, complete to the thick tooled-leather belt with a big round buckle. In case there was any doubt who he was, his name was etched on the buckle in fancy brass script.

I would have expected him, for some reason, to be fat. In fact, he was just the opposite. Lean to the point of skeletal, darkly tanned, black hair and eyes as if he had Mexican or

Indian heritage, though I knew he'd swear he didn't. Big weathered hands with gold nugget rings like brass knuckles—hands that had once worked, those rings said, and didn't have to any more.

The three Mexican mechanics looked away, mumbled excuses, and picked up tools. Hector bent to work with the air wrench again, and its shriek tore the air in half. Cal kept walking, not even acknowledging the men, until he was toe to toe with me.

"You're that new one," he said, unsmiling. "Sparkman brought you in."

"Deputy Dan Fox," I said, and offered my hand. He took it and tried to squeeze the bones to powder. I squeezed back. We finally declared a truce, and he let go and took a step back. "Nice to meet you, Mayor Worthen."

"Sure is nice to meet you, too," he said with the hearty, unfeeling insincerity of a car dealer. Or politician. "And the little lady—"

"Meg Leary," she said flatly. "You remember me, Cal."

He must've, because he shut up, staring at her. After a minute he took a deep breath and said, almost reverently, "Old Hillyard must be having a shit fit."

"Must've been a hell of one," she said. "He's dead."

Worthen did a good facsimile of surprised, but then, I wasn't sure I was going to see any genuine emotion out of him. He was just too much surface.

"You come here askin' about Sheriff Hillyard?" he asked, disbelieving. "What my Mexicans got to do with that?"

He said it the same way he might've said my car lot or my tools. They were possessions, pure and simple; Cal Worthen was the lord of this castle, and by God, he was worth it. The first day I'd come to Exile, shell-shocked by small-town differences, Jimmy had driven me around the east side of town, and pointed out Cal Worthen's rustic ranch house estate, complete with dead animal skulls over the gate and split-rail fencing. Cal Worthen, he'd said. And his wife Barbie. Whatever there is left in Exile, he owns half of it and can buy the other half.

Including the Mexicans, apparently.

"Do you really think I'd give a damn about Hillyard?" Meg asked coolly. "We were asking about Aurelia Galvan."

He looked blank. "Who?"

"High school girl, missing since Halloween," I said. "Maybe you saw her."

I took out the photograph and passed it over. Worthen glanced over it, shrugged, and handed it back. His silence indicated that they pretty much all looked alike to him.

"One of your mechanics said she was here," Meg said. "Right before payday, which was November first, right? So that puts her here the day she disappeared."

"You think one of my Mexicans did her in?" Cal looked interested in a beady-eyed kind of way. "Well, that's possible, get a snootful in 'em and God only knows what they'll get up to."

"So you let them get a snootful during working hours, there, Cal?" I said pleasantly. I wanted to punch him in the mouth. He shrugged.

"I run a good shop, but I can't watch 'em all the time. Got enough trouble just making sure they get here and stay working for eight hours a day. Maybe sometimes they sneak off and have themselves a little party, I don't know. What the hell was some schoolgirl doing out here, anyway? Where were her parents?" He said it triumphantly, like he'd just discovered the secret to teenage delinquency. Meg's eyes turned just a shade more gas-flame blue.

"Her father's dead," she said softly. "He died of cancer after never missing a day of work for twenty years at the Delta plant. Her mother works two jobs to support the family. That's where the parents are. Oh, except Rosa's not working right now, she's sitting in her house grieving and waiting for the phone to ring to tell her her daughter's alive and well, Cal. So did you see her around here, or not?"

"Hell no," he snapped. "And I'll thank you to get out of here and let my people work for a living."

I could tell that nobody was going to have anything more to say, not with the Great God Cal breathing fire. I nodded to Meg, and we walked out into the watery sunshine. The wind had a damp edge to it, as if clouds loomed somewhere just the other side of the horizon. A tumbleweed drifted lazily across the parking lot, paused to consider a shiny aluminum hot dog wrapper, and picked it up like a kid's toy to twirl in its branches. Meg and I, by common silent consent, did not go back the way we'd come. We walked around the direction Roberto Cruz had pointed, to the other side of the garage where Aurelia Galvan had disappeared off of the face of the earth.

It was a blank space of pavement with chain-link fencing at the side and end, heavily braided through with more tumbleweed. There was a gate at the far end. We strolled in that direction, casual as a couple of lovers on a Sunday stroll, and I watched the ground for anything out of the ordinary. Nothing. Nothing at all.

The fence at the end of the lot had a man-high gate, but it was fastened with a shiny new lock. I considered it carefully, looked at Meg, and we both stepped up to look through the chain link at what was on the other side.

On the other side of the fence were new cars. A blank shining lot of new cars with stickers in the window. I wondered why they weren't out front, being hawked by eager salesmen; there seemed to be a lot of them, maybe a couple of tractor-trailer trucks' worth. Odd . . .

"Inventory," said Cal's voice from behind us. I flinched, but kept from whirling around; Meg wasn't quite so controlled. I turned slowly to face him and saw him grinning like a rat terrier, his teeth oversized and blindingly white. Cal had himself a fine, though not very natural, set of choppers. I wondered about the thick dark hair that squatted on his head, too. In the sunlight it didn't look quite right.

"Always lock up your cars where people can't see them?" Meg asked. Cal shrugged and produced a key; he unlocked the gate and swung it open with a screech of metal. From the garage came the sound of metal hammering metal.

"Matter of fact, I do, when they haven't been properly logged in yet. Just unloaded these babies day before yesterday, my accounting girl hasn't come in to write down the VIN numbers and get 'em entered in the computer yet. We keep 'em in quarantine back here until everything's ready. Look around. If you see something you like, well, make me an offer, we'll see what we can do."

I checked the invoice on the Ford F-150. I didn't see how, on my salary, we could do much of anything. When I wasn't driving the town's cruiser, I had a perfectly good 1976 Vega that was only mostly rust-colored. A classic, which meant I laid out more for parts and upkeep than I ever had on the original payments.

I noticed that the invoice had shipping information on it. "These come in from Mexico?" I asked. Cal nodded and put a possessive hand on the truck's hood.

"Assembly plant's in Mexico," he said. "Built of U.S. parts, though."

Reflexive marketing, but his heart wasn't in it.

There wasn't anything to see, except the cars; I had the maddening feeling that there was something here, something just out of sight, that was going to answer my questions, but I couldn't put my finger on it. Nothing moved among the cars except a wispy rustle of sun-faded plastic and the rattle of a forgotten piece of tumbleweed. The cars all had a fine coat of dust on the hoods, which meant nothing; the drifting of sand around here was constant. You could set your coffee cup down and pick it back up, there'd be a thin film of dust. It flavored every bite of every meal, every sip of every drink. The cleanest house, left ten minutes, would begin to show invasion by the dust.

So why was I bothered by that?

"You unload these here in the lot," I said. "Off the truck. What do you do to them?"

"Not a damn thing," he said. "We park 'em and forget 'em until they're ready to put out front; we run 'em through the car wash then, and give 'em a spit shine."

That was it. It snapped into focus for me with a feeling like a plucked string.

The cars weren't that dusty. Not if they'd been unloaded two days ago off of a long-haul truck coming from Mexico. These babies had been washed down, shined, and made ready. But why, if they weren't ready to be put out on the lot?

I glanced at Meg, but I couldn't tell if she was thinking it or not. She looked bored, her eyes half-closed, staring off into the distance. She walked around a black Lincoln Town Car, scuffed her shoe against the pavement, and bent down to pick something up. I couldn't see what it was, and neither could Cal; I sensed him straining to find out, but he wasn't about to ask.

"Dan," Meg said. "Let's go."

Cal was obviously amused. "You let the criminals tell you what to do, Deputy?"

"Well, you told us to get the hell out of here," I said. "Guess I'm paying attention to one of you. Afternoon, Mr. Mayor."

I nodded to Meg and we sauntered out, nice and easy, with Cal's black oily eyes on us all the way out the gate, around the garage where the three mechanics continued working, only the flicker of their eyes betraying they knew we were there. We were all the way back into salesman country when I asked her, as casually as I could, "What'd you get?"

She held out her hand to show me. On her palm sat a clod of West Texas dirt, completely unremarkable.

I didn't get it until I saw her razor slice of a smile.

"Nothing," she purred. "Makes him think, though."

That may have been the moment—although I really can't be sure—that I actually fell in love with her.

Chapter Ten

By noon we were at the Wandora. It was still early, and except for a couple of pickled drunks surgically grafted to their barstools, the place was empty. I held up two fingers to the bartender and guided Meg to a back table near the pool area. Under my arm was the file folder Joetta had given me; Meg didn't ask about it. I didn't tell. We called a curiosity truce for the space of a frosty mug of beer apiece.

Meg licked foam from her upper lip—believe me, I watched—and said, "So go ahead, you're dying to look at it."

"What?"

"The file. You know. The 'parking tickets.'"

"Speeding tickets."

"Whatever." She flipped a hand at me. "Go ahead."

I pushed over a bowl of pretzels as a reward and opened the envelope. Inside was the manila folder with LEARY, MEGAN written in black magic marker on the tag. I started to pull it out, then hesitated. Meg was watching me over the rim of her mug.

"Dan, I know what it is," she said. "And you're just eaten up with curiosity."

"Partly eaten," I said. "Look, I won't look at it here if you don't want me to."

She put her mug down and pressed her hands flat on the table. Short fingernails, her manicure broken and chipped by her short friendly visit. Vulnerable hands, with a storm cloud of a bruise across her right knuckles. She slowly

155

closed that hand into a fist, then deliberately relaxed it.

"Read it," she said. Even in only two words, I felt the tension, the reluctance, and the trust. She settled back in her chair and lit up a cigarette, the second one of the day as far as I remembered. Something for those bruised, hurting hands to do.

I opened the file and read Megan Leary's complaint, and it became clear to me why this town hated her, and why it had been so achingly important for her to come back here to face her demons.

When I'd read it through, every page, I felt as if I'd been eating ashes. I closed the folder, took a deep drink of beer to wash the ugly taste away, and finally looked up at her. I didn't say anything. She offered me a crooked, impenetrable smile.

"Another beer?" she asked huskily.

"In a minute," I said. "Gotta make a pit stop."

She nodded and avoided my eye as I rose. I signaled the bartender for another round on my way to the hall where the rancid bathrooms were. I went to the telephone and dialed the number of the phone on Jimmy Sparkman's desk.

He picked it up on the second ring.

"Damn it, Jimmy, don't fuck me like this," I said. "You didn't tell me."

"Tell you what?" He sounded tired. Exhausted. "Give me a break, Dan, I've had a bitch of a day."

"The rape charge," I said. "Jesus Christ, Jimmy, there were four deputies involved and Joe Hillyard did his level best to cover it up. You send me walking around with her like a second fucking shadow and you don't tell me? I'm wearing a goddamn deputy's badge!"

"It was a long time ago—"

"She was fifteen years old," I said. "They handcuffed her

156

to the cell bars. Peyser's dad raped her while the others—Have you read this goddamn thing?"

He was silent. I didn't wait for his conscience to wake up.

"She knew nobody would believe her. Even then, she knew."

"The only evidence they had was Meg's statement," Jimmy said. His voice was colorless as glass, curiously slow. "And the bruises. Peyser was the only one who confessed, and he said it was her idea."

"Ever met a pedophile who didn't? She said the other ones stood there and watched, cheered him on, and Hillyard knew about it—it's pretty damn convincing, Jimmy. And it's a motive for murder. You know it is."

"Sure it is." Jimmy took a deep breath. "File doesn't show what happened to this town later. Peyser did six months, came home, and ate a shotgun shell. Gillford shot himself and his wife and two little children a year later. Lyle Martins is still around here someplace, a sad old broke-up drunk. Don't know what happened to Terry Wallace, but last I saw he was sacking groceries at the Piggly Wiggly. Forty-year-old man, sacking groceries. Meg's lawsuit took every dollar out of this town, Dan. Schools closed down. Public services folded. Lot of people consider her responsible for the death of the town, not to mention the deaths of those men."

"Do you?"

"I don't know what I think anymore. Until I saw her face, I'd managed to put all that out of my mind, but I guess it never really goes away. Not really."

I looked down at the drunken scrawl decorating the wall behind the telephone. Not surprisingly, the hooker's number was there, along with the number for the Best Inn

Towne. What surprised me—and made me feel an eerie lurch, given what I'd read in that file—was the drunken, aging notation, "Meg sucks and swallows, along with a phone number." Peyser's handwriting. I'd recognize it anywhere. How long had he been nursing his hate? Since his daddy was taken away in handcuffs? Since they'd found the torn bloody corpse lying in a stew of its own blood, shotgun beside it?

"She was the victim, Jimmy."

"Probably," he agreed. "And it was good that she left town. But now? Is she still a victim now? You prepared to swear she didn't put a gun to Hillyard's head?"

It was a good question. I cut the connection and hung up the receiver, felt in the coin return for change, and just before I turned to head back to the table I felt a presence behind me, wild animal heat, menace blazing like molten metal.

I tried to turn around. Pain exploded in my kidneys, sent white bolts of fire up and down my side. My knee went loose, and I fell. I caught myself on the telephone.

A hand grabbed my hair and slammed me face-first into the enameled metal case. I thought crazily, dial 9-1-1, and then it was blood, and dark pulsing spots of agony, and a strange, disconnected sense of surprise. I went down.

Time blurred like running water. Sometimes I only felt pressure, then things would snap crystal-clear and agony would explode in some part of my body, fresh as a shiny icepick. I was on the floor and he was using pointy-toed boots. After one huge crimson burst of pain somewhere in the vicinity of my ribs, I sank into that watery state that means something very wrong here but the pain was distant and strangely cool to the touch.

I missed the moment that he stopped killing me and walked away.

When I opened my eyes, I was lying on the filthy floor of the Wandora's hallway, and I felt cold. Nobody around. I tried to get up, and ribs screamed. Something deeply wrong with my fingers on my left hand. I didn't look at them long, the view made me dizzy. I dragged myself up to my hands and knees, swaying and thinking stupidly that there was a lot of blood on the floor.

"Easy there, partner." I half-recognized the voice, but it wasn't until a pair of strong hands hauled me to my feet and steadied me I was able to place it, and the cold-eyed, hound-dog face.

Texas Ranger Jonathan Gentry

He kept hold of me, which was good; I wasn't sure I could manage walking upright just yet. "Want to tell me what happened?"

"Got me from behind," I mumbled, and spat out a clotted mouthful of something that didn't bear close inspection. No teeth, at least. "Didn't see."

His hands were a whole lot kinder than his smile. "I continue to be impressed by high-quality local police work. Sit down. You're going to need a doctor to take a look at that hand if you want to play piano again."

"Violin," I croaked. The humor was a reflex. Inside, I was a howling, wounded animal. Somehow—I didn't remember walking—I was sliding into the blessed soft comfort of a rickety wooden chair. My head was spinning off into the dark, but I dragged it back, opened my eyes, and looked around. Something was missing. Something—

"Meg."

Gentry didn't frown, exactly; his face grew more lines. "I was about to ask you about that. I came looking for her."

"She was out here—waiting on me." He stared at me, one hand tapping the table top. "Bartender?"

"He's gone. It's open bar," he said. "Nobody around when I came in, except for some drunks helping themselves. Either he was one of 'em, or he saw what was going on and took a five-minute break."

"Felt more like thirty." I let my eyes drift closed. Gentry tapped me on the hand, waking moist hot pain, and I struggled out of it.

"Stay awake," he said. "Probably got a concussion to go with that scalp wound. If he'd beat you for thirty minutes your sheriff would've had another murder to cry over. Can you walk?"

"Sure," I whispered. It was wishful thinking, anyway. Gentry got an arm under my shoulders and walked me like a puppet out of the Wandora, past those same unmoving drunks, who didn't look at me at all, out into the parking lot. Gentry's pickup truck was parked blocking my cruiser. Had he thought Meg would make a run for it?

I was trying not to think about the pain in my ribs. It was a knife sharpening itself on bone with every breath I took. Something wrong with my knee, too. The muscles felt loose and watery.

"You believed her," I said. Gentry looked at me sharply as he opened the truck door. It was a Rocky Mountain-size step up into that cab, and I didn't feel prepared to take it. But I was less prepared to be carried like a sack of dry dog food by a Texas Ranger. I gritted my teeth and hobbled up a white-hot painful mile to the safety of the bench seat.

Gentry hadn't closed the door. He was looking at me, measuring whether or not I was going to kick the bucket on him.

"I believed her about the rape," he said. "Some towns,

160

the cops forget there's any other law outside the city limits. Exile was like that. I could smell it on 'em."

"And her mother?"

He started to close the door, then said, "Don't bleed on my seats, son. I just had it detailed."

One broken rib, two cracked. Torn ligament in my knee. Mild concussion. Twelve stitches on my scalp.

Oh, and three broken fingers on my left hand. My doctor looked like he was about fifteen years old, complete with pimples, but he had the cheerful contempt for pain of a true medical professional. I sat there and tried not to grunt as he moved broken bones, poked, prodded, and made delighted sounds of discovery.

"He gonna live?" Gentry asked. He'd sat quietly in the corner of the room, arms folded, as if I was the fugitive he was guarding. The doctor gestured at the array of X-rays on the light boxes.

"He's not in any danger," he said. He clicked a ballpoint pen and scrawled something on a chart. "You're going to be hurting for a while, deputy; I can't give you any pain relief until we're sure about that concussion."

"How long do you want to keep him here?" Gentry asked.

"Two hours under observation. He can sit in the waiting room. Mr. Fox, if you feel faint or dizzy, call for a nurse."

He was out of the room before I could tell him to shove it up his ass. The nurse lingered, cleaning up after him. Gentry exchanged a look with her. She was a large Mexican woman, I didn't know her name except by the tag that said FERNANDEZ, M.A., R.N.

"What did he write on the chart?" I asked. Her lips twitched.

"A.F.U. All fucked up," she said, "but you didn't hear it from me. You're not going to sit in the waiting room, are you?"

"No," I said. She nodded and pulled a business card out of her pocket.

"Call me in four hours or I start calling everybody on your papers, including your mama."

"Yes ma'am," I said humbly, and found a pocket for the card that wasn't blood-spattered.

"No lifting, no twisting, no fighting," she continued. "You put that rib through a lung and I'll be very disappointed in you."

"Yes ma'am."

She leveled a finger at Gentry. "Take him straight home."

He ignored her and stood up. I eased myself off of the treatment table in a crackle of crisp paper. I'd gotten used to the bitter, astringent, cold smell of the room, but I was surprised, as M.A. Fernandez bent closer, at the warm rose scent of her perfume. She traveled in a cloud of flowers.

"You be more careful," she said to me. I nodded, which woke up one bitch of a headache, and shuffled behind Gentry out of the hospital treatment room.

In the tiny waiting room—a linoleum box cheered up by faded orange plastic chairs and a few tattered magazines— sat two men. One of them had a busted nose. Trails of drying blood snaked over his cheeks, disappearing behind the ice pack he held on his face; both eyes looked like they were in the process of developing black-and-orange Halloween shiners. It took me a second to place him, given the swelling, but the rancid oily hair was a dead giveaway.

I walked past him, then reached over with my good right hand, took a fistful of that hair, and yanked him six inches upright. My ribs argued about the strain, but I won. He howled, dropped the icepack and grabbed my wrist. Fresh blood exploded down his chin and spattered his greasy t-shirt.

"Mr. Gentry," I said, "Meet Joe Wilkerson. He's the bouncer at the Wandora. He was mysteriously AWOL at the time I was getting the shit beat out of me."

The speech left me feeling sick and weak, but I wasn't going to let either of them know it. Not yet.

Joe was howling things that only a dog could hear, or understand. I let go of his hair and dropped him back in the chair; I kept my eyes focused on his face and braced myself on the back of his chair so I wouldn't fall down. Pain rumbled through my body like a gravel crusher.

"Pleased to meet you, Joe," Gentry said, his voice a low, silky growl. He put one booted foot up on the chair next to Joe—he had cowboy boots on, I noticed, but they had no bloodstains on the tips. "You want to tell me how you came by that little boo-boo?"

"I fell," Wilkerson said, his voice thick and surly. "Fuck you."

"He fell on Meg's fist," I said, and grabbed him by the broken nose. He howled again, this time more of a high-pitched Pekinese howl. "Where is she, Joe?"

"Fuck you!" He'd exhausted his repertoire after only two sentences. Gentry reached out and gently tapped me on the shoulder, shaking his head. I let go.

"Nice lady nurse said you weren't to strain yourself," Gentry said reproachfully. He focused back on Wilkerson's face, and his benevolence curdled into menace. "Son, I'm going to do you a favor and explain myself, so don't make me say it again. I'm looking for Megan Leary. If you have any knowledge of where she is—and I mean any—you'd better cough it up now or I'll be reserving you cell space with a big inbred mouth-breather named Bubba who never met a knothole he didn't like. We agreed?"

Wilkerson nodded mutely, both hands hiding his nose. "I'm listening."

"She—she was at the Wandora," Wilkerson said. He threw a panicked look at me. "She took off, though. All I know about it."

"She didn't take off," I said. "She was taken."

"Easy," Gentry scolded me. "Far as I know, Deputy, you couldn't see a lot, being as how you were face down on the floor in a pool of your blood. Joe, you think your cousin Lew Peyser might have an idea where to find the girl?"

Joe looked as if he'd been punched in the forehead. A born career criminal, he simply couldn't believe he wasn't more clever than the opposition.

"Lew?" He tried shaking his head, then gave it up. "Naw. Lew don't have nothing to do with—"

I grabbed his nose again. Gentry sighed. Joe howled and batted at me ineffectively. I held on until Joe gave a little-girl shriek and blurted, "Yeah! Yeah, he left with her, I told him not to and he punched me in the fuckin' nose—"

I let go, turned to Gentry, and said, "Looks like we'd better get out there and track down Lew Peyser."

"For leaving a bar with a woman?"

"For assault," I said. "On his cousin."

"What about your assault on me, you nose-twisting son of a bitch?" Joe interrupted. Gentry barely spared him a glance.

"He did you a favor," he said. "I'd have twisted it off." Gentry suddenly revealed his cold, eerie shark-smile.

"I still ain't pressing no charges against Lew," Joe said. We ignored him.

★ ★ ★ ★ ★

Gentry hadn't told me why he was looking for Meg. He didn't enlighten me now, and I decided not to ask. Gift horses and mouths. It wasn't as if I was qualified right now to go out and take on Peyser—or Old Lady Perlman, for that matter—by myself. One bone-breaking ass-kicking a day is my limit.

I fastened the seatbelt, swallowed a hot bubble of pain as my ribs shifted, and tried to take a good breath. The wrapping they'd put on me would have done the Egyptians proud. Half use of my lungs was the best I could hope for. Adrenaline was starting to wear off, and now I just felt tired, sick, and cold. If it hadn't been for Meg, I would've gone home, crawled in bed, and slept the day away.

The radio crackled in Gentry's truck. He had a nice built-in unit, wood-grain face inset in the black faux-leather dash. The truck gleamed of careful use of Armor-All. It reminded me suddenly of my father's car, of Saturdays spent spraying and wiping down the dash, the steering wheel, the seats. Of washing and waxing and detailing. Cars had always been my father's first love, his children only competing a distant second. He'd died in a NASCAR speedway crash, well on his way to finishing last.

Gentry had answered the radio while my mind drifted. I snapped back when I heard Jimmy Sparkman's voice asking, "How bad is he?"

I reached for the handset, clicked the button and said, "Death's door, Jimmy. Better pony up those bereavement benefits."

"Lucky for you that you put me down as beneficiary," he said. "So? You okay?"

"Sure. Couple of cracked ribs, bruises like a county map of Texas. And now I'm pissed."

Silence, and the hiss of static. Finally, Jimmy punched the button and said, "Then this won't matter. We just located Aurelia Galvan's body, Dan. Couple of kids horsing around the graveyard found it."

"The graveyard?" I had a stunned instant image of her body cradled in the arms of a marble angel.

"In that big marble crypt on the west side. The Patterson crypt."

Something about the crypt—Meg. I'd followed Meg to the graveyard, and after she left I'd looked around. The lock on the crypt had been broken. I'd gone in and looked around.

I keyed the radio and said, "She wasn't there two days ago, Jimmy."

"Well, she's there today. I'm on my way to see Mrs. Galvan."

I was glad it was him, not me. I'd always found it easier to look into the eyes of the dead than the ones they left behind. I held the handset for a few seconds longer, then keyed it and said, "Meg's missing, Jimmy. She was gone when I came to at the Wandora."

"I heard." He didn't say where. "Let Gentry look for her. She's his problem now anyway. You go on home and rest, Dan, you're no damn good to me beat half to hell."

I signed off and hung up the mike, turned painfully to look at Gentry. He started the truck. It shivered and purred like a stroked cat. Under the hood, I knew, the engine would be polished and gleaming, not a speck of spilled oil or dirt anywhere. He'd spend his weekends at auto shows and swap meets. Or races.

"We searched Meg's Lexus," Gentry said. "Came up with a recently fired Smith & Wesson .38 caliber, same caliber as the slug in your famous former sheriff. I've got to ask her some questions, Dan."

I thought about the report I'd read, about the brutality of what she'd endured at the hands of this town. About Gentry, the stone-faced Texas Ranger, witnessing most of it.

"You don't really think she did it," I said. He didn't look at me. He put the truck in gear. "Do you?"

He didn't answer. He applied gas to engine and eased the truck out of the hospital parking lot onto Main Street.

"Did you know about the rape?" I asked. I didn't think he would answer me. It took him a while, muscles bunching and relaxing in his jaw.

"Not at first," he said. "They said she'd tried to kill herself, gotten the bruises from being restrained."

"But you didn't believe that."

"She was—she was a surly little firecracker. Right up to then. Then she just sat there, staring straight ahead, eyes like pits to the bottom of hell." Gentry shook his head. "I couldn't prove it until then. Tried to get her to talk about it, but she—she didn't say. Couldn't or wouldn't, I don't know which."

"Somebody must have."

"Not then. Marlon Leary turned himself in for his wife's murder, said he'd done it in a drunken rage. The case against Meg went to shit, and she was acquitted. Marlon pled guilty and went straight to lockup. After she left town, she felt safe enough to tell the truth."

I wanted to cough, but I knew it was going to hurt. The impulse took over, and I was right, it did hurt like the devil; I hacked and bent over and grabbed his dash with sweaty fingers while the pain did a black-and-red dance inside. When I could talk again, I croaked, "Shit."

"You are in no shape to go looking for anybody," Gentry

said. "I'm taking you home."

"No," I half-whispered. "Graveyard."

"You're on your way there whether I take you or not," he muttered.

I kept my eyes shut, drifting on a hot sea of liquid pain, as the truck rumbled and bumped and turned. Against my eyelids a silent movie flickered. It wasn't of Meg Leary's rape, all those years ago; it was of her huddled silent and alone in the cell afterwards, her knees drawn up to her chest, fresh bruises on her body and that broken look in her eyes.

Lew Peyser's father had been the weak link, the one who confessed first, the one who'd killed himself and brought nothing but pain to his family. Lew Peyser was full of mis-placed rage against the girl who, in his opinion, had brought it all on herself.

He had Meg, and I couldn't do a damn thing about it.

"End of the line, partner," Gentry said just as the truck braked to a gentle stop. I opened my eyes, blinked against a bright and shifting world, and saw a blur of flashing lights and moving people. The silence of the cemetery had been smashed like a glass bulb with a hammer. I opened the door of Gentry's truck and stepped—or fell—down to the gravel drive, clung to the door for a few breaths of support, and then stood straight and waved to him gravely. He stared back, frowning.

"Find Meg," I said.

"Count on it."

"When you do—" What could I say? Be gentle with her? He smiled slightly and nodded in recognition.

"I won't shoot her," he said, "unless she shoots me first."

I had to be content with that as he pulled away, a bright

candy-apple blur on the winter day. I stuck my hands in my coat pockets and took a couple of deep breaths, felt shattered ribs shift uncomfortably, and walked to the gothic arched entrance of the cemetery.

Jimmy had pulled in everyone, including Harlan Wilson, who was an honorary deputy, really—he was seventy if he was a day, gnarled and weathered and with a good case of the trembles in his gun hand. Harlan was standing guard at the gate. He stared at me in open-mouthed horror as I limped toward him, then reached out to help me. I shook him off.

"Jesus on a stick, boy, you look like somebody tied you to a tackle dummy for football practice! Hang on, there, just hang on. You got no business here."

"The hell I don't, Harlan," I said. "Jimmy!"

He was in conference with a knot of other men, but at my yell he turned and shaded his eyes, shook his head, and walked over. He surveyed me sadly from head to foot.

"I told you to go home," he said.

"I want to see her."

"Dan, this girl's been dead for days. She was probably dead before her mother called us. You didn't let her down."

"I want to see her."

He shook his head again, this time in frustration, and gestured for me to follow. We picked our way through the timeworn gravestones, legacy of Kev Miller and Doc Larkin, through whispering dried grass, to the Patterson family crypt.

Men parted when I limped up. I knew most of them, and nodded when nods were given, but my attention was on that open door, on the glare of floodlights inside. Photographer's strobes exploded silently every few seconds—he was shooting quickly, he wanted out. I didn't blame him. I didn't really want in.

I stepped inside anyway, braced myself against the right-hand marble wall that held two of the Pattersons in their marble-capped drawers. Opposite me was a sealed tomb for Arledge Patterson, dead in 1974. In the uncapped opening lay Aurelia Galvan.

Weather had been cool, but time had begun its work; her skin was pallid and threaded with dark blooms of decomposition. Her eyes were closed and sunken, her face composed. As I watched, the photographer snapped a couple more halfhearted shots and cleared out, nodded to me on the way. I limped closer, lowered myself to my uninjured knee, and looked into the drawer at eye level.

A scrape of footsteps behind me told me Jimmy had joined us.

"Hands folded on her chest," I said. "Somebody tried to make her look nice. Her clothes are straight, her hair combed. There's a rosary around her fingers. Did your guys unwrap the sheet?"

"No, the kids who found her said they did that. She was wrapped up tight when they came here."

I nodded, thinking, then climbed laboriously back to my feet. Something stabbed me wetly in the side. No lifting, no twisting. "Jimmy, help me roll her over a second."

She was limp, no rigor mortis at all. Jimmy was right, she'd been dead for days now. No sign of what killed her, not immediately, but when I checked the skin of her back it was only lightly livid. The blood had pooled on her right side.

"She was originally put someplace else, someplace small," I said. "On her side. I'll bet she was dumped, or going to be dumped, but somebody had an attack of conscience. Somebody cared, Jimmy. They laid her out and wrapped her up for God."

"Not Javier Nieves," Jimmy said.

"No," I agreed. "Not Javier. He'd dump her like a dead dog. This is somebody who knew her. Somebody who loved her. When the coroner looks at her, they may be able to take a look at the lividity and match it to a dump site—"

I broke off and bent over to look again at the rosary wound around her hands.

"Jimmy," I said, "did her mother say Aurelia took her rosary when she left?"

"I don't know."

"I saw it. I saw it in her room the day after she left." Hanging from a pin holding up a Marilyn Manson poster, to be exact. Maybe not the same rosary, though. I reached in and carefully, using a fold of the sheet, turned the cross of the rosary to look at the back.

There was a name engraved on the back. I dug a penlight out of my pocket and tried to get a look, staggered, and almost went down. My knee sent a bolt of blue lightning up my spine, warning me I'd better not try it again.

"Let me," Jimmy said, and leaned in with my flashlight for a look. "It's hers."

He straightened up, clicked off the penlight and handed it back. I put in my pocket. "It's somebody with access to Rosa Galvan's house."

Jimmy drove me home. I wanted to go to Rosa's, try to find out who might have been in the house lately, but he wasn't having any. "You're not dying in my arms," he said. "People would talk."

"Anybody find Lew Peyser yet?" I asked. Jimmy shook his head. The cruiser hit a bump, not a bad one but enough to make me feel my bones had shifted south in my chest. I groaned and put my head back against the seat.

"You okay?"

"Sure." Nobody had bothered to tell me how a punctured lung would feel. I could still catch my breath, so I was probably not going to bleed out here in the cruiser.

"Lew do this to you?"

"I don't know." The truth was, I didn't know for certain, and even if I thought I did, I didn't want Jimmy in the middle of it. "We had words in the squad room yesterday. Over Meg, partly."

"If he did it, and we can prove it, I'll toss his ass in the state prison," he said. "I won't have this going on in my town, Dan. So you're not going to look for him, either. Gentry's got that covered for now, and if I have to I'll get some men on loan from Killing Rock. Lew can't hide. Not in Exile."

Probably true, but it only took him thirty seconds and a good pair of pointy-toed boots to half-kill me. He'd had Meg for more than two hours now. Two hours.

I closed my eyes, but that didn't stop the visions.

"Dan?" Somebody was shaking my shoulder. I grunted and straightened up, blinking away ghosts and gummy eyelids. "Home."

Somehow I'd fallen asleep. Waking up reminded me I had a pounding Mike Tyson of a headache; I groaned and reached up to my forehead, half expecting to feel a swelling where the skull was about pop open. Nothing but solid bone under abused skin.

"Listen, are you going to be okay by yourself?" Jimmy asked. "I'm not asking as your boss."

"I'm not answering as your employee," I said, and found

a dusty smile lying around. "I feel like a big pile of shit, Jimmy, but I'll live. Couple hours of rest and I should be nearly back to normal."

"Except for broken ribs and a torn-up knee, you'll be right as rain," he agreed. "How many times he kick you in the head?"

"Couple."

"I thought so." He watched me open the door and step out, then leaned over to say, "I'll call you the minute I know anything about Meg."

I managed to slam the door and wave him on. He ignored me. I fumbled in my pocket for keys, found them, and walked slowly to my apartment. It took me four tries to get the lock and key to mate successfully at my door. When I looked back, the cruiser was gone.

Inside, the room was cool and dark. A light gleamed somewhere in the bedroom at the back, but all the curtains were drawn and my eyes were still attuned to winter sunlight. I closed the door, locked it, and froze with the keys in my hand as I breathed in a ghost of perfume, warm and spicy.

My apartment still smelled like Meg.

All of a sudden I felt exhausted, as if gravity had just doubled; my head throbbed sickly, and my broken ribs caught fire. I had no idea where I'd found the strength to yank Joe Wilkerson by the hair and run around playing detective, but I was paying for it now. I made it to the counter that separated kitchen from living room, tossed my keys down, fumbled my gun off, and added it to the pile.

The bedroom was too far away. I found the couch and stretched out. It hurt. A lot. Then, slowly, it started to fade away.

I wasn't supposed to sleep, was I? Concussion . . .

Too exhausted to care.

I had let the dark tide carry me far, far out when the light next to the couch flicked on, turning the black of the inside of my eyelids a screaming warning red. That's not right, I thought, exhausted and fumbling for an explanation. I cracked open my eyes, squinted against the light, and for a few seconds I couldn't believe I wasn't dreaming.

Meg Leary was sitting on the edge of the couch, hands folded in her lap, looking down at me. The light glimmered in her eyes, revealing an expression I didn't recognize and didn't know how to interpret. She raised a hand, started to touch my face, then let it fall back in her lap.

"I didn't know," she said softly. "I swear to God, Dan, I didn't know anybody had hurt you."

I moved my hand and touched hers. It was warm and real. She was warm and real. Something tight and painful unknotted in my guts, and I sucked in a breath to fill the void.

"I thought Peyser—" I began. She interrupted as if she hadn't heard me.

"He came in with Joe Wilkerson and some other guy I didn't recognize," she said. Her eyes never left my face. "Joe had a knife. He took me outside and put me in the back of Lew's squad car. They told me I was under arrest."

"Anybody read you your rights?" I asked, and winced when I tried to sit up. She pressed my shoulder and kept me down.

"No. Lew argued with Joe, and then he and the other guy went back inside the Wandora. Joe took off whining." Her eyes shimmered with sudden rage. "Which was when they jumped you, I suppose."

"Where did he take you?"

"Nowhere," she said. "I smashed out the cruiser window

after I heard on the scanner that Gentry really was looking for me."

She was silent for a while, still cataloguing my bruises. That had shaken her pretty hard. "I didn't know, Dan. I would have come back for you, but I thought I'd better run."

"If Peyser had gotten hold of you—"

"I know," she said. "He wasn't taking me in. Not until—not until he'd gotten even. He thinks I killed his father."

"His father committed suicide. Not your fault."

"So far as I know, he did, but Peyser doesn't believe it. He thinks I hired somebody to blow his dad's head off and leave the note. He thinks I made it all up to get back at the deputies and Sheriff Hillyard."

"Did you?" I regretted it as soon as it was out. Apparently, I thought, my tact bone was broken too. Too bad they hadn't warned me about that.

She was silent for so long I thought she was too angry to answer, but then she said, in a tight, controlled whisper, "Sure, I made it up. Right after I killed my mother and got away with murder."

I closed my eyes against the lash of her fury. Too tired to fight.

After a moment of silence she said, "At least you can testify against him now."

"Testify to what? I didn't see him," I said. "He sucker-punched me from behind, then kicked the shit out of me while I was down. I never saw his face. He meant it that way."

She was silent. After a few seconds she raised her hand, and this time she let it rest very lightly on my forehead.

She didn't answer directly. Her eyes were dark and far away. She finally said, "I was always surprised it was old

175

man Peyser who crumbled. He was the hard one, you know. The one who grinned while he did it. He looked right into my eyes and grinned. I never thought he'd be the one to have an attack of conscience."

"So you think somebody did kill him?"

She shook her head in silence. We sat for a long time, two people in a pool of light surrounded by darkness.

"Did you kill Hillyard?" I asked her. Her eyes darted sharply to mine, then looked away.

"Official question?"

"Do I look official right now?"

"No comment, officer."

"They've got a gun out of your car," I said. "Recently fired. Same caliber as killed Joe Hillyard. Gentry didn't say, but it's probably registered to you."

She went very still, no expression on her face, her eyes wide and empty.

Slowly, she smiled. Not a nice smile. Not a smile I took any comfort in at all.

"That's odd," she said, "because I tossed that gun in a Dumpster behind the courthouse about eight hours ago."

Chapter Eleven

I forgot about my ribs and concussion. Meg made coffee—
better than I made it—and looked over the contents of my
refrigerator. She settled for two frozen chicken pot pies and
refused to talk to me while they were baking in the oven I'd
hardly ever used. We ate them in silence, staring at each
other, and she was right, the food and coffee helped. I no
longer felt half dead—more like a third. Sitting up seemed
like heavy bag training, only I had been used for the heavy
bag.

As she took her last bite of crust and sauce, she finally
answered me about the gun.

"It's mine," she said. "It's the one I keep in a hideout
holster under the dashboard. I found it lying on the seat this
morning, and it had been fired since I last cleaned it. Didn't
take too much imagination to see the setup. So I dumped
it."

"Your other gun?"

She shrugged and moved her coat to show me that she
was still wearing her sidearm.

"Any other guns we should worry about? Rocket
launchers in the trunk?"

She gave me a quirky grin. "Sue me. I overcompensate."

"I can alibi you most of the time."

"Peyser's not going to let that get in the way. And there
are periods where I'm unalibied, you know it as well as I do.
Want some dessert? You've got ice cream bars in the
freezer."

"Not for me. Look, Peyser's not the one I'm worried about, he couldn't do real police work if he was handcuffed to Joe Friday. But Gentry's in this now, and he's coming for you," I said, and took another sip of coffee. Meg scooted her chair back from the table, went to the freezer, and pulled out an ice cream bar. She sat down again, unwrapped paper from hard chocolate coating, and then nibbled a bite. Another one. I watched her in utter concentration.

She knew I was watching. A smile warmed her eyes. She took another bite. "Dan."

"Yeah?"

"It'd probably kill you right now."

"I know," I sighed. "Let me have my fantasies."

"Just so long as I don't have to hear them," she said. "It'll take them a while to think about looking for me here, I think we're okay for a while."

"Not that long. Gentry's no fool. He knows you haven't got too many places you can go to ground here. Where's your Lexus?"

"Still behind the Dairy Queen, as far as I know," she said. "If they haven't impounded it yet."

Which they would have, if they found the gun in it. She had no car, no friends in town except me, Rosa Galvan, Dolores Sanchez, maybe a very few more. It was just a matter of time.

Meg took another bite of her ice cream. "I was just thinking about Gentry," she said. "Did you know he protected me after the acquittal? There was a mob outside the courthouse that wanted to beat me to death, and he put himself in front of me. Not because he believed I was innocent, because the court said I was innocent. That's pure, Dan. Gentry is the one pure man I've ever known."

"Do you think he'll believe you shot Hillyard?"

"Doesn't matter," she said. She got up and carried plates to the sink as if she was too restless to sit still. "As soon as he finds me, he's going to try to take me in."

I had a bad feeling. The word "try" had a neon trouble sign attached to it. Meg wasn't going back into that cell, with all those memories, without a bloody fight. It was going to be bad for somebody, maybe for everybody. As an officer of the law, I was obligated to get up from the kitchen table, turn her around, and put cuffs on her. Drop a dime to Gentry to come pick her up.

What I said was, "I have a car."

"You call this a car?"

She wasn't joking. She stood there in the parking lot, hands in her pockets against the increasingly cold wind, and stared at my primer-colored 1976 Vega like it was a milk crate with whitewalls. It didn't help that at this particular hour of the day the parking lot was nearly deserted; the Vega, parked not far from the Dumpster, looked as if somebody with lousy aim had tried to toss it in.

"It runs," I said. I sounded defensive, even to myself. "And you're not in a position to be picky, goddamn it. Take the keys. If anybody asks you where you got them, they were on a hook in the kitchen."

"I'm not driving that," she snapped.

"It's that or jail, Meg."

"Jail or a rolling death sentence. Assuming it rolls."

I'd made my case. She knew the choices. I dangled the keys out to her and waited. It was a long thirty seconds of gimlet-eyed silence, and then she reached out and grabbed them with a frustrated groan. I opened the door for her—it squealed piercingly—and she bent down and looked inside at the worn, patched upholstery and the cracked dashboard. She straightened up, looked at me, and widened her eyes. She had expressive eyes. There was no mistaking her utter snobbery.

"Anything I need to know about it? Does it blow up when a tumbleweed hits it from behind?"

"That's a Pinto, and no. It's all my ex-wife left me with, so you could show some appreciation; you're driving off in half my net worth."

She did a double-take that was just almost funny. Expressive eyes pitied me. She gingerly lowered herself—physically and mentally—into the car, adjusted the seat, slammed the door, and rolled down the window. I didn't say anything. The wind was getting colder, the sky a white-steel blur. Texas weather. There was a storm coming, and fast. Out here on the flat plains, there was no place to hide.

I hadn't told her about Aurelia Galvan because I knew if she found out, she'd stay. If she stayed, she'd be back in a jail cell, maybe for good. Maybe the Vega would get her far enough, maybe not; maybe by the time she dragged the lame-ass rustbucket into Odessa or Big Spring there'd already be a warrant for her arrest.

I could be helping a cold-blooded murderer. She could have driven over to Joe Hillyard's house, put a gun to his head, and slammed his brains out the back of his skull. Maybe I didn't know her at all. Maybe I was, as Jimmy Sparkman was sure to point out, thinking with my dick.

She didn't say anything. Neither did I. She turned the key, and the Vega's starter ground and groaned and finally caught. The car frame shuddered with vibration. Meg closed her eyes for a few seconds, misery on her face. She wasn't thinking about going to jail. She was thinking about the indignity of driving a Vega.

I slapped the cold metal of the door panel, as if I'd just loaded an ambulance, and she forced the tranny into gear. All that was left was for her to step on the gas and be gone.

And for whatever selfish reason, I really didn't want to let her go. The moment in the squad car came back to me, seconds of memory so real it was like stepping through a time warp. The heat between us, the taste of her mouth, the ripe swell of her breasts against my body. Ah, God, I was tired, my head ached, my bones felt like I'd been run through a blunt buzz saw, and all of a sudden I had a hard-on like the Washington Monument. Which, because of the low-slung Vega, was just about at her eye level.

She hadn't stepped on the gas yet. The Vega was still idling and coughing white smoke. I shifted uncomfortably to relieve pressure on my bad knee. She was still staring at me.

"Go," I finally said. Just the one word.

"I can't," she said. "I'm sorry."

I didn't know what the hell she was sorry for until her eyes shifted minutely, and I turned to look over my shoulder to see Jonathan Gentry's polished and beloved pickup truck pulled up on the street, blocking the exit from the apartment parking lot. I couldn't see him, but I knew he was looking straight at us.

Too late. We were too late.

"Get in," Meg said. I frowned. "Just get in, Dan. And trust me."

Which Meg was real? The one who might have killed Joe Hillyard, or the one who'd been with me in that cruiser, panting my name? Both? Neither? Which one was she asking me to trust?

I limped around the Vega and got in on the passenger side. Meg applied gas, and the Vega started crawling slowly out of its Dumpster-shaded parking space. It turned directly for Gentry's truck.

"Meg," I said.

"Shut up," she snapped, and hit the gas. The Vega shuddered hard and leaped forward, spraying gravel against the Dumpster with a sound like rapid gunfire. The shiny truck loomed up, close, closer, too close. At the last possible second, Gentry gunned the truck and pulled it just far enough out of the way as the Vega flew out of the parking lot. Meg leaned on the steering wheel and achieved a two-wheel screaming turn in the opposite direction from the way Gentry was facing. I grabbed for the cracked, dusty dash.

Meg whooped, a war-yell that gave me cold chills.

"Stop!" I yelled. She laughed. "Meg! Jesus, stop! What're you doing?"

She was doing about fifty, I figured, when she blew through the stop sign at the corner. I turned to look over my shoulder—not painless—and saw that Gentry had turned the big pickup around. He was closing the distance, fast. It wasn't like he was alone, either—he had a radio, and he'd be stupid not to use it. He could have deputies cut us off whenever and wherever he liked.

The thought of Lew Peyser actually arresting Meg made my stomach lurch. Or maybe it was the dip she slammed the Vega over at fifty-five miles an hour.

I tried again. "Meg! There's nowhere to go now! It's too late!"

"There's always someplace to go," she said. She made another right turn, racing down Sycamore as if she actually thought there was freedom at the end of it. "I didn't shoot Joe Hillyard, Dan. I need you to believe that."

"I'll believe you if you stop the car."

The light at the corner was flashing red. So were the

cherry lights on the police cruiser sitting in the intersection, waiting for us. Gentry's front grille was taking up the entire rear view mirror. We weren't going anywhere, but we were going there very fast.

"Hold on," Meg said. I grabbed dashboard. She bootlegged the wheel, somehow kept the Vega under control as the bald tires shimmied and screamed and slid. The back bumper missed the squad car in the intersection by inches. We'd made a left so sharp it wasn't possible for Gentry, in the massive pickup, to duplicate it.

He didn't even try. He went wide, around the squad car, ran up on the sidewalk, slammed back down to the pavement and roared after us.

But Meg wasn't going any further. She signaled—signaled—a left-hand turn, slowed down to twenty, and cruised into the parking lot of the courthouse. She parked, shut off the engine, and handed me the keys. Her eyes were bright, and beautiful, and oddly satisfied.

"Not a bad heap of junk," she said, and leaned over and kissed me, a flash of warm lips so sudden and short it was as if I'd imagined it. "Arrest me."

"What?"

"I don't want it to be any of them."

She meant it. I reached around to the holster at the back of my belt and pulled out handcuffs. I snapped on the right wrist. She turned to let me secure her left behind her back.

"You have the right to remain silent," I said. "For God's sake, Meg, take advantage. You have the right to an attorney . . ."

Meg's door flew open.

Lew Peyser had a look I'd hoped never to see on a lawman's face as he reached in, pulled her out by her hair, and shouted, "Did you kill Joe Hillyard, you fucking bitch?"

"Peyser!" I yelled, and clawed my way out of the car. Gentry had pulled his truck to a smoking stop beside us, and he was just in time to grab my arm and drag me back. Meg twisted in Peyser's grip, then went limp. He threw her against the car and let go.

More cops appearing now—Jimmy Sparkman, pelting down the courthouse steps, the part-time deputy Frank Carroll, even Joetta coming out to see the show. I tried to shake Gentry off but it was like shaking off a vise clamp.

"Let go!" I yelled.

"Wait," he whispered in my ear.

Peyser grabbed Meg by the hair again, bent her neck back at a painful angle, and spat in her face. Literally. I flinched and tried to get loose again, but Gentry stood solid as a rock, watching and waiting.

"Did you kill Joe Hillyard, you fucking bitch? Answer me!"

Meg looked Peyser right in the eye, eerily calm, and said, "Absolutely. He cried like a baby before I pulled the trigger and blew his fucking brains out."

Then he hit her, a hard punch to the face, and Gentry let me go. In two long loping steps he had Peyser by the arm and was slamming him back against the limestone of the courthouse wall. I turned back to Meg. Her nose was bleeding, her lip cut, and in her eyes I saw absolute, soul-deep terror, but then she blinked and it was gone, hidden behind that hard, brilliant wall of strength.

She'd orchestrated it perfectly, pushed his buttons, even pushed mine. Half of the cops were looking at her, half over at Peyser.

She spat out a mouthful of blood and said, "You can finish reading me my rights now, Dan."

Believe me, that got everybody's attention.

* ★ ★ ★ ★

It was mostly impressions after that. Gentry's cold-eyed hound dog face as he carefully read Meg her rights and sent somebody for Merle the paramedic to see to her face. Lew Peyser's dirty-gray expression as he sat alone on a stone bench, turning his cowboy hat in his hands, wondering where it had all gone wrong for him. No badge on his jacket now, and no gun in his holster. Every once in a while, he remembered to hate me or Meg, but he did it from a distance.

It started raining, a gray driving rain that held the promise of sleet. Lew Peyser stayed out in it, unmoving. The rest of us went inside. I had to take my time with the stairs and cursed the whole way, with Jimmy hovering near me like a mother hen. My knee felt swollen to basketball size, but it didn't look so bad, just sausage-tight in my blue jeans. The ribs didn't bear thinking about.

Meg was in handcuffs, and I wanted to go with her, I wanted to be with her when they put her in a cage again. But I couldn't keep up. I saw her look back once, at the top of the steps, her face a white-pale blur in dark wind-whipped hair. Too far away to see her eyes.

I struggled to the top of the steps five minutes later, soaked to the skin and hot with pain. Inside the courthouse the air smelled musty and thick with ghosts. The civil servants were clustered in the hallways buzzing gossip. I looked at the winding staircase leading up to the tower and swallowed hard. Jimmy tugged on my elbow.

"Elevator," he said.

"Oh, Jesus, Jimmy, I hate that thing."

"Just do it."

To call it an elevator was charitable. Pushing the button revealed a tiny cubicle, just wide enough for two skinny people if they were real friendly. It was more like a moving coffin than an elevator, and it dated back to the twenties, at least. As did the cables holding it up.

"See you at the top," Jimmy said, and the grimy industrial green door slid closed between us. In the little aluminum box I braced myself against the wall and pressed the number 3. The box jerked. It didn't make me feel better that I could brace myself in all four directions without even straightening out my arms. The jerking continued, slow and painful. I held my breath and tried to tell myself the walls weren't really getting closer. There weren't any indicators to tell me how far I'd gone, how far I had to go. One more especially big jerk, the kind that I half-expected to come with the sound of snapping cable, and then the door creaked open on the third floor.

True to his word, Jimmy was waiting. I almost knocked him over getting out of there. Through the double doors I saw there was a knot of people struggling, and Jimmy looked over his shoulder toward it, too.

"She doesn't want to go," he said. "Dan, just let it be. She has to go in the cell, you know that."

"Let me try."

"She'd kill you. You can barely stand up."

"Jimmy." I met his eyes. "Let me try."

He opened the door for me and bellowed for everybody to clear off of Meg. Everybody did except for Gentry, who wasn't taking his orders from the locals. I limped up to her, saw the blind sheen of rage and terror in her eyes, and stopped just out of touching range.

"Meg," I said. That was all. What else could I tell her that would make any difference at all? Her eyes focused on me, and so did Gentry's.

Amazingly, she managed to smile. "How's the knee?"

"Not so bad," I lied. "Don't make me kick your ass."

186

Such a fragile smile. Merle the paramedic had closed up the cuts and the bruise was just a dark promise for the future. She took a deep breath, and some of the feral shine left her eyes.

"You do it," she said, and it came out just a husky whisper, invisible to anybody except Gentry. "You and Gentry, nobody else."

I looked at Gentry's face. It had no opinion. I reached in and gently took hold of her other elbow, and together the three of us limped down the hall to the holding cells. Meg stopped dead in the doorway, facing the row of bars. I started walking her toward the nearest empty cell.

"Not that one," Gentry said. "Put her in the one on the end."

I was glad he'd steered me away from the one with bad memories. Meg didn't say anything at all, stayed quiet and composed but vibrating under my hands like a machine running too high.

She walked into the cell on her own, let me take the handcuffs off without any words at all. Once she'd sat down on the narrow bunk—collapsed, more like it—she rubbed her wrists convulsively to get rid of the feel of cold metal. The place smelled like a cell, the ghosts of sweat and piss and vomit still lingering behind a layer of lemony disinfectant. Clean cot, clean blanket. No amenities except a full roll of toilet paper by the toilet.

I hadn't shut the cell door. Gentry stood in the opening, blocking it like a solid door of flesh.

"Meg?" I asked. She stared straight ahead at the blank stone wall, full of the scratched graffiti of other occupants. "You okay?"

"Peachy," she said. Nothing in the word at all. She'd never been so closely guarded. "What now?"

I opened my mouth to answer but Gentry beat me to it.

"Now we talk about you and Joe Hillyard, Meg. You know we got to do that. Ballistics will have a result back on the gun we found in your car in the next six hours. I think you're going to want to say something before then. Get ahead of this thing this time."

"Did you have a warrant for my car?"

"Didn't need one. Gun was in plain sight on the front seat, all the doors locked. Meg, I've also got an eyewitness that says your car was parked in front of Joe Hillyard's house two days ago between three-thirty and four o'clock. According to the way his rigor was passing off, that fits the time of death."

That froze both of us in place. Not that I hadn't suspected it would happen, but it had the rancid taste of a well-thought-out setup. She looked at me.

"She was with me, Gentry," I said.

"Don't think so, Dan. You came back to the office to voucher some evidence. It's in the case file that you were taking a phone call from a runaway right around then. I also have a time-coded videotape that shows you here until after four."

Of course he did. I'd brought back Javier's ring, I'd taken the call from the fake Aurelia, and on Jimmy's instructions I'd closed the case files. And Meg hadn't been with me.

I looked at her. She was still studying the far wall.

"Meg?" he prompted.

She didn't turn her head. "I've been abducted, shot at, and beaten while in handcuffs in front of witnesses, including you, and I confessed to the murder before being read my rights." She suddenly looked right at him. "You should know when you're licked, Jonathan."

It gave me a bad moment. She seemed too cool, so in control. Could she have planned it this way? Known what would happen? Manipulated Peyser to be sure he'd queer the arrest? Manipulated me to be sure I didn't do my job too well?

But then I remembered Gentry holding me back as Peyser dragged her out of the car. As Peyser spat in her face and screamed at her.

As Peyser hit her.

I had a sudden, very weird feeling that Gentry had manipulated Peyser. But why? Why would he want Meg's confession called into doubt?

Gentry wasn't giving anything away. He stepped back, holding the cell door open, and jerked his head at me to get out. I didn't want to, but he was a Texas Ranger and I wasn't even in the minor leagues. I stepped out.

The door shut between us with a hollow bang. Meg flinched.

"I'll give you some time," Gentry said. "Cell's a good place to think."

"If people leave you alone," she said. God, her voice, hollow as an empty grave. "Leave me the fuck alone, Gentry."

He turned and walked away, down the hall, out of sight. I stood there and looked at her, at the bars between us.

She didn't look at me at all. After a while, she said, "I was wrong about him."

"Did you go to Joe Hillyard's house on Tuesday?"

"He's as much of a bastard as he ever was," she said softly.

"Please tell me if you did."

"I think he knew. I think he knew all along."

"Meg!" I slapped the bars hard with my good hand. Unfortunately, it was connected to bad ribs. I wrapped my fingers around the metal and held on tight through the stabs of pain. "Did you go to Joe Hillyard's house on Tuesday?"

She jumped. The vibration in her was visible now, a light tremor all over her body. She slowly turned her head toward me, but her eyes were somewhere else, far away, looking into darkness.

"It's the same cell," she whispered. "He wants me in the same cell. Think about that for a while, Dan."

She wouldn't say another word. I sat there until I realized what it was I had to do. One of the worst moments of my life. So, Danny, who are you putting first? You, or her?

Her. I walked to the other end of the cells, where Earl Brenner was sleeping off the excitement of exposing himself to Pastor Franks of the Central Baptist Church. Nobody else to listen. I pulled out my cell phone, the one I so rarely had a use for anymore, and pushed a speed dial number I had programmed in dusty years ago. The phone had been a gift, I remembered suddenly. A Christmas gift three years ago. It seemed longer than that.

On the other end of the phone my ex-wife René answered on the third ring and said, in her smooth pleasant voice, "René Morgan."

"Don't hang up," I said. "It's—"

She hung up. Immediately. I sighed and hit END for the call, then redialed.

"René Morgan." A shade less warmth in the tone.

"I have a job for you," I said, and managed to get the whole sentence out before the click of disconnection. "Damn it!"

"Keep it down out there," Earl murmured from his cell. He turned over and wrapped his pillow over his head. "Damn cops."

I hit redial. She didn't bother to announce herself this time, but the fact she'd picked up the call instead of directing it to her assistant told me she might be willing to listen.

"René, it's not for me," I said, still talking fast. "I've got a woman here who needs the best defense attorney in Texas. I figure that's still you, regardless of how things stand between the two of us. Listen to the message, not the messenger. Give her a chance."

She didn't hang up. After a few long seconds she said, "This had better not be a trick, Danny."

"No tricks. Believe me, the last thing I want to do was open old wounds." Mine hadn't healed. Probably never would. René, on the other hand, was an overachieving survivor. She'd gone from law clerk to an attorney of international reputation in record time, had missed being a member of the Simpson defense team only because she'd been defending a twelve-year-old gang banger in El Paso for a triple homicide. She was a fast healer, but slow to forgive. "Her name's Megan Leary."

"Megan Leary?" Her voice sharpened. She had phenomenal recall, nearly eidetic. "Murder case, about fifteen years ago? Someplace in Podunk, Texas? She was acquitted. Greg Chapman was her lawyer."

That was René. She knew the wins, losses, and appeal stats of every attorney in the state the way football fans knew the Cowboys. "She was acquitted then, but she's been arrested for another murder now, same town. She didn't do it."

"Really." Only a lawyer could sound that cynical and dry on one word. "If you're interested, she must be pretty."

I had no defense for that one. I stayed quiet. She hated that.

"What's your involvement?" she asked.

"Friend," I said. "I hope. Truth is, I just can't stand by and let this happen. It's wrong, René. Real wrong."

I'd managed to get Earl's attention. As I paced a narrow path between the cell bars and the wall, I glanced over and saw he'd dropped his pants to show me his equipment. He put his hands on his hips and modeled for me.

"Nice, Earl," I said. "Save it for the pastor."

He pouted and zipped up.

"I'm losing interest, Dan," René said. "I bill out at three hundred an hour, and you're costing me money. Tell me why I should care about a friend of yours."

"They've got her locked in the same cell where she was raped by cops fifteen years ago," I said. "Interested now?"

Pause. "I'm still listening."

I told her a rapid-burst version of the story, up to Meg's cool confession and the screwed-up arrest. She didn't speak, but every once in a while I heard the scratch of pen on paper.

"Well?" I said. I'd finished talking, and she hadn't started. On the other end of the phone, I heard the pen tapping the desk. "I'm on the cell, René. You want to pay the roaming?"

She snorted. "You always were cheap."

"I'm driving a rusted-out Vega and living in a concrete box," I said bitterly. "I can't afford to be anything else."

"Don't blame me for your stupidity," she shot back. "We both know this is your fault."

My fault. René was in the business of laying blame. In that first few seconds of silence after the gunshot, with the two of us face to face and stopped in mid-argument, the first thing she'd said was, "My God this is your fault," even before we'd both turned and run for the stairs.

Before our lives had ended.

I made an effort to pull myself back from that black whirlpool that always formed between us. "Listen, this isn't the point. She needs help. Will you do it?"

"Can she pay me?" René laughed, short and bitter. "No, of course she can't. She's a friend of yours."

"She's got money," I said. I didn't know if she did or not, but she'd won three million in the lawsuit against Exile, and she drove a nice enough car. "How soon can you get here?"

"Hmm—I have a deposition this afternoon, but I can catch a plane tonight for Midland. I'll rent a car from there. Book me a hotel, nothing cheap, Hilton or Marriott would be fine."

"There's a motel," I said. "You'd better pack your own champagne and caviar. Whatever time you get in, come to the courthouse. I'll be waiting."

After a second of silence, René said, "You really do care about this, don't you?"

"Believe me, I wouldn't have wasted the phone call if I didn't."

I hung up before she could insult me back. Petty victories were better than no victories at all.

I catnapped uneasily on a bunk in an empty cell next to Meg's, listening for the sound of footsteps. She wasn't disturbed. She didn't make a sound. When I looked in on her she was awake, lying on her side with her back to the wall. She looked at me, but I couldn't tell what she was thinking, and she didn't respond when I asked her.

Jimmy came to get me to tell me the autopsy was in on Aurelia Galvan.

Exile wasn't big enough to have a coroner, in and of itself, but it was the county seat, so we had a miniscule crime lab and a forensic pathologist who spent most of his time puttering around in his garden and training his show dogs. Two autopsies in two days, I would have thought, would strain his abilities to the limit.

I was wrong. He was a cheerful middle-aged man with a thick belly and a close-trimmed dark beard, a rich singing voice, and undeniable enthusiasm for his work. He sat in Jimmy Sparkman's guest chair with the file folders and told us what he'd found.

"First of all, it seemed fairly obvious what happened to Joe Hillyard," he said. "Bullet went in at close range, came out the back of his skull, and took most of his higher brain functions with it. His autonomic functions continued for a while, probably about fifteen minutes or so, before he expired. The temperature in the house was unusual—about seventy-eight, according to the record of the scene. The thermostat was set on eighty. I'd venture to say somebody tried to throw off the time of death."

"Without success, though," Jimmy said. The coroner nodded.

"Even with the acceleration of the decomposition process, that much was pretty clear-cut. He died mid-afternoon on Tuesday, probably between three and five o'clock. He'd eaten a good lunch, which was mostly digested. Nothing else remarkable about his physical condition at all. Fatal gunshot wound to the head, murder by unknown assailant." He frowned and shifted in his chair. "Here's the funny part. Our corpse was shot twice. The second time was hours after he was dead."

"What?"

"The first wound killed him. No trace of that bullet, which plowed in and out—there was some evidence of a slug dug out of the wall, however."

"You said you found a .38 caliber bullet," Jimmy protested. "That's why Megan Leary's in jail right now! Ballistics matched it to her gun."

"We did. A .38 caliber bullet went in and stayed in, but all of the wound track related to that bullet appears to be post-mortem." Slaughter shrugged. "I'm not saying the first bullet wasn't a .38—it certainly could have been. But without the slug I can't say for certain. All I can tell you is the first bullet was fatal, the second ornamental."

"Jesus," Jimmy said.

"Well, I consulted him, but he didn't have anything to add." The coroner switched folders. "Aurelia Galvan's just as complicated. My best guess is that she died sometime between noon and four o'clock five days ago. She had a shrunken stomach, so she hadn't eaten in at least eight hours before her death. As to how she died, she had a crushing head wound hidden by her hair. Very little bleeding, so death was probably instantaneous. Difficult to say whether it was homicide or accident, but the concealment of the body—two times—leads me to think homicide."

"Two times. So she was moved," Jimmy said.

"She was a world traveler," the coroner agreed. He took a sip of the coffee that Jimmy had provided and was polite enough not to cough it back up. I knew better. I'd shared a dorm room with Jimmy in college, and his coffee-making impairment went back further than that. "She had post-mortem lividity on her right side, and was put in that position before rigor set in, probably immediately after death. I can't tell you too much about where she was concealed, but the way the blood pooled it looks like it was probably a car trunk. We found fibers on her clothing and skin consistent with automotive carpet fibers, but we're sending them for further testing. I'll be able to give you a color soon, and maybe some makes and models of cars if we're lucky."

Jimmy was outright grinning in satisfaction. "Great. That's great. Thank you, Doc."

"I'm not done," he said. "We found oil in her hair. Used automotive oil. Also some gravel fragments and soil. Find me a place to test, we can probably match to it. I hope that helps you."

Jimmy stood up and shook his hand solemnly. The doctor turned to me. "I'd shake your hand, deputy, but I'm afraid you might come apart. I've seen better-looking corpses."

"Thanks, Doc. I'll try to stay off your table for a while."

"Do that," he said. "We haven't been introduced. I'm Jeff Slaughter."

"Dr. Slaughter the coroner?" I raised my eyebrows. "Planned it like that, did you?"

"Mea culpa," he laughed. "In my defense, my family's been out here for more than a hundred years. My great grandfather was the first coroner in the state of Texas. Just carrying on the family joke."

I liked him. He had warm brown eyes and strong hands, and looked like he could relax like a regular guy. He'd also be a perfect trial witness, if it came to that. We shook hands, carefully, and he headed back to his garden and his dogs.

"Automotive oil," I said. "Meg and I traced Aurelia to Cal Worthen's car dealership on the day of her disappearance. She probably went to see her cousin Hector, but he says he never saw her. She was definitely back in the mechanics' area, though. Plenty of gravel and dirt back there, not to mention oil."

"You still like Javier for this?" Jimmy asked me. I nodded. "How does he fit into the mayor's car dealership?"

"Hell if I know, boss. I'm just a small-town deputy."

"That'll be the day," he sighed. "Look, is Meg talking?"

"Not to me. Not so far." I hesitated. "Her lawyer's on the way."

"Well, I guess that couldn't be helped," he shrugged. "Gentry's been out getting his forensic results, but I don't doubt they're going to come back matching to Meg, do you?"

"No. Somebody went to a hell of a lot of trouble for this. Somebody wants her in prison and not asking any more questions. I thought that was because of Aurelia, but what if it's because of her mother?"

"Her mother?" Jimmy echoed, frowning. He poured himself a cup of coffee and didn't bother to offer me one. "Don't let her tie you up in conspiracy theories, Dan. Either she killed her mother or she didn't. Either way, nobody's got any reason to launch a cover-up this late in the game for that."

But there was something strange about the way he said it. Jimmy had always been a bad liar.

Farlene knocked on the door and stuck her dyed-blonde head inside. She'd already seen and exclaimed over my damage, so she dismissed me and focused on Jimmy to say "Meg Leary wants to talk to you."

"To me?" Jimmy asked, surprised. He looked at me, then quickly away. "Be right there."

"Move her to another cell, Jimmy," I said. "I tried to get her to move about an hour ago, but she wouldn't. She'll do it if you order it."

"Why?"

"Because Gentry had me put her in the same cell as before," I said. I still felt a twinge of bitterness about that. "It's not helping things."

Jimmy considered that in silence for a few seconds, then shook his head and took a big gulp of coffee. He didn't make a face. I did.

"I'm not messing with Jonathan Gentry," he said finally. "If you're smart, Dan, you won't either."

He walked off to talk to Meg. I sat back down with a sigh, stretched my leg out, and waited.

I didn't have long to wait. Five minutes later, maybe less, Ranger Gentry opened the door to Jimmy's office and stepped in. He looked at me in silence for a few seconds, then went to Jimmy's desk and picked up the handset of the phone.

"I don't like being used," I said. He put the handset back in the cradle.

"Something you want to say?" he asked, and leaned against the desk. He crossed his arms and fixed me with that cold stare.

"I think I just did. You had me put her right back in the cell with bad memories."

"Nothing personal, deputy," he said. "It's her weak spot. Believe me, she doesn't have too many. The faster we get this done, the better off she is."

"So if she was claustrophobic, you'd put her in a hole in the ground?"

"If I thought it would close the case and get this behind us, I'd swing the shovel," he said. He uncrossed his arms and stood up. "I'd like this to be a private call. We done now, or do you want to piss around the desk some more?"

"We're done," I said tightly, and got up from the chair. I tried not to limp on my way out. Gentry kicked the door shut behind me.

Jimmy Sparkman was walking back down the hall from the cells, hands in his pockets, looking thoughtful. He almost walked past me without speaking, but I caught his elbow and dragged him to a stop.

"Jimmy?" I asked. He looked at me like a stranger for a few seconds, then blinked and focused.

"I can't tell you, Dan," he said. "I have to go check something out. You stay with her until I get back. Don't let anybody alone with her, anybody, you understand?"

"Where are you going?" I asked. He hesitated. "Damn it, Jimmy, don't go getting protective on me. Tell me."

"Doc Larkin," he said. "He called. He says he knows who killed Joe Hillyard."

Chapter Twelve

I dragged a faded orange plastic chair back to the hallway and put it in front of Meg's cell. She was awake, walking around—pacing the length of her cell, her fingers knotting together, twisting apart. Her head was down, her shining dark hair hiding her face. She didn't look up at the creak of plastic as I settled down and stretched out my leg more comfortably. She paced to the back wall, turned and did a diagonal that led her close to my chair. She didn't pause. Didn't speak.

"Anything you need?" I asked.

"No," she said. The first word she'd spoken to me in hours, and not from lack of trying on my part. "You shouldn't have called anybody for me, Dan. I don't need a lawyer."

"Crazy talk from a lady behind bars."

"When's my bail hearing?"

"Ten in the morning," I said. "You should get some sleep. She'll be here in about an hour, I expect."

"Your ex-wife." Meg stopped pacing and sat down on the edge of the bunk facing me. "What's her name?"

"René Morgan."

The eyebrows went up, the blue eyes opened wide. "Well," she said. "Aren't you just full of surprises?"

"She'd be the first one to say so."

"Then why'd you divorce?"

"She didn't like surprises," I said, and got up. My turn to pace, though I pretended I was trying to work the kinks out of my injured leg.

"Any kids?" Meg asked. Such an innocent question. I stopped, turned, and kept my head down as I paced past her cell back to the chair. "Dan?"

"It was in the papers," I said. "We had one son. Sean. He was six when he died."

She got up off the bed, closed her hands around the bars. She was staring at me now. I avoided her eyes. "I remember now. That was you?"

I nodded. My knee felt hot and liquid, and I put my full weight on it just to have the satisfaction of that white-hot burn. I needed pain. I needed it to give me limits, because otherwise that black whirlpool my conversation with René had started would suck me down again.

"I'm sorry," Meg said. Her hand reached through the bars to touch my shoulder, but I stepped back. "It was a terrible accident."

"No," I said. "It wasn't. I left the gun on a side table, I was too tired and distracted to put it in the safe. René and I had a fight at the dinner table, just like usual, and Sean ran upstairs. He took my gun and we didn't even notice. We didn't stop yelling until we heard the shot."

The papers called it a tragic accident with a firearm, but René and I had always known the truth. The truth wasn't convenient to René's career, though. She'd always been a passionate advocate for gun control, and an accident would help her; being the mother of a six-year-old suicide victim begged too many delicate questions.

I'd been the one who'd always made the arguments for safe and responsible ownership. Safe and responsible ownership, sure. I'd thrown the gun on the table fully loaded and walked away. Not drunk—I was rarely drunk—but just irritated and tired. A moment of human weakness, with inhuman results. I didn't want to think about Sean. I couldn't think about Sean. When I tried to, the whirlpool closed over my head and I went down into the darkness, gulping despair.

It had been better not to think about any of it. Better to get out of Houston, leave my job, leave my friends, leave everything for nothing. Nothing was what I needed. What I suppose I deserved.

"Anyway," I said, "René's the best. She'll rip this case apart like wet tissue. You'll be on the street five minutes after she walks in the room."

I sat down in the chair again with a groan of pain, rubbed my knee, and slowly straightened it out.

"Aren't you supposed to take it easy on that?" Meg asked. She sat down, too, but kept holding on to the bars.

"I am taking it easy," I said. "I'm not kicking Peyser's ass with it. Anything you need? Anything I can get?"

"Fresh underwear would be nice," she said. "And coffee."

"You look like the last thing you need is coffee," I said. Her hands wouldn't stay still, kneading the bars, adjusting her hair, picking at lint on her wrinkled pants. Dark circles under her eyes told me she hadn't slept, not for long.

"Thanks. Well, you're looking better," she said, which was a lie, my bruises were turning a nice ripe blue. But maybe she wasn't talking about the bruises. "Where's Jimmy?"

"Jimmy's gone to talk to Doc Larkin. Listen, you asked me to believe you. I didn't. I'm sorry," I said. She stared at me for a few seconds, then sat down on the bunk and leaned forward as if I'd punched her in the stomach. "You didn't kill Joe Hillyard. I shouldn't have doubted that."

"I wanted to kill him," she said. "He walked in here that night—he walked in here and saw the cell door open, the four of them inside—he just stood there. I looked at him and he just stood there. He didn't say anything to me at all, he just told them to get out. He sent his wife in here to—to put my clothes back on. And then he lied about what he saw to save those men. I had to fight, Dan. I had to fight to make anyone hear me. I've been fighting ever since."

I didn't say anything. There was nothing I could say that would make any difference. She leaned forward, pressing her hands against her stomach until her head touched her knees.

"I didn't kill my mother," she whispered. "Oh God I didn't kill her, Dan, I didn't."

"I know that."

"I was high but I would've known, I would've remembered—"

"I know."

"But I was glad she was dead."

And for the first time since I'd met her, she cried, quiet wrenching sobs that were torn out of her by the roots. I stood up and went to the bars, put my hands around the cold metal because I couldn't put my hands around her face. She cried without seeing me. Without seeing anything.

Gentry, I thought. You bastard. But how long had she needed to cry like this? How many years of bitter rage and dry eyes? Maybe he was right. Maybe.

I said, finally, "Fresh underwear, coming up. With a side of coffee."

She lunged up as I turned to go, reached through the bars and grabbed my unbandaged hand. Our fingers laced together without either one of us meaning it to happen, and all of a sudden we were close, nothing but the cold bars between us.

There was just enough room for me to kiss her. I did,

long and slow and sweet, careful of the cut in her lip, my bruises, the world between us.

I pulled back just far enough to whisper. "Look out for yourself in here. Don't trust anybody, Meg. Not even me."

"Too late," she said, and took in a deep breath. "Don't be long."

It wasn't far to Madie's Fashion Barn, so I walked, limping but getting used to the pain. Madie was huddled in the coffee bar with four of her cronies, heavy-featured, heavy-hipped women with only slight differences in hair color and skin tone to tell them apart. Two of them, in fact, were wearing the same dress. All of them stopped talking when I opened the coffee shop door, and Madie tried her best to look as if my name had not been part of the suddenly deceased conversation.

"Deputy," she said. Sweet as poisoned honey. "I was just about to close up for the night."

Actually, she was already closed, but she'd forgotten to turn the sign and lock the doors. I didn't tip my hat. Over the years I'd cultivated the cop stare, and I gave it to her now full force. Her face flushed. She looked away.

"Coffee?" she asked brightly. "I'll make you some hazelnut, on the house."

"Two," I said, "to go. And I'll need some things in the shop, too."

"For the prisoner?" The question escaped her before she could think better of it. I didn't smile. I didn't respond at all. She stood up and scraped her chair nervously on the tile with a chalk-squeak that set my teeth on edge. "Right this way, Deputy."

In the dress shop, surrounded by blind mannequins with blue eye shadow, I gave her a list of what I wanted. She

bustled around gathering up bras and panties and present-
able clothing for tomorrow's court appearance. I knew what
to get. I'd been married to René long enough to remember
how to dress a defendant.

"You ought to get her some thongs, Dan," a woman's
voice said from right behind me, close enough to bite a
chunk out of my ear. I jumped and turned and backed
away, because it was Jimmy Sparkman's wife Kitty. Kitty
Cat, to her friends, Alley Cat to those of us who really knew
her. She'd been to the beauty shop recently. Her auburn
hair still smelled of chemicals, its curls too tight to be natural. But then there wasn't much about Kitty that was natural. From her tinted hair to her padded bra, from fake
fingernails to a tan out of a bottle, Kitty was a tribute to
modern beauty tools. The one natural thing about her was
her eyes—large, protuberant green eyes that never looked at
anyone without seeing herself reflected. A pale sort of
green, like peridot. As she got older, the green got paler. By
sixty she'd look like a blind snake. At thirty-eight, she
looked unforgettably dangerous.

"Thongs," she said again, more slowly. "I have Madie
order me a stock every couple of months. They're just so
comfortable. And men find them so sexy."

"Kitty," I said, and tried to keep the distaste out of my
voice. She was standing too close. Kitty always stood too
close, and came closer the more I tried to back away. I kept
my feet planted this time, but she edged her breasts closer
to my chest. "Just running an errand."

"That's what you are, Dan, an errand boy. Didn't used
to be that way, did it? Back in the day, you and the high-
and-mighty . . ." As much as Kitty despised me, she loathed
René. René had taken one look at her and seen straight
through to the filthy muck clogging up Kitty's soul, and

from that moment on, there hadn't been a cease fire in the war. "How is she these days? Still rubbing up against murderers and rapists?"

"I heard you were leaving town," I said. She blinked those eerie sea-green eyes and pulled her head back slightly, as if I'd threatened to slap her.

"Who said so?"

"Your husband. I guess he'd know."

Her ruby-red lips curled into a sneer of contempt. "I don't know how the hell he would, he's never home. Well, as it happens, he's right. I'm leaving. Soon."

Sooner the better, I thought. "Good luck," I said. "Have fun."

"I can't take another year in this coffin of a town. Honestly, it's like being buried alive! Jimmy may like the taste of dirt, but not me. Not for long." She had a secret and she was itching to share it. I watched Madie bag up bras and panties, nothing fancy, just day-to-day stuff. I didn't think Meg wanted presents from me of lacy lingerie. Not yet. Not now.

"I'm not going alone," Kitty said. I nodded absently, as if I didn't care. One thing about Kitty, she never could stand being ignored. If she couldn't grab the spotlight with her looks and charm, she'd grab it by the balls and drag it into focus. She stepped in my line of sight, her peridot eyes glittering with menace, and said, "I'm leaving with Cal Worthen."

"Have a nice life," I said, but she'd caught my attention. Cal Worthen? I could see Kitty as his partner in spending all that money, but Cal was the mayor of Exile. Politicians were generally stupid, but they were rarely that stupid. Running out of town with the sheriff's wife? Not something a man with a political future would consider for a second.

So either he was lying to her—I wished him the best of luck, in that case—or something was happening in Exile that I needed to know. "When's the happy day?"

"You won't tell Jimmy?" It was a don't-throw-me-in-the-briar-patch question. She meant for me to tell Jimmy. It would make things just perfect for her to have that kind of scene—Jimmy, still in love with her for whatever godless reason, confronting her and her rich lover on their way out of town. She'd love to humiliate him one last time.

"Not a word," I said. She smiled.

"Tomorrow night," she said. "Cal's got some business matters to finish up, and then we're going to Midland. We're catching a flight to Cozumel. Cal has a condominium on the beach."

"Why would Cal leave town?" I asked. "Reelection's in another four months. No reason to think he wouldn't win."

"Cal's tired of politics." Kitty patted her hair, reached into a rack and picked out a skin-tight polyester dress with a snakeskin pattern. "What do you think? Is it me?"

She pressed it up against her body. I smiled gently and said, "It's you."

"You always were a prick, Dan."

"One you couldn't get your hands on."

"I wouldn't spit on your dick if it was on fire."

"Saves me from having to have it amputated later," I shot back. Kitty, fuming, stuck the snakeskin dress back in the rack at random, clutched her Fashion Barn bags, and threw a poisonous look at Madie. Madie was pretending she hadn't heard a thing.

"At least when I get to Midland I can go shopping in a real store," Kitty spat. "The next set of clothes you buy for that mother-killing bitch will be for her funeral. Don't think you can do a thing about it, because you can't. They won't let you."

She turned and started out, hips swaying, tinted hair bouncing.

"They who?" I asked.

She paused in the doorway to the coffee shop, raised her plucked eyebrows, and smiled. "For me to know," she said. "Say hi to Jimmy for me."

I watched her click her heels on tile through the coffee shop. She stiff-armed the door and disappeared outside, leaving the rattled bell tinkling in her wake.

"Ninety-seven thirty," Madie said. I handed her my credit card. "Don't come back in here with that kind of nonsense, Dan. I don't need your business that bad."

"You need her kind?"

"Don't get smart with me, young man." She ran the card, punched numbers, handed it back. "As a business owner in this town, I think it's disgraceful what kind of circus you people are running. Meg Leary, back in town! That never should have been allowed to happen. Never."

She passed over the credit card slip. I signed it. The old-fashioned plastic handled bag she gave me was surprisingly light, for $97.30. I looked in it to check the contents. All there.

"Dan," she said, and leaned forward over the counter. I leaned over, too. "That Lew Peyser's got it in for you. If I were you, I'd do what Kitty's doing. Get out of town before things get worse. That stuff about Meg . . . I have to say that. You understand."

I understood just fine, she had an audience to please. When I left, burdened with two hot hazelnut coffees and the bag, Madie was back at her table with her cronies, all of them quivering with the need to gossip.

I left them to it.

René hadn't arrived by the time I got back. Farlene was still on duty—unusual for her, but then these were exceptional times. A collector of town trivia like Farlene wasn't about to leave without all the facts she could carry away. She winked when she saw the bag on my arm.

"For me?" she asked sweetly, and pressed her hand theatrically against her chest. She'd gotten a new nail design in magenta and chartreuse. "Darlin', people will talk. And Lester would just beat whatever ass you have left."

"What's in the bag, Danny, those silk boxers?" Harlan laughed, and coughed into his handkerchief. "Hear the girls go crazy over those."

"You should know, Harlan," Farlene said. "I heard you got your Viagra prescription refilled. Well, Dan, I hope you didn't get any of those thong undies. Only a man could think that having your underwear up your crack like that was sexy."

"Next time, let me go, I'll buy the undies," Harlan said.

"Why are you still here, Harlan?" I asked, and pushed through the swinging wooden gate that separated the bullpen from Farlene's receiving area. "Isn't it past your bedtime?"

"Yep," he sighed. "Thanks for reminding me. Watch out for that hellspawn of a girl, now."

"Don't talk about Farlene that way," I said. He cackled. Farlene tossed a wadded up piece of paper at my back.

Harlan was on his way out when the outer doors swung open, and Hurricane René arrived.

She was tired, rumpled, and annoyed, and the sight of me didn't do her disposition any favors. She'd never been a thin girl, but the last three years had loaded her down with stress and extra pounds. It had never mattered to me, but she had always complained bitterly about outgrowing a size twelve. She was probably an eighteen now, maybe more. Still flawlessly dressed, though. Her hair was longer than I remembered, brushing her shoulders now, naturally thick and wavy. Bright brown eyes that fastened on me like Velcro.

"Nice town," she said, and dropped her Italian leather briefcase and purse on Farlene's desk. "Let's get the preliminaries out of the way, Dan. Nice to see you, blah blah blah, whatever. Where's my client?"

Harlan's jaw dropped. Farlene rolled her chair back from her desk in an alarm squeak of wheels. It wasn't anything René said, it was just how she was. Some people were nurturers, born to heal the sick and comfort the distressed; René was all about confrontation. The only other profession for her would have been something where she got to wear combat fatigues and carry a rocket launcher.

God, it took me by surprise to realize I missed her.

"René Morgan, this is Farlene Gibbs," I said. "Farlene will get you anything you need while you're here in the office, at least until ten minutes before her quitting time."

Farlene hesitantly offered to shake. René accepted with the brisk efficiency of someone who'd given a thousand similar hand jobs. She turned her gaze to Harlan, who was still frozen in the act of shrugging on his old pea coat.

"Harlan Wilson. Just leaving," I said. She nodded. No offer of hands.

"Dan?" she prompted. "The Howdy Doody show is over. I want my client."

"Come on."

She grabbed her briefcase, left her purse—which was

probably worth a month's pay to Farlene—and moved past the wooden gate into the bullpen. Her gaze flicked to the two coffees I held.

"One of these for you?" she asked. I nodded. She took one. "Mine now."

Our divorce agreement in a nutshell.

I took her back down the hall to the cell. René put her briefcase down, looked at Meg Leary for a few seconds, then said, "Two things. First, have there been any pictures taken of the injuries to her face?"

"Not that I—"

"Go get the Polaroid," she said. "I'll need them for the million-dollar civil suit we'll be filing later."

"Second thing?" I asked. René stepped up to the bars, extended her hand, and focused her attention entirely on Meg.

"I'm René Morgan," she said. "I understand you need the best attorney in Texas. I'm the best. I bill out at three hundred an hour, plus expenses—and you just bought a plane ticket and rental car, by the way. I'm also cranky as hell. Because Dan asked me so nicely, I'm going to give you the special rate for Dan's friends."

"Three hundred an hour, plus expenses?" Meg guessed. Blue eyes locked on brown, and the assessment was short. Meg took her hand and shook it. "You're hired."

"Damn right I am," René said. "When's my hearing?"

"Tomorrow, ten a.m.," I said.

"Who's the judge?"

"Ted Hepplewhite."

"University of Texas, 1982. Fine. I know him." She pulled out a cell phone the size of a credit card and speed-dialed. "Leslie? I have a hearing tomorrow morning, ten a.m., Judge Ted Hepplewhite, Exile Courthouse. Move it. I want to be out of this godforsaken desert by nine. Set up the computers in my room, we're going to be working through the night. If there isn't a night number for the clerk, and there probably isn't in this hellhole, call the judge at home. Tell him René says hi, and I'll owe him a favor." She said it without any doubt that it was going to happen. She wanted it done; it would be done. She hung up without saying goodbye.

"Leslie?" I asked.

"My clerk," she said. "I only brought the one. Which reminds me, Leary, you're also getting billed for the clerk's airfare and hotel. Not to mention the overtime."

Meg smiled, but it was a fragile thing, brittle and ready to crack. René saw it, put away the cell phone, and walked back to the bars.

"If money's a problem, we can work that out," she said more quietly. "Money I've got. Interesting clients I need."

"No," Meg said. "Money's not a problem. I have three million in the bank."

I'd expected it. René, who was used to hearing figures in that ballpark without warning, recovered quickly.

"Then I'll expect you to pay on time. Now, we're going to talk. Privately."

She stepped back and gestured for me to open the cell door. I unlocked it and swung it open.

"You can use Jimmy's office," I said.

"I'd rather use an interrogation room."

"It's Jimmy's office or the box room," I said. "We don't do a lot of interrogating here."

I was still holding a cup of coffee. I handed it to Meg. She met my eyes and smiled again. Something strange in her eyes, something I hardly recognized because I'd never really seen it in her before.

Hope.

"Thank you," she whispered, and brushed her lips against my cheek. I didn't look at René as I put the Fashion Barn bag on the bunk.

"I wouldn't bother," René said. "My client is not going back in that cell."

"She'll have to when you're done."

"Not into that one," she said. "Not unless you want me to call Judge Hepplewhite right now and make you unemployable in this state."

I held up my hands in surrender. A bit of playacting on both sides. Now I couldn't be blamed for the change, and René could establish her credentials as the person with the biggest, brassiest balls in the room.

Win-win. A lawyer's favorite term.

Jimmy came back fifteen minutes later, looking tired. He took off his coat and threw it on the stand, looked at Farlene, looked at the clock, looked back.

"I'm going, I'm going," she muttered, and picked up her purse and fake ermine coat.

Gentry took the coat and held it for her. Farlene giggled and called him a gentleman, which made him smile a bit. His eyes followed her out of the doors as he shrugged on his own jacket. "I'm going to take some dinner time. Did Doc Larkin make any sense?"

"Not too damn much," Jimmy said. "Have a good night, Farlene. Gentry."

"I'll be back," Gentry said. He went after Farlene.

"Somebody should have told him about Lester," Jimmy said. "Ah well. Gentry won't be the first man led down that particular path of thorns."

I thought of Kitty's poison-green eyes narrowed in satisfaction. You won't tell Jimmy, will you? No, Kitty. I won't. Stick that in your pipe and smoke it.

Jimmy pushed through the gate, nodded to me, and started for his office.

"Jimmy," I said, and put out an arm to stop him. "Meg's in with her lawyer."

"Who'd she get?" He wasn't too concerned, more preoccupied than interested. He crossed over to the coffee maker and checked the pot. There was a thin layer of thick sludge left, which he poured into a chipped mug with the Texas state flag on it. "Darby?"

"No."

"Vargas, from over across—"

"René," I interrupted. The coffee cup paused halfway to his lips.

"Not—"

"Yes."

"Well, Jesus."

I nodded. Jimmy sank into the chair Harlan had abandoned, rubbed his face, and sent me a questioning look.

"I'm fine," I said. Which I was, oddly enough. All this time between us, all this anger, and it was damn strange I didn't feel worse at the sight of her. I wasn't thinking of Sean, of the sound of the shot echoing through the house. I was thinking of how hard it had been to close the door of that white house behind me and walk away from my life.

"Those two are a lot alike," he said. He sounded surprised. So was I, a little. "Having both of them in this town, though . . . something's going to blow up. I just hope it's not one of us."

"Amen, brother. What about Doc Larkin?" I asked. "Anything?"

214

Jimmy remembered his coffee. I winced as he swallowed a thick mouthful, but it didn't seem to faze him. Nothing much did.

"Couldn't find him," he said. "Poked around out there until it got too strange. You know about the tombstones?"

"I saw."

"Then you know how it feels out there. I turned the corner, next thing you know I was looking at my own goddamn grave." Jimmy shook himself like a dog shaking off water. "Cold out there tonight. Rain's still coming down, it might freeze before morning if it keeps up. Anyway, Doc wasn't anywhere to be found. It's just like him these days, to make a call like that and then hide out. His dogs aren't all on leashes."

Right then, the door to Jimmy's office opened, and René stepped out. She closed it behind her, saw Jimmy, and nodded to him. He nodded back.

"Food," she said. "I've been on a plane that served peanuts for dinner, and my client hasn't had anything since lunch. Order us something; we're going to be here for a while."

"Italian okay?" Jimmy asked.

"Unless it's from Chef Boy-ar-dee." René transferred her attention to me. "I understand you can alibi my client for most of the day in question?"

"Most of it. I lost her from about noon until after two, then again from three until after four. Other than that, I was with her the whole day."

"And night?" Coming from René it was a loaded question, but I didn't have any room to dodge.

"Yes."

The stare transferred itself to Jimmy, who shifted uncomfortably. "You can confirm she didn't leave his apartment that night?"

"I can."

"So the only times my client doesn't have an alibi is during the time the victim was killed? Well, that's suspiciously convenient, isn't it?"

"It's convenient if she did it," he said evenly. "You know that as well as I do, René. It's real good to see you, by the way."

"Don't try your small-town sheriff charm on me, Jimmy, I've known you too long." Still, she smiled, a quick controlled flicker that vanished back into business. "The gun was found on the front seat of her locked car in plain view."

"Yes."

"Found when? By whom?"

"It was reported by a waitress at the Dairy Queen, who walked past the Lexus on her way to work. She saw the gun on the seat and called it in. The gun was recovered by my deputies."

"Which one?"

"Lew Peyser," Jimmy said. René smiled.

"The one who beat my client. By the way, Deputy Fox, I need that Polaroid."

I silently got up and found it. She took it, checked the film, and turned to go.

"Oh, Jimmy?" she asked. "I understand Lew Peyser also found the body of Joe Hillyard. Any reason why he would have been there at that time of the morning?"

"You'd have to ask him," Jimmy said.

"Oh, I will," René purred. "I will. Italian's fine, by the way. Fettuccine Alfredo, pesto on the side. Caesar salad. My client will have the same."

She shut the door again. Next to me, Jimmy stretched

out in his chair, tilted his chin toward the ceiling, and started to laugh.

"Oh, Jesus, this is weird," he said when he'd caught his breath. "Throw me the directory."

I did. "You didn't ask, but I'll take spaghetti."

He was dialing the number when the dispatcher's radio squawked for attention. I limped over to Farlene's desk, turned the knobs, and keyed the mike.

"Dispatch, go," I said. Nothing but the crackle of static. "This is Exile Sheriff's Office Dispatch, come in."

"This is Gentry." It was certainly Gentry's voice, but there was tension in it I'd never heard before. "Lew Peyser's disappeared from his house. Nobody's seen him all day. His mother says his gun safe was hanging open. I thought you ought to know."

The good humor I'd been storing up inside flared and burned itself out. "Yeah, roger that. Thanks for the heads-up."

"We don't know if he took it out of the safe, but if he did he's got some kind of rifle, too. Could be an assault rifle."

"You looking around for him?"

"Thought I might," Gentry said. "Just in case. I'd recommend you and Meg stay in the tower and don't go wandering around in the dark tonight. And stay away from the windows."

Jimmy had joined me at the radio. He leaned over and keyed the mike. "Gentry, are you telling me I've got a potentially dangerous armed deputy driving around out there?"

"Looks that way."

"Keep looking. I'm taking my cruiser. I'll keep in touch."

He keyed out and pushed the microphone back. We looked at each other, old friends who didn't need to say too much to be understood.

"I don't think he would," Jimmy said, "but I don't dare take the chance I'm wrong. You stay here. Keep your heads down. If Peyser comes in here, armed or not, I want you to take him into custody. If he comes in shooting, you know what to do."

I pushed back from the desk and went to the filing cabinet at the end of the row. I unlocked it, reached in, and pulled out two of the four Kevlar vests the Sheriff's Office owned. I tossed one to Jimmy.

"I never knew small towns could be so dangerous," I said. He pulled the vest over his head and Velcroed it in place with brisk efficiency.

"Stick around for the annual county fair," he said, and pulled his sidearm and checked the clip. "Swear to God, Dan, if I live through Meg Leary I'm going to retire and take your job with me."

I offered him a closed fist as he passed to go out. He tapped it with his own. No goodbyes. I hadn't told him about Kitty. I was suddenly glad about that. The last thing he needed to have on his mind was that manipulative bitch. Let her scat out of town with Cal Worthen, run through his millions, and indulge herself with the pool boys. Jimmy would be much the better for the loss.

He'd hate me for it later, but I could live with that.

I went to the front and locked the double doors. Peyser would have a key, of course, but if he came he'd hit them hard enough to rattle them, and give me some warning. If he came, which he wouldn't. Gentry had broadcasted on the police frequency knowing damn well Peyser would have a scanner and hear it. He was giving him fair warning we knew what he was up to. Lew was a mean son of a bitch, but he wasn't stupid.

René asked for the police reports on Meg's cases. I gave her all I had, including the folders Farlene had pulled for me. I made coffee. I turned on the small black-and-white TV set in the corner to give us some companionship in the cold. Italian food arrived forty-five minutes later: two Fettuccine Alfredos, two spaghettis. I ate mine with garlic bread and radioed Jimmy to tell him his food was getting cold. He cursed at me with cheerful disregard for FCC regulations.

"Anything on Peyser?" I asked. "By the way, the spaghetti's damn good."

"Screw you, son, and no. Don't eat all the garlic bread. Out."

I pushed back from the desk, but as I did his mike keyed again. No more joking now. All business. "Danny, come back."

"Right here."

"I'm on the east side. There's a light in Joe Hillyard's house. Peyser might be inside."

"Don't go alone," I said. Maybe it was the cold, the night. My own worked-up nerves. "Gentry, do you copy? Come back if you copy."

Static. Wherever Gentry was, he wasn't answering.

"Gentry, if you can hear me, get over to Joe Hillyard's house and back up Jimmy. Jimmy, do not go in there alone."

"I've got a vest," he said.

"You've got a headstone out at Doc Larkin's place, too," I shot back. "Do not. Give me time to get there."

"Don't be stupid," Jimmy said. "You can't leave a prisoner and a lawyer alone in the damn jail."

"I'll call Harlan to come in here."

Jimmy's mike clicked, then clicked again. Finally he said, "Call him. Hurry up. It's damn cold out here."

I dialed Harlan's number, woke him up, and told him to get his ass to the station. Something in my voice told him not to argue. I knocked on the door of Jimmy's office, then stuck my head in.

"Out," René said flatly. She was standing up, staring down at the color photos of Doris Leary's body. "I mean it, Dan. Don't interrupt us."

"I need you out here," I said. "Now."

Her head snapped up, and for a few seconds she thought about taking me apart one bone at a time. Instead, she closed the folder, nodded to Meg, and came outside with me. I closed the office door behind us.

"René, I've got a situation. Harlan is on his way back here. He'll stay here with you. I'm going to tell him this, but I'll tell you, too: don't let Lew Peyser in here. Harlan has orders to shoot him if he has to stop him."

She went very still, and some of the color went out of her cheeks.

"I don't think anything's going to happen," I said. "I have to go. Jimmy could be in trouble."

"This is fucked, Danny."

"It's fucked," I agreed. "Be careful."

"Oh, yeah," she said. "I'll be so glad to have Harlan protecting me. Hey, Dan? Try not to get killed. I'd just have to represent your killer, and the publicity would be terrible."

She had her priorities straight, as always.

It took Harlan fifteen long minutes to arrive, and ten more for me to make it down to his cruiser and drive it to Joe Hillyard's house. Another silent night in Exile, the shadows full and waiting. I pulled the cruiser to a silent stop right behind Jimmy's car, cut off the engine, and listened.

No sounds at all. There was a light on in Hillyard's house, all right, a dim flicker where I remembered the kitchen to be. I got out of my car and walked over to Jimmy's prowl car. Empty. Jimmy hadn't waited, damn him.

Somewhere in the distance, a dog barked a sleepy alarm. Another one answered him out of tune. The wind shifted and blew dry leaves down the street gutters, past silent houses and unmoving cars, and it was cold, very cold. My breath clouded the air like cotton.

The sound of a single gunshot pop shattered the air like crystal.

I spun toward the Hillyard house, pumped the shotgun I held, and ran as fast as my damned torn knee would let me. Not fast enough. Not nearly fast enough. The front door was locked and solid. I ran past the boxwood hedge, around the corner into darkness. I found the wooden fence by touch and lifted the gate latch.

Somebody else rounded the other corner at a flat run. I skidded to a stop, planted myself in shooting stance and yelled, "Police, stop!"

He froze. In the cool blue moonlight Lew Peyser looked scared. Scared to death. He held out both hands—empty—and said, "Where's Jimmy?"

I didn't know. Peyser's eyes flickered, and I thought he might run for it.

"Behind you!" he yelled. He had to be kidding, or wildly optimistic. I didn't turn around.

Something hit me hard in the back the head. I sprawled on wet grass, tasting blood and seeing stars, and realized I'd dropped the shotgun. I tried to shake it off, but my head was numb as a watermelon.

When I did manage to look behind me, there was no one around. I remembered Peyser.

He'd already reached the back fence. I grabbed for the shotgun, fumbled, tried again. "Stop!" I yelled. I wrestled the gun back into firing position. He dropped over on the other side of the fence. He'd known I was out of range for a shotgun, my knee would never let me keep up, and shooting blind in the dark was too risky. Damn him.

The back door of the house was open. I managed to get to my feet and circled in, shotgun held ready. Golden light from the kitchen spilled over pebbled linoleum, glittered on a couple of bowling trophies. The house was full of the smell of fresh gunpowder.

"Jimmy?" I called. I crossed the ten carpeted feet of living room and saw the kitchen. There was still fingerprint powder on the counters, dried blood on the floor.

Jimmy lay on his back, his hands flung out to the sides. Powder burn on his temple, both eyes open, and he was still breathing, still breathing, the small black hole in his skin didn't look like much, really, nothing to die from.

His hands were trembling. There wasn't much blood on this side. On the other side there was something (red and gray) that my eyes didn't want to comprehend, the way they hadn't seen what was wrong with Sean that dark night in Houston. But there was something (red and gray and white slivers of bone) wrong with Jimmy's head on the right side.

His eyes were open, staring straight up at the ceiling. He looked so puzzled, so utterly baffled, that for a second I looked up to see what he was staring at. Nothing up there, of course. Nothing at all.

This wasn't happening, it couldn't happen. Not to Jimmy. He was wearing his vest.

222

Contact burn on his temple. Someone standing kissing-close. Killed where Joe Hillyard had died.

"Dan."

For an insane second I thought Jimmy had called my name, and then I realized the voice was coming from behind me. I looked back to see Ranger Gentry standing there. His dark eyes were holes into hell. Full of fury.

"Goddamn," he said. His voice was shaking. "Goddamn it, what happened? What the hell—"

"9-1-1," I said, in a voice I hardly recognized. I'd used that voice before, to René. All of Sean's blood on the carpet, my gun gleaming in his hand like a steel jewel.

"Who?" he demanded. Maybe he thought I'd done it—but no, I was carrying a shotgun, he'd know the wound profile.

"Lew Peyser went over the fence," I said. "Get the ambulance here. Now."

He went. I knelt down next to Jimmy, put the shotgun down and put my fingers on his carotid pulse.

Dear God, he was still alive.

"Hold on, Jimmy," I whispered, the way I'd whispered to my son. "Please stay here. Please stay here."

But like Sean, he didn't listen to me.

A sheriff had never been killed in Exile, not since pioneer days. It had been one of the selling points Jimmy had used in his recruitment pitch. Just like the bad old days, Danny boy. You and me against the town.

He'd been wearing his vest. He should have been safe.

We found a gun in the back yard, a .45 caliber Glock. Lew Peyser had been proud of his ownership; he'd carefully inscribed his name in copperplate script on the butt of the gun. One round fired, and as I looked at the cheerful, well-

Roxanne Longstreet Conrad

cared for gleam of the weapon I knew we were going to find Peyser's fingerprints on the gun and bullets.

I hadn't taken the shot. I'd watched him go over the fence with Jimmy's blood on his hands, and I hadn't even taken the shot.

Before long the scene could have been straight out of Houston, or Austin, or New York City. Flashing lights and sirens. Police from Westgrove and Killing Rock and Lover Falls, come to honor Jimmy and help in the search. Two more cold-eyed Texas Rangers. Noise and confusion, and in the middle of it Jimmy lay dead on Joe Hillyard's kitchen floor.

"Dan?" Somebody was talking to me. I looked up and saw that two ambulance drivers were bent over Jimmy. I started to get up, but a strong hand pressed me down. "Dan, I need to take him away now."

It was Jeff Slaughter, the cheerful coroner. He wasn't so cheerful now. His eyes were wounded and bloodshot, his voice gentle but sad. I nodded silently.

"You should go home," he said. "When's the last time you slept?"

Sleep sounded like a dream I'd once had, one I'd never have again. Not without hearing a gunshot, seeing blood on the floor, seeing Sean or Jimmy lying dead.

"I have to stay," I said. My voice sounded rusty and raw. "Do right by him, Jeff."

"I will." He looked over his shoulder at the hallway behind us. There was a commotion at the door. "Who's in charge now?"

"Me, I guess." It should have been Lew Peyser, he had seniority. Maybe I should find him and make him scene commander. Maybe I should find him and hold him close and put a bullet right through his brain. I shook myself to get the image out of my mind. "Do what you need to do, Doc."

I got up and went to the door, where two burly young linebackers from the Killing Rock police department were holding back a knot of people trying to get in. One, I saw, was Mayor Cal Worthen.

The other, cringing in the wide circle of his arm and looking like she'd rather be anywhere else in the world, was Kitty Sparkman.

"Let them in," I said. The two linebackers looked at me in surprise. "Come in, Mayor. Kitty."

Cal wasn't shy about it. He shoved past the cops and stepped in, looked around, and said, "Joe Hillyard's house. I haven't been here in years. Deputy, I'm damn sorry about Jimmy. Hard to believe a boy like Lew Peyser could go off the mark like that. Don't know what's going on in this town these days—Joe, then Jimmy."

"You forgot Aurelia," I said. His eyebrows pulled together. He smelled like fresh cologne and shower soap. He and Kitty had probably been making it at the Best Inn Towne when Jimmy was dying, laughing about her stupid cop husband. "Aurelia Galvan."

"That your missing Mexican girl?" he asked. "I told you, I don't know—"

"She's not a missing girl anymore," I interrupted. "She's a homicide victim, and maybe tomorrow I'll stop by and we'll have another little conversation about car trunks and where you dumped her body."

I'd surprised him. Scared him, too. Something flared in his eyes, then shut down. He bared his teeth.

"I got no idea what you're referring to, Deputy, but lawmen are always welcome out at my place. Any time, day or night."

"Their wives, too," I said. Kitty flinched.

"Jimmy—" she faltered. I stepped back and let them go ahead. Kitty took one look and started to scream, a high, grating sound that made me want to throttle her senseless. She buried her face against Cal Worthen's whipcord-lean chest—not much comfort to be found there, I thought; he was as burled and solid as a piece of petrified wood. He didn't do more than glance at Jimmy, either. Not worth his time.

"Oh my God, Jimmy!" Kitty wailed. The two ambulance attendants, supervised by a stone-faced Dr. Slaughter, were zipping up the body bag over Jimmy's face. "Jimmy, don't leave me!"

"Shut up," I whispered tensely. She looked sharply at me, and her eyes were full of crocodile tears. "Don't you dare, Kitty. Don't you dare."

She gulped back whatever else she might have wailed and watched in silence as the gurney wheeled past us, down the hall and out the door. Nothing left of Jimmy now but a drying pool of blood and color photos that would fade in a file folder.

"Anything I can do," Cal said, and offered his hand to me. I looked at it, at him, and turned my back.

"You can leave," I said. "Plenty of reporters out there to talk to. I'm sure you'll take the opportunity."

They left without another word. I felt so alone, standing in the house with nothing but Jimmy's blood to talk to. Lots of police, nobody doing a damn bit of good. I missed Meg, I realized. I missed her like I'd miss oxygen in a vacuum.

"Dan." Gentry was standing in the kitchen doorway, looking in at me. "Nothing else we can do here. I'm organizing the search for Peyser outside."

I followed him out, struck by the cold wind and the

colder stars overhead, caught in the branches of Joe Hillyard's old oak tree. There were a lot of gawkers on the street, some in pajamas with coats thrown on for warmth. There were TV crews from the local station and from Killing Rock. Not enough time yet for the out-of-towners to arrive, but they'd be along. Too many people dead in Exile too quickly for it to escape the press.

Cal Worthen was standing in the glare of halogens giving an interview. Kitty was playing the grieving widow for another camera. Either she'd taken the time to change into a black dress, or she'd just gotten lucky. I felt sick watching them, and I did the only thing I could. I turned to work.

Gentry had a knot of badges waiting around the hood of a police cruiser. Jimmy's, I realized belatedly. He unfolded a map of Exile and started marking off search grids. It was only when he'd named everybody off that I realized I wasn't on the list.

"This man could be armed, folks, and he's shown he's willing to shoot to kill," Gentry said. He had complete attention. "A vest did not save Sheriff Sparkman. Don't get careless. Find him, call for backup, and let's take him down by any means necessary. Put him in handcuffs if you can. Put him in the morgue if there's any doubt."

"Gentry," I said. He held up a hand to stop me.

"Deputy Fox is going to coordinate the search from the Exile Sheriff's Office," he said. "He'll have the map. Once you finish a grid, report in to him and he'll reassign you. By the end of the night, gentlemen, I want Lew Peyser's skin hanging on the wall of my den. Go."

They went, heading for their own cars. Gentry turned to face me.

"No," he said before I could say anything. "I don't think so, Dan. You were Jimmy's friend, you've got personal issues with Peyser, and you're walking wounded. The worst thing I could do would be to put you up against him right now. I need a man on the radio, and you're it."

"Fuck you!" I shouted. He smiled.

"I can't order you," he said. "You can go haring off on Mr. Toad's Wild Ride if you feel you must. But if Peyser's on a killing spree, he'll be looking for you. He'll also be looking for Meg Leary, and this looks to me like a perfect opportunity for him to make a move. All of us out in the field . . . her sitting there all alone in a cell. Your call, Dan. But if I were you, I'd think about that."

I was thinking about it. Gentry made sense. Worse, I hadn't thought of it first. I stared back at him, both of us shivering in the bitter cold wind, and I finally nodded. He nodded back.

"Smart boy," he said, and handed me the map. "Better get moving."

I went back to my cruiser and started back to the station. On the way I keyed the radio and called in.

"Harlan, this is Dan, come in."

"Dan!" Harlan sounded flustered. "Dan, I got reporters outside trying to get in. I kept the door locked like you asked."

"You do that," I said. "I'm coming back. Just hang tight."

"Ten-four. Is it true about Jimmy?"

"It's true," I said. "Dan out."

I was hanging up the radio when I heard something moving behind me, not equipment shifting, a stealthy animal move. My eyes darted to look in the rear view mirror.

Lew Peyser was sitting up in the back seat of the cruiser, his face pale and shiny with sweat. He was holding another gun.

Chapter Thirteen

I hit the brakes. A sudden screaming stop slammed him into the mesh that separated us, tossed my broken ribs into the steering wheel and made all the stars in the sky dance in front of my eyes. I got my gun out of my holster.

"Don't," Lew panted. "Swear to God, Dan, don't you try it or I'll blow a hole in you the size of my fist."

I believed him. I'd seen Jimmy. I froze.

"Roll down the window and toss your gun out," he said.

"I'm not going to do that, Lew," I said. I sounded calm, which was funny because it felt like my blood was boiling in my veins.

"Do it or I'll shoot!"

"You'll shoot me anyway," I said. "I saw Jimmy."

"I didn't fucking kill Jimmy!" he yelled. "Man, you have got to believe me, I didn't do that!"

He sounded so desperate I almost did believe him. Almost.

"Drive," he said.

"Why should I?"

"Because I want to tell you the truth, okay? I got nobody else to turn to, Dan. I'm all alone out here. I know there ain't no love lost, but you owe me a hearing. You owe me that."

I didn't, but it didn't seem like the time to debate it, either. I put my gun down on the seat and took my foot off the brake. We started rolling again, slowly, toward the Exile Courthouse.

"If you want to talk," I said, "you'd better start. You've got from now until we get to the courthouse to convince me I shouldn't blow a cap through your skull."

He looked like a ghost back there behind the mesh—pallid, shrunken, all the fight gone out of him. There was nothing ghostly about the gun, though. It was a snub-nosed .38 revolver, straight out of detective stories of the forties.

He tightened his grip on it when I shifted in my seat. "Sit still," he said.

I snorted. "I'd like to. You're the one who stove in my ribs."

He let that pass without comment. "I got worried," he said. "Something's going on around here, Dan. Something big. First I'm told to keep Meg Leary out of town—that came straight from Jimmy Sparkman—and then I'm told she's hands-off. And then Joe died, and I knew she done it. She always hated him. She comes back in town, and he's dead a day later? No coincidence."

"Was burning down her house part of the plan to get her out of town?"

"I didn't burn it," he said. "I think that was Jimmy."

I saw red mist. If my blood was boiling before, it was steaming now. God, I wanted my hands around his throat. Broken fingers or not, I'd snap him like a chicken.

"Why the hell would he?" I pushed the words out against the pressure.

"He thought there was something in the house. Newspaper clippings. I heard him talking to Cal Worthen about it."

"You're a goddamn liar."

"No! Jimmy went down to Cal's office, I heard them through the door. Somebody organized it, Dan. Who better than Jimmy? You can ask the Fire Chief, he'll tell you who told him to delay answering the alarms. They went out there and soaked the other houses, you know. Before the fire."

Jimmy. That wasn't possible. It couldn't be possible, unless he'd counted on me to keep her distracted and the timing of the fire was accidental. I could believe Jimmy might set a fire to destroy property if he thought things were bad enough. I couldn't believe him capable of murder.

"What in the hell could Jimmy have to hide?" I was wondering it out loud, not expecting an answer. I didn't get one. Peyser shrugged. "You say you didn't kill Jimmy. Who did?"

"I don't know," he said. "Look, I was running when it happened. I was in Joe's house looking for papers, anything to tell me what was going on. Joe was part of it, I know that much. But the house had been cleaned out. I looked out and saw Jimmy's cruiser. I ran. I was running when I heard the shot."

"News flash. It was your gun that shot him."

Lew froze and went dirty-pale, his eyes wide and blind.

"We were looking for you because you'd cleaned out your gun safe and gone out roaming the streets."

"Bullshit!" he protested. "I just took this one out. Why would I clean out my safe?"

"The one that killed Jimmy was a .45 Glock," I said. "It's got your name on it in nice neat script. Where'd that one come from?"

He looked sick. "My car. It was in the floorboard of my car. Somebody's trying to set me up, Dan."

"Lot of that going around," I said.

Meg and Lew had the same story, now that I thought about it. The murder of a law officer, up close and personal, with a single shot to the head. Personal guns used to implicate, left either at the scene or in an equally compromising location. Somebody had a plan, and they weren't afraid to go for double bonus points with it.

It wasn't the first time, either, I realized. Meg's mother had died of a single shotgun blast. So had Peyser's father. If it hadn't been suicide, maybe it was something else.

A pattern.

Peyser was right in this one thing, at least: there was something going on. If I accepted the idea of a pattern, Peyser didn't fit. He hadn't killed Joe Hillyard; I'd seen him discovering the body, and I knew he was innocent of that. If he hadn't killed Joe, maybe he hadn't killed Jimmy either.

And Meg couldn't have, because she'd been in jail for the second murder.

"Who hit me from behind?"

"Don't know," he said. He was lying. He was absolutely lying. I wondered why. "Dan, you got no reason to trust me," Peyser said. "I got a bad temper, you and me were never friends. But I did not kill Jimmy. They'll kill me if they find me out here."

"Guess it's your lucky day," I said. "You're under arrest."

Of course, that was easy to say, but the fact was Peyser had a gun. He'd been smart enough to hide in the one place no cop would be looking for him—the back seat of a cruiser. But he was stupid enough not to realize right off the bat that he was trapped. That meant he might be stupid enough to blow the head off the only man willing to help him, just out of sheer panic.

I pulled up in the courthouse parking lot, killed the engine, and picked up my gun.

"I'm getting out of the car now," I said. "I'm going to open your door. You're going to drop your gun out on the pavement, and I'm going to kick it under the car. Then you're going to get out and lay face down, hands behind your head. You got it?"

"I don't like this," he said. He was sweating a river, and shivering at the same time. "You put me in a cage , they're sure to kill me."

"I let you go, it's open season on Peysers in three counties," I said. "Statewide manhunt. FBI alerts. If you're in a cage, somebody can watch over you."

He glared at me, narrow pig eyes back to Peyser normal for just a second. "Who? You?"

"Same way your father watched over Meg Leary," I said. I turned and pointed the gun at him through the mesh. I caught him by surprise; the .38 was down by his side. Neither one of us breathed for a few seconds, and then I said, "Don't you fucking push my buttons, Lew. I watched Jimmy die. Your doubt benefits are running out."

He didn't move. I opened my door and slid out, keeping the gun trained on him through the window. I opened the back door.

"Drop it," I said. "Now. Or by God you'll be explaining all this to God."

The .38 hit the ground. I kicked it to the other side of the car.

"Out," I said. He came out carefully, trying to stare everywhere at once. "Down on the ground."

He knew the position. I got my handcuffs out and snapped his wrists behind him. He didn't resist. I kicked the cruiser door shut and we went around the car, where I retrieved the .38 and put it in my pocket.

It seemed like an eternity climbing stairs. Peyser was rank with sweat, muttering under his breath; I could feel his muscles twitching with the urge to bolt. We were clear targets out in the cold moonlight as I limped along.

"Sorry now you screwed up my knee?" I asked him. He cursed. I said, "I can always slow down."

He shut up. When we achieved the doors and looked at the spiral steps up to the tower I felt him relax; I didn't. It was going to be all too easy for Peyser to shove me off balance on these steps, send me crashing down to break my neck while he ran wild. I could see it flashing through his narrow eyes.

"Elevator," I said. Peyser looked stricken.

"There ain't room for two!"

"Sure there is," I said. "If they're real friendly."

I'd been claustrophobic in that ancient coffin before, when I'd been by myself and had plenty of breathing room. Once Peyser was inside, there was just enough room for me to squeeze myself in next to him. His breath was rank, his sweat pungent enough to qualify as nerve gas. I breathed shallow and hit the button for 3.

"Not a lot of room," I said. "If you move I can't be responsible for this gun going off."

The gun, as it happened, was pressed up against his bulging stomach, right on top of a pearl button on his plaid Western shirt. Peyser hugged the wall.

It was a long, creaking trip. I didn't like the squeak the cables were making. When the door opened on the third floor, Peyser muttered something under his breath that might have been the Amen to a prayer I hadn't heard.

The elevator jerked hard as we stepped out of it. I looked back and saw it had dropped three inches. The door slid closed again, waiting for the next victim.

I went up to the door and yelled through the frosted glass. "Harlan! It's me, Dan. Open up."

A shadow slid over the glass. I tightened my hold on the

gun, and tried not to be twitchier than I had reason to be.

Harlan fumbled the door open, blinked at me and Peyser in handcuffs, then stepped back. "Damn, Lew," he said. "You're in a mess of trouble, boy."

"No kidding," Peyser said. "I got that."

"Where are they?" I asked Harlan. "Lock the door again, would you?"

He looked confused, but he did it. "Leary's back in the cells. That lawyer lady took off back to her hotel, she said she'd call. You going to lock Lew up?"

"Safest thing," I said.

"For him or us?"

"Maybe both." I walked Peyser back down the hall, to the cells. Meg had been moved to the cell in the center, and as I came that way she sat up on her bunk and brushed dark hair back from her face. Her lips parted at the sight of Peyser in handcuffs.

"Guess what, Lew?" I asked. "We've got just the cell for you tonight." I walked him over to the one on the end, the one where his father had assaulted a fifteen-year-old girl. "Happy dreams."

He sat on the bunk, staring down at the floor between his boots, his head held in both hands. I slammed the cell shut and pulled up the battered orange chair I'd left there from before, when I'd talked to Meg.

"We haven't got much time," I said. "Who hit me from behind?"

He didn't look up. "Sam Larkin."

Sam? Again, a piece that didn't fit. I sighed. "Tell me everything you know. Everything."

By the time he was finished, I wished I hadn't asked.

I should have known better than to leave Harlan with the

radio and news to spread. When I went back up front I found him sitting in the dispatcher's chair looking pleased as an alley cat in a pigeon coop.

"Called off the search," he said. "Did that for you. No sense in having all those cars disturbing the peace all night long looking for somebody already in jail."

Unfortunately, it was sensible. I couldn't tell him why I hadn't wanted it done. Instead I smiled and thanked him and told him to go on home. Which he did, gratefully. I locked up behind him, went back to my desk, and dialed the number of the Best Inn Towne. The clerk was wide awake. I had the feeling most everybody in Exile was awake tonight.

René certainly was.

"Is it true?" she asked before I could get a word out. "Jimmy's dead?"

My silence must have told her. She sighed. "I'm sorry, Danny. I'm really sorry. But I can't let this change my focus. I have a hearing at eight a.m., and I intend to have Meg out and walking around by eight-fifteen. Business first."

Business had always been first. "You think you've got enough to release her?"

"I've got enough to make bail for her. Making them drop the case is going to be a little more difficult."

"What do you need?"

On the other end of the phone, René went quiet. I could picture her expression, that wary calculation as she weighed benefits and risks. "What are we trading for?"

"Use of your law clerk," I said. "I need to do some research, and I don't have time."

"Leslie's asleep."

"Wake her up. I'll pay her for lost sleep."

She seemed to find that amusing for some reason. René in negotiation was a wonderful thing. Her voice dropped into a seductive warm purr, and her personality came through so clearly I could almost feel her touching my shoulder. "My take on the case is that they have the basics—method, motive, and opportunity. No eyewitnesses that saw Meg go into the house, but two people who saw the car. No alibi for Meg. No direct evidence she was there, either. What I need, Dan, is somebody who can testify Meg wasn't there when Hillyard was shot. Or I need the shooter."

"One or the other," I said, "I need Meg. I need her free and ready to come with me by nine in the morning."

"You'll have her," she said. "Want to give me a hint?"

"Ask Leslie to look up anything in the Texas newspapers that centers in this area of the state from January to March 1984. I'm looking for something big. Something involving a lot of money."

"In the county?" René asked.

"No, I don't think so. Just in the southwestern part of the state. Call me when you have something."

"You know, you could search the Internet," she said.

"I could if the Sheriff's Office had the budget for an Internet connection. Just do it for me, René. I'll owe you."

"You already owe me more than you can ever pay," she said. No seduction in that, no teasing. It was a bald statement of fact. And it was true. How could I ever pay for leaving my gun on a side table, fully loaded?

"Please," I said. She let out her breath in a disgusted rush.

"Meg will be released on bail by nine, guaranteed. I'll get your information. And you're going to deliver me an alibi, or a perpetrator, by the end of today, because I so do not want to spend another night in this wretched excuse for a town. There is no continental breakfast, Daniel. Do you understand me?"

There was no small value in having René out of town and off my back; I'd seen her, we hadn't exploded into flames, so the suspense was all over. Nothing left now but finding out we were still angry at each other, deep down, and that whatever little friendship had blossomed so far was bound to wither in the heat. I should let her get out of Exile, and I should, I knew, never darken her field of vision again.

I knew all that.

"I brought in the man they're going to say killed Jimmy," I said. "Only problem is I don't think he did it."

"Do not ask me for another favor, Dan."

"Wouldn't dream to," I said. "Happens he's not a friend. Happens he's the one who beat me half dead yesterday. He's also the son of the man who was sent to prison for raping Meg."

I didn't have to dangle the bait for long. She snapped. "Can he pay?"

"Meg didn't turn out to be pro bono. I figure you've already come out ahead."

"I figure nothing can compensate me for staying in this fleabag for long, and a murder trial could drag out for months, you know that."

"I hear the magic words 'change of venue.' "

"I hear the magic word 'no.' "

"Suit yourself," I shrugged, and started to hang up. The receiver was halfway to the cradle when I heard her voice making a trapped-bee buzz. I put the phone back to my ear and said, "I'll tell Peyser his lawyer's on the way."

"Prick," she said, but without any real malice.

"Good morning to you, too."

The office filled up. Gentry arrived first, leading a fleet of police and sheriffs' deputies from surrounding counties; they all came up, milled around, drank Farlene's coffee, and generally had nothing to say. Lew Peyser, according to the low-toned gossip, had never been that well liked among his peers.

We didn't have enough chairs for all his peers to sit in. I cornered Gentry, who was busy talking on Jimmy's phone, making reports to some faceless authority in Austin. When he hung up he sank down into Jimmy's battered chair, put his hands over his eyes, and rubbed so hard I thought he might rupture his eyeballs. The hound-dog face took a load of mileage without any bad effects, but it was starting to show now. Dark circles under a red, unfocused stare.

I had a flash of irrational anger at seeing him there, where Jimmy had been sitting less than eight hours before. Where Jimmy would never sit again. I reached out and captured Jimmy's autographed baseball in one hand, turning it like a worry bead. The hide felt cool and slick against my skin.

"Send them home," I said to Gentry. His stare focused on my face.

"Who?"

"The men out there. They aren't needed anymore."

He nodded slowly. "I'll take care of that. I have two more Rangers coming in tomorrow to take charge of things around here."

That rocked me, because I hadn't thought past the day. But with Jimmy gone, with no sheriff in place, I would only be sheriff pro-tem, and not even that unless I got blessed by the powers-that-be. And who did I have on staff? One old man who'd probably never put bullets in his gun in his life; one middle-aged deputy who'd taken his wife and kids for a vacation in San Antonio for the week and wasn't due back for days yet. Farlene. Joetta. That was the sum of my resources.

It was odd to realize that I needed Lew Peyser.

"Your job doesn't change, Dan," Gentry said. He sounded exhausted, drained hollow by the night's work. "Just keep doing it."

"You're not staying on?" I asked. He smiled slightly, and it was the bitterest, most cynical smile I've ever seen.

"No," he said. "I'm retiring in fifteen days. Going to buy a fishing boat and get out on a lake somewhere, catch trout for a living. I'm done, Dan. I'm just about all done."

Somebody tapped on the door. An oversized Smokey Bear hat looked in and said, "Lady lawyer out here wants to see her client."

"That'll be René," I said, and put the baseball back on Jimmy's desk. "Meg's got a hearing this morning."

I turned to go. Gentry's voice stopped me.

"Dan," he said. I looked back and saw nothing but sincerity on his face, a shadow of warmth in his eyes. "Don't trip over the lies. You're liable to end up like Jimmy."

Crowded as it was in the bullpen, René had claimed her own space, with a healthy margin of respectful distance. She was like a glittering Ann Taylor stone dropped in the center of a khaki pond.

"Morning," I said to her as I held open the swinging gate. She gave me a filthy look.

"So it seems," she said, and swept by me. She trailed a wake of subtle perfume and adrenaline. Court days were the worst, with René. Always had been. I let the gate swing shut and followed her down the narrow hall past Jimmy's office—Gentry still sat behind closed doors—and into the holding area.

Meg looked stretched past her limits. Her blue eyes were ringed with dark circles, her face so pale it had taken on a blue undertone. She hadn't changed clothes from the rumpled shirt and pants of the day before. The Fashion Barn bag still sat untouched in the corner.

I almost forgot about René standing behind me, briefcase in hand, as I weighed the keys in my hand and looked at Meg.

"Do I have to ask for a postponement?" René snapped. I fumbled keys and found the right one. Meg got up off the bunk and came toward the door, her hands wrapping the bars. As I swung the door open, she reached out to me and pulled me inside. Her arms went around me. I fell into the hug like falling into a feather bed. Her hair felt silky soft to my fingertips. I rested my head in the hollow of her neck and pressed my lips to soft skin, and felt her shudder.

René said, dryly, "Why don't I give you a minute." When I looked back she was gone, pacing back toward the outer office.

Meg captured my face between her hands and stared at me, long and hard. I stared back.

"I'm sorry, Dan," she said. "Jimmy never deserved this."

For some reason that made it real again, in a way that even Jimmy's bloody body hadn't. The compassion in her opened up wounds in me that shock had neatly cauterized. I didn't need the pain. I couldn't face it.

I stepped back away from her and turned away.

"You should focus on your own problems," I said. I felt her reach out a hand to me, then pull it back. The private Meg retreated behind the armor.

241

"All right. What about Doc Larkin?" she asked. "Any word?"

"Jimmy was supposed to talk to him, but as far as I know he never did," I said. "He was there when Jimmy was killed, so maybe they were supposed to meet there. We'll find him as soon as René gets you sprung."

"You think she will?" Meg asked archly. I heard the bunk creak and turned again to see her sitting down, back braced against the bars, knees together, hands flat on her thighs. As I watched, she methodically scraped her palms against the fabric of her pants, wiping off sweat or the remembered feel of my skin. No, this wasn't the place for intimate moments. It wasn't even the place for a civil conversation.

"If anybody can."

"Damn right. Minute's up," René announced from behind me. "Come on, Meg. It's time for a makeover."

At eight-forty-three, Meg Leary walked out of the courthouse with her charges dropped. I had a lot of statements still to put down on paper—Jimmy, the surrender of Lew Peyser—but it was all too much. Sitting in the back of the courtroom as René worked her evil magic and made the judge dance on the head of her Mont Blanc pen, I'd suddenly been overwhelmed by all of it. Meg. Peyser. Jimmy. Burning houses and devastated families. Aurelia Galvan lying dead in a tomb not her own.

All I wanted, in this death-state of exhaustion and grief, was to go home and huddle in my bed for three days. And I knew I couldn't.

Judge Ted Hepplewhite was in his early middle age, maybe forty, with prematurely graying hair that was an asset for a man sitting in judgment. Nothing particularly imposing about him, except the combination of his level stare and his thin smile. I'd been told he was sharp, but he'd have to be a new scalpel to get the better of René.

She had him from her formal, "Good morning, Judge Hepplewhite, thank you for seeing us so early this morning." If Hepplewhite didn't know her, he knew of her—she'd been on "Court TV" enough to qualify as a network star. He was well aware of how foolish she could make a judge look if she had to, and that she wouldn't break a sweat doing it to a county judge in Exile, Texas.

He smiled and sat back and let her make her arguments. It took fifteen minutes. The poor bastard of a prosecutor was more used to arguing drunk-and-disorderly than murder, and he made a bloody mess out of it. René listened with a Mona Lisa smile. No rebuttal. None needed.

Meg was released on a fat $100,000 bond. She wrote a check.

"Well," René said, as we walked down the courthouse steps. "That was entertaining. One down, one to go. You will bring me a shooter or an alibi by tonight, Dan? I'd really hate to have to go to trial with this. Your girlfriend is not a sympathetic witness."

"Not my girlfriend," I said.

"Not for lack of trying, I bet. Oh, and here's the stuff Leslie pulled off the Internet for you last night. Happy reading. What are you looking for?"

I took the sealed envelope she handed me. A nice hefty bundle of papers inside promised for a long night of study.

"Wish I knew," I said. "I'm playing a hunch, that's all. It's things Jimmy was saying and doing. They just don't add up."

"Hunch," she said, in that cool tone that could freeze and shatter opponents standing at the bar. "Uh-huh. Well, try not to bet your life, Dan. You still owe me favors."

Good old René. She was still beautiful, still self-centered, still arrogant and prickly and fond of her own opinion. And I was glad, now, that I'd been able to see her again. I stopped on the steps and looked at her. She looked back. I had a perilous urge to tell her I was sorry, that I'd been a prick, and I should have handled my grief and rage better. But she knew all that. No point in saying it.

She gave me a little half-smile, full of bitter amusement, and continued down the steps.

I turned to look as Meg came out of the doors above. The makeover attempt had been masterful, concealing dark circles and pallor, and she looked almost like the perfected woman who'd rolled her window down to jab words at me on State Highway 114. She was wearing the clothes I'd bought for her, and standing there in the weak sunlight, her face turned up to drink in the warmth, she was so beautiful it hurt.

She sensed me watching her, and her eyes opened and focused. She came down the steps and stopped, toe to toe with me. So much to say, and I had no idea how to go about saying it.

"Congratulations," I said.

"I'm on bail, not having a birthday."

"Beats sitting in a cell next to Lew Peyser, doesn't it?" I asked. She swept dark hair back from her face as the wind ruffled it, and nodded. We started walking down the steps. I saw her glance down at my knee.

"It's better," I said. Which wasn't quite a lie. I was going to limp for a while, but anything was better than the swollen mess my knee had been before. "I need you to help me find out what happened to Jimmy."

"Lew Peyser happened."

244

I shook my head. "Lew's selfish, arrogant, and butt-stupid, but he had no grudge against Jimmy. I know something about desperation, and believe me, Lew's desperate right now to prove he didn't put a bullet through Jimmy's head."

As I talked, a bleak look came into her eyes. She'd thought Jimmy's death at least had been settled, his murderer safely caged. "So somebody put Peyser in that cell."

"Same way they put you there," I agreed. "Gun stolen out of his car and disposed of to incriminate him. Only Peyser's motive for killing Jimmy isn't as clear as yours is for killing Joe Hillyard. René's going to make short work out of that."

"René?" We'd reached the sidewalk. My knee accepted level ground with a creak of gratitude. Out in the parking lot sat two identical patrol cars—mine and Jimmy's. I supposed Gentry had detailed one of his Smokeys to deliver it back from Hillyard's house.

"René's taking Peyser's case, too," I said. "Since she's here. It's the two-for-one defense lawyer special."

Meg laughed. It didn't have a lot of humor in it. "So I'm out, Peyser will be. What now?" she asked.

"I know who killed Aurelia Galvan," I said. "Want to help me bring him in?"

Chapter Fourteen

Sometime during his night of roaming, Lew Peyser had found time to vandalize my poor old Vega. That had slipped his mind when confessing to me in the cell, apparently, but I had no doubt it was him. The seats had been slashed to pieces, yellowed foam rubber bubbling out of rips, the rusted springs exposed. There was a definite smell of urine in the car, and the driver's side seat was still wet. I could picture Peyser walking over to my car, a knife in one hand, his dick in the other. I cursed quietly, went to the trunk, and rummaged through junk until I came up with a garbage bag and two threadbare blankets. The bags provided me a condom-like layer of protection against Peyser's body fluids; the blanket made the raw springs bearable. I spread the second one over the passenger seat.

Meg watched all of this in shell-shocked silence until I wriggled out of the space and gestured it was all right to get in. She took a step back.

"No."

"We can't take the cruiser," I said. I'd taken the time to change out of my bloodstained khakis into blue jeans and a black t-shirt with a tweed jacket. Gun and handcuffs went under concealment. "I don't want to draw attention. Not yet."

"This rolling pile of crap was bad enough before. In no universe am I getting in it with urine stains all over it."

"Fine," I said. "Stay here."

It was an effective threat. After pacing and muttering,

she got in, and we endured a horrible drive out to Cal Worthen's. I kept the windows wide open and breathed shallowly through my mouth, and Meg did the same. Not much conversation. Funny, the stench of Aurelia Galvan's decomposition hadn't bothered me this much. Maybe it was the idea that it was Peyser's piss, I don't know. It sure smelled worse than a cat.

Cal's statue was still booming his praises at the top of its ragged mechanical voice. The dealership was a three-ring circus of salesmen in shirtsleeves and ties, loudspeakers crackling messages, flags flapping. Funny that people get their backs up about protesters burning the American flag, but they don't care about car dealers exploiting the symbol of their freedom. I cared. If what I suspected was true, it was bad enough Cal was mayor; hiding behind the flag was as stomach-turning as the stench of Peyser's urine.

For all the bright carnival flurry, there were no customers. A salesman attached himself to me like a lamprey the second the Vega's engine coughed itself silent. I shook him off and left him to scratch his head in dismay at the state of my current wheels.

"What now?" Meg asked.

"We see if Hector's at work."

I tried to make my limp as casual as possible while we meandered around; when no salesman's eyes were on us, we ducked around the corner and down the side of the building toward the mechanics' area.

There was a giant Dumpster ten feet from the corner, the perfect cover for an observation post except for the smell—there wasn't a Dumpster in the world that didn't stink of rotten milk and fly-blown meat. This one had a new, metallic odor, too. Worthen was violating state regulations about the disposal of waste oil. It was leaking out the bottom of the Dumpster in a thick, black stream, soaking into the greasy dirt. And from there, into the shallow water table that was all this town had to live on.

Another reason to leave Exile. As if I needed another one.

The mechanics were tearing apart a shiny black car. The banging and hammer of the air wrench covered any noise we could have made, including screaming at the top of our lungs. Meg braced herself against the Dumpster and leaned out to take a look around.

"Well?" I prodded. She shushed me with a wave of her hand, then pulled her head back around the corner.

"They're loading the cars in the fenced lot back up onto a rig," she said. "Shipping them out. Cal's out there giving the orders personally."

"Why bring in new cars from Mexico, never enter them in inventory, and then ship them on to someone else?" I asked. We stared at each other for a few seconds, and then she said the answer for both of us.

"Because there's something in the cars."

"Drugs?" I guessed.

"Hold on." She looked around the Dumpster again, then flinched back. "Guess who's visiting."

I edged around to take a look.

Javier Nieves strolled into view with two of his dead-eyed friends. Worthen talked to him for a few seconds, then turned his back. Javier didn't take it well. He reached out to grab Worthen's arm. Worthen shook him off like a fly.

The air wrench stopping screaming as if somebody had cut its throat. In the few seconds after, Worthen and Javier kept talking at full volume, the way people do.

"—how'd she end up in the goddamn crypt—"

"—fuck you, puta, I took her out to the Rock like you told me—"

They both stopped, temporarily embarrassed to be caught yelling. Worthen lowered his voice to an indistinct buzz.

"They killed her," Meg said bleakly. "They killed her and dumped her like a bag of garbage."

"We're going to need a warrant," I said. "Let's go."

We prepared to beat a hasty retreat. Taking on Javier and his gang, Cal Worthen, and a bunch of mechanics with wrenches didn't much appeal to me in my present condition, gun or no gun—and Meg still unarmed.

"Wait," Meg said. Hector Galvan came out of the mechanics' shop wiping his hands on a dirty paper towel. He was walking in our direction. "Of course. Hector."

Hector was Aurelia's cousin. He'd been genuinely surprised to hear his fellow mechanics say that Aurelia had showed up looking for him on the day of her death. Maybe they hadn't told him the identity of the dead girl. Javier had dumped her somewhere—Killing Rock, maybe? It was deserted enough out there. Then we'd come along and inadvertently told Hector he'd been a party to his cousin's death.

Hector had access to Rosa's house. He could have gotten the crucifix. It would have been the act of someone who loved her to wrap Aurelia so carefully and put her on hallowed ground.

A profile that definitely didn't fit either Javier or Cal Worthen.

As Hector tossed his paper towel at the Dumpster on his way past, I grabbed him and slammed him up against the brick wall of the building. He opened his mouth to yell. I pulled my gun.

The air wrench started hammering again.

"You put Aurelia in the crypt," I said to Hector. His dark eyes widened. "Don't fuck around, Hector. Did you see her killed?"

"No!" He shoved me off, but he didn't run. Meg circled like a stalking lion. He watched her, breathing hard. "I didn't know she was here. I didn't know."

"Somebody killed her."

"She fell," he said. "She hit her head."

"And then she dumped herself out in the desert," I said. He flinched. "Come on, Hector. I know you want to believe that, but she came out here looking for you to get a loan, and somebody smashed her skull. Who?"

"I don't know!" he cried. I was grateful for the continued whine of the power tools. "Victor told me some girl hit her head and they were going to get rid of her. He didn't tell me it was my cousin. I didn't know!"

"Javier took her away."

"Yeah."

"You didn't wonder? After Aurelia disappeared?"

I watched his eyes flicker. Oh, he'd wondered, he just hadn't been able to believe it. It would mean, after all, that he was responsible for her death.

"What did she see, Hector?"

"Nothing! She just fell and hit her head!"

"What if she didn't? What if they crushed her skull? You work for them, Hector! You take their money! What's in the cars they're shipping out?"

He shoved me back. Hard. I hit the Dumpster with enough force to make the partially open lid slam shut.

Unfortunately, the sound of power tools cut off just before the boom hit the air.

My eyes locked with Hector's as I heard Cal Worthen's

voice—much closer now—tell Javier to check out the noise.

"Your move," I said. I had the gun, but all he had to do was raise his voice. "How'd she look when you found her, Hector? Peaceful? Or did they hurt her before they smashed her skull?"

That slammed home. His face contorted in reaction, and he shoved past me and walked toward Cal and Javier. I heard footsteps slow and stop.

"Sorry," Hector told them. "I was just cleaning up."

He kept walking, back to the mechanics' shop. I didn't dare look around the Dumpster, but I didn't hear Worthen or Javier making any effort to follow him. Meg pressed tight against my shoulder, listening.

"It's a mess," Cal said tightly. "A complete goddamn mess. You should have told me she was his cousin."

"I was fucking her, not tracing her family tree." Javier sounded amused. "She showed up here, I thought she was looking for me."

"Does Hector know?"

"Nah, he doesn't know nothing or he would've gone to the cops. When's the truck going out?"

"Tonight," Cal said. "Once the boys are finished cutting down the Continental, I want you to take the carpet and upholstery out and burn it. Make sure there's nothing left they could match to forensics."

"Hey, man, I'm not your Mexican janitor. Burn your own fucking carpet. Give me what we agreed on."

"Later," Cal said. "You burn the carpet first. You get your stuff when it's done."

"You don't want to mess with me."

"No," Cal said. I could imagine the big, fake smile, the false glitter in his eye. "You don't want to mess with me, you stupid punk wetback. I been doing this more years than you been alive. You're not the first little spic who tried to threaten me, but the way you go on, you may just be the most stupid. I'm the mayor of this town, you dumb shit."

"Gonna be the mayor of the boneyard if you don't watch your mouth," Javier said. "Get it ready. I'll burn your fucking carpet, but only because she was my problem."

"You do that," Cal said. I heard one set of footsteps crushing gravel in the opposite direction. "You do that."

In the silence, Cal's mechanical doppelganger told me again that Worthen Was Worth It. I listened carefully, waiting for footsteps. I didn't hear anything. I waited for three long minutes, listening, and then peered around the corner.

Worthen was gone.

"Go," I said to Meg. We limped quickly back around to the business side of the car lot. Once we were there, admiring the latest in Lincoln engineering, I leaned closer and said, "Buy a car."

"What?"

"Your Lexus is impounded. It'll take days for it to be cleared up. You've got three million, buy another car. Start your own fleet."

"As if they had a car here I'd drive to a dogfight," she said.

"I was thinking something in a sport utility vehicle. For off-road use." I steered her gently in that direction. "We still need to find where Cal Worthen buries his bodies."

"Do I look even remotely outdoorsy to you?" she snapped, and then turned a blinding white smile on the new sales rep who closed in on us like a lion cutting antelope out of a herd. The rep was female, red-haired, and wearing her navy suit and short skirt like someone born to it. She had hazel eyes and a delightful smile. Meg hung onto her own goodwill with an effort. "Hi. I'm looking for something in an SUV."

"Great!" The saleswoman was perky, too. "Come right over here, I'll show you some very—"

"You go ahead, honey," I told Meg. She threw me a look that could break bone. "I'm going to get Hector to take a look at my car."

I opened the door to the rustbucket Vega. The sales rep's smile suffered from bad reception.

"Your car?" she repeated. I managed a knowing smile. She turned to Meg. "You're not trading it in, are you?"

Meg shook her head.

The sales rep could not have looked more relieved.

I drove the rustbucket around the corner and parked it right at the entrance to the mechanics' shop. Hector came out again, still wiping his hands. I wondered how much of it had to do with grease, how much with imaginary blood.

"Hi," I said when he leaned in the window. He flinched and started to back up. "Pretend we're talking about car repair."

"Not much pretending," he said, and made a face. "Phew, what cat pissed in here?"

"A big one. Hector, my friend and I are coming back here with a warrant to search this lot for evidence that Aurelia died here. When we come back, where are we going to find what we need?"

"I don't know," he said. He glanced around. "Pop the hood."

I did. He raised it with a squeal of metal, bent over the engine, and tinkered for a minute or so before he came back.

"There was a black Lincoln," he said. "We just got done parting it out."

"And?"

"It was new, man. New car."

I got the drift. "Blood anywhere in the car?"

"Stains on the trunk carpet."

"Where'd the carpet go?"

His eyes slid around again, looking for listeners. "Around back. But they're going to burn it."

"Shit." I thought hard, trying not to breathe through my nose. My eyes were stinging from the ammonia. The smell was getting worse, not better. "Your friend said she hit her head. Do you know where she was when it happened?"

"In the lot." He gestured vaguely over his shoulder.

"The locked lot?"

"Yeah. Car bumper or something."

Which meant that one of the cars being loaded on the truck for transport had evidence of Aurelia's death on it. Leaving tonight, Cal had said.

"Hector, where are the cars going?"

He didn't say anything. He went back to stick his head under the hood, did something, and yelled "Give it gas!"

I did. The Vega roared and shivered. He shook his head and came back.

"They're watching me," he said. "They don't trust me no more."

"Where are they taking the cars?"

"North, to a place outside of Killing Rock. They unload the stuff there and ship it out in trucks. The cars go on someplace else." Hector's grease-smeared face was absolutely still, his eyes like chunks of coal. "Mr. Worthen says I got to drive the truck tonight."

"You ever drive the truck before?"

"No," he said. "We leave at ten."

That was all he had time for, because around the corner came the petrified man, Cal Worthen, and his little widow Kitty Sparkman. Hector bent over the engine again. I revved the motor. Cal and Kitty walked by without a second glance, but I slumped down anyway to give them the smallest profile possible. I jumped when Hector slammed the hood down.

"Fifty-two dollars," he said.

"You're kidding, right?"

"No way." He held out his hand. "Gotta account for my time."

I dug out cash and handed it over. He shoved it in a pocket of his coveralls and walked away, a bent and troubled man with a short future. He knew it as well as I did.

I put the car in reverse and went back to the front. Cal Worthen, the white all-father of Exile, the man who owned the town. How much money could a car dealer make in a town with less than five thousand people in a good year? Not enough to own the town, not hardly. Jimmy had described him as a self-made man.

So how had Cal gone about making himself?

I ripped open the envelope René had given me. Inside were twenty-six articles culled from regional papers throughout Texas, all relating to big events in the southwest region for early 1984.

Wildfires, tornadoes, lots of natural disasters. Corporate mergers. Oil booms and busts. I picked out the likely suspects and began to narrow the list. When I'd finished reading, I knew which one was important.

In November 1983, a tornado had ripped through the small town of Sweetland, about seventy-five miles from Exile. The only thing in Sweetland of any real value was the

Sweetland Box Factory, which had employed nearly everyone in town and had been in business since the turn of the century. The first article showed a devastated facility, workers huddled together in shocked clumps, and a picture of the owner Fred Parman promising "We will rebuild." Parman, whose family had been part of Sweetland since pioneer days, had recently moved to St. Louis, the better to spend the millions his family had accumulated over the years.

Parman didn't spend it on rebuilding. The follow-up article showed that he'd announced the closing of the Sweetland Box Factory. No comment from Parman when asked about the hundreds thrown out of work with no prospects for anything better. His corporate spokesmen offered words like "self-sufficiency" and "individual motivation." None of which was paying any bills for the hundreds left homeless and jobless.

In February of 1984, Parman's daughter Chelsea had gone missing from her exclusive St. Louis daycare center. Chelsea was six, a regular angel in the photos the family had provided to the police. Ransom notes followed. A major FBI operation went into effect to track the ransom money—all ten million of it—that had an ironic drop site: the devastated Sweetland Box Factory.

The money vanished on that dark, icy night. So did Chelsea Parman. Her body didn't surface for more than a year. Cause of death was dehydration and malnutrition. She'd been found still bound and gagged in a shack out in the desert somewhere between Sweetland and Exile.

No money. No kidnapper.

No nothing.

Ten million in portable cash, and nobody had ever found a single dime of it.

I sat in my rusting Vega in the parking lot of Cal Worthen, the Car King, and wondered how much of it I was looking at all around me, carefully laundered through the everyday operations of the city of Exile, Texas.

I knew how much of it was paying my salary.

Meg's SUV, a spanking new Ford Explorer, had the same silver finish as her Lexus. Power windows, power locks, a six-CD changer, satellite navigation, and enough cargo space to haul my Vega, if she'd been willing.

She wasn't. When she pulled to a stop in it and looked down at me from the taller vantage point, she'd smiled.

"I could get to like roughing it," she said. "Hop in."

"I need to drive my car home."

"Piece of advice, drive it to a mortuary and have it cremated." She raised an eyebrow. "I'll follow you home. For God's sake, try to keep downwind."

Driving at the Vega's top speed of sixty, with all the windows down, the stench didn't seem so bad. Meg stayed right on my tail, an enigmatic shadow behind tinted windows. We pulled into the parking lot of my apartment at ten-thirty in the morning, and found we had a welcoming committee.

Jonathan Gentry. Of course.

He was leaning against his truck, arms folded, as I got out of the Vega. He didn't say anything about the car, but he frowned when he caught the smell.

"Cats," I said. "What can I do for you, Gentry?"

He started to say, but paused when Meg stepped down out of the Explorer. He tilted his head to consider her for a few seconds, then nodded slowly. She nodded back.

"Congratulations," he said.

"Better luck next time," she replied.

"There going to be a next time, Meg?"

"Hope to hell not, but around this town you can never tell."

Gentry's smile was almost human. He liked her, I realized. He liked her about as well as he liked anybody. "I have some good news for you," he said. "You're going to want to put Dr. Slaughter on your Christmas list."

"Coroner," I said to Meg. She nodded, waiting for the shoe to drop.

"Joe Hillyard wasn't killed by your gun," Gentry said. "Dr. Slaughter found a fragment of the first bullet still in Joe's brain. He matched it to a gun we found in his desk drawer, one shot fired."

"You're telling me Joe really did commit suicide?" she asked blankly.

"No. No powder residue on Joe's hands. He never fired the gun. But somebody did, and put the gun back where it belonged. The shot from your gun came post-mortem, according to Slaughter. Somebody found the body, figured to throw suspicion on you."

"Pretty accurate throw," Meg said. "My car was parked in back of the Dairy Queen. Somebody must have seen who took it and drove it to Joe Hillyard's house."

"Nobody we've been able to find," Gentry said. "DQ wasn't too busy that time of the morning, and all anybody remembers was seeing it drive away. We got a bit luckier on the drop-off; witnesses say the driver was a man. I don't suppose they'd ever mistake you for that, Meg."

A gust of wind broomed leaves across the parking lot, rattled branches in the bare trees across from us. The temperature was dropping again, and the sky already clouding over. Snow clouds, this time, pregnant and ready to pop. We were in for it.

"What about Jimmy?" I asked. Gentry's expression went blank. "Come on. You don't really think Peyser shot him and dropped a gun with his name on it, do you? Lew's stupid, but he's not a moron."

"It had to be Peyser. You saw him going over the fence."

I hadn't told Gentry about Sam Larkin. I had reasons for that, good ones, and I wasn't going to go against my instincts now.

"It's not Peyser," I said. Our eyes locked. "I'm going to find out who it is."

Gentry straightened up and unfolded his arms. "Afraid that isn't going to happen," he said. "You're out of it. Texas Rangers are in charge of the investigation now. Dan, trust us. Let us take care of Jimmy."

He wanted me to go back to patrolling Highway 140, to writing up tickets and shepherding tourists. He wanted me marginalized. It occurred to me to wonder why. I shot a glance at Meg, but her face was unreadable, her eyes fixed on Gentry. How did she feel about him, anyway? Hate? Love? Respect? All possible. None evident.

"They're screwing you, Dan," she said. "This is just the first step. Put you on the sidelines while they do the investigation, come back later and ask for your badge and gun. Or come back with handcuffs."

Funny how these things don't occur to you, no matter your experience and training. There was a vast, cold silence in the air, and I felt the world shifting under my feet.

"You were there, Dan," she said. "You left the station looking for Jimmy. You were the first one to find the body. You were there right after someone killed him. If it wasn't Lew Peyser, you're the next logical suspect. Right, Gentry?"

He didn't say anything. Meg took a step toward him.

"Motive?" she asked. Whatever she saw in his face, I didn't see it. "You have something. Something big."

"You know this isn't the way to do this, Meg," he said. "I'm still investigating. I can't discuss the case with you."

"You'd better discuss the case with somebody, because you're making a mistake," she said. "Don't let them manipulate you the way they manipulate everybody in this town. Think for yourself, Gentry."

"Who's 'they'?" he asked. A soft-voiced question, an intense stare behind it. "You'd better tell me if you know. People been killed around here long enough for their secrets."

A cold wind blew down my neck. Overhead, clouds scudded and collided, and the sun disappeared. The day went lead-gray.

Meg didn't answer him.

"If you don't know, I can't arrest them," he said. "Dan, I need you to give statements about how you arrested Lew and exactly what he said to you. Need them as soon as possible, Dan. Right now."

I opened my mouth to reply, but Meg got in the middle. "He'll be in tomorrow," she said. Her black leather jacket wasn't built to keep out the kind of cold wind cutting us now, but she wasn't shivering. She didn't look like she'd ever shivered in her life. The armor was firmly back in place.

"Can't wait until tomorrow," Gentry shrugged.

"Can," she corrected. "Because he's dead on his feet, can't you see that? Give him a break. You've got Peyser in a cell with my name on it."

"And I don't damn well want to put him in there, too!" Gentry burst out. He sent me a troubled look, shook his head, and jammed his hands in his coat pockets. "Today,

Dan. It's in your best interest."

I nodded. Gentry climbed into his truck and left, trailing white exhaust and implications on the cold wind. Meg stood watching him with dark, intense eyes. I touched her arm.

"Come inside," I said.

She followed.

Meg read the articles without any comprehension at all. "So?" she asked. "It's D. B. Cooper all over again. The guy grabbed his ten million and ran. Nobody ever caught him."

"Think so?" I asked. "Maybe. And maybe the guy and the ten million are still here in Exile."

She thought for just a fraction of a second before she said, "Cal Worthen."

We were sitting in the cold cinder-block living room, curled up on opposite ends of the couch. Meg had stripped off her shoes and settled a blanket around her shoulders. I had skinned off my coat and t-shirt and put on a thick sweater that didn't do too good a job of keeping out the chill. The heater in the apartment was working overtime just to keep frost from forming.

Outside the window, the parking lot was swirling with white. It was too cold for the snow to stick yet, so it blew like confetti, drifting against the wheels of our parked cars. It would feel like Styrofoam, I knew, crunch in the hand like packing material before it melted. Even the snow in Exile was empty.

"How much money did your mother leave you?" I asked. Meg, who had been sipping hot chocolate from one of my two mugs, stopped.

"What?" she whispered.

"How much?"

"What the fuck does that mean?"

I stared at her. She stared back.

"No," she said. "It was insurance money. The rest if it came from the lawsuit."

"How much was the insurance?"

She hesitated, then said, "Two hundred fifty thousand dollars."

"For a nurse out at the ass-end of nowhere? Double indemnity or not, that's a hell of a lot of money. Premiums for that must have bankrupted her."

We were going into territory Meg didn't want to travel, I knew. What had she said the first time I'd mentioned her mother's name? Saint Doris. I hadn't thought she believed it, but maybe the conscious mind and the part of her that was still a child mourning weren't in agreement.

"There's more. Doc Larkin gave me a bequest, said my mother wanted me to have it," she said slowly. "He put it in trust for me."

"How much?"

"A million dollars."

Doc Larkin, the man who'd been having an affair with her mother. And where would Doc get a million dollars? He wasn't a Beverly Hills plastic surgeon. It made no sense viewed that way, either. I couldn't have it both ways—either Cal Worthen was a kidnapper and murderer with ten million unclean dollars, or Doc Larkin and Doris Leary were . . .

Or they all were. Cal, Doc, Doris . . . Joe Hillyard. Larkin had called Jimmy to say he knew who killed Joe Hillyard. Had Joe been about to spill something to Meg?

"You think Doc and Cal Worthen kidnapped this girl," Meg said. "And my mother found out."

"Nope. The FBI was all over this case, and they never so

much as glanced at Exile. I don't think anybody in this town had a thing to do with it."

"So it was just stealing," Meg whispered. "All that money, and nobody to see them take it. But the FBI would have tracked anybody suddenly coming into money. How'd they get around that?"

"Easy," I said, and took a mouthful of hot cocoa. Sweetness clung to the roof of my mouth as I swallowed. "Cal Worthen was the mayor of Exile. Maybe the money never went into their pockets. Maybe the money went into the town treasury, where it stayed, all legal and above-board, paid out in the form of salaries and business loans and tax breaks. Ten million makes a big splash for any one man, but it's just a ripple for a town. Especially during the oil boom, when Exile was still a growing concern."

Meg wrapped her long, elegant hands around her cup for warmth. We both drank and thought about it.

"My lawsuit," she said.

"You wondered why they hated you so much," I said. "It wasn't just your mother, it wasn't just the deputies whose lives went to hell. It was the money. You took part of their hard-earned blood money."

"They must have known," she said. "The case was all over the news. When the ransom went missing, they must have known what they had in their hands. If they'd just spoken up, the FBI could have concentrated the search, maybe found the girl—"

She was looking at the article, at the picture of Chelsea Parman. Six years old, left tied in an abandoned shack, dead of thirst because no one had bothered to save her life. I put my cocoa on the rickety coffee table and slid over closer to her, took the cup from her fingers and put it down, too.

Her eyes were full of tears.

"My mother," she said in a shaking voice, "my mother tried to save her life. That's why they killed her. Oh, God, I know it. I know it."

I put my arms around her. Under layers of bandage my ribs flexed and ached and reminded me I was supposed to be the comforted, not the comforter.

Then her body fitted itself against mine, and none of the aches mattered anymore except the heartache. Fifteen years of murder and greed, and the bodies were still piling up. Aurelia Galvan, who'd been in the wrong place at the wrong time, seen too much. Joe Hillyard, a man who'd had too strong a stomach for evil to ever have been good.

Jimmy. According to Peyser, Jimmy had been in this with Worthen, part of the machine that ran on regular infusions of blood money. But Jimmy had had his limits, too. And he'd reached them sooner than Joe Hillyard.

Meg's breath warmed my neck. Her soft hair brushing my face, smelling of vanilla and flowers. She was the key, the key to everything. To Doris Leary, to Joe Hillyard, to Doc Larkin.

To my heart.

Her hands slid up my arms, over my shoulders, touching me in an unmistakable way. I pulled away just far enough to see the confirmation of it in her midnight-blue eyes.

No words, not this time. I leaned close and put my lips on hers, tasted cocoa and Meg. Heat snapped through me like live current, heated me deep. Her lips moved under mine, wet and hot, then opened to give me entrance. Her body arched against me. Our mouths trapped a moan that could have come from either one of us. Her hands were hot on my skin under the sweater, and she was pulling it up, breaking the kiss to drag the rough wool over my head and throw it aside. Nothing but bandages now to stop her hands from tracing my shoulders, my chest, down.

She put her hands on the hips of my blue jeans and pulled me closer. The jeans were pressure enough, but the feel of her body on the other side was enough to make me shudder. I took deep breaths while I unbuttoned her white raw silk shirt, dragged it open to reveal a bra that hadn't looked nearly as sexy when I'd bought it at Madie's Fashion Barn. Meg writhed to shed the shirt. I reached behind her to unsnap the bra just as her hands unbuttoned the fastener on my jeans and moved to the zipper.

I swore when the hooks refused to cooperate. My hands were shaking. I hadn't been this turned-on since I was a teenager, wrestling with nubile high school girls in the back of my dad's Armor-Alled Mustang. Two of the hooks came free. The third one refused.

Meg opened the zipper on my pants just as the third one snapped loose. Lace slid away from satin skin, and I gently pulled her hands away from exploring the gap in my jeans to drop the bra on the floor next to her shirt and my sweater.

She sank back to the cushions of the couch, one hand falling across the firm swell of her breasts to conceal a pointed, rose-colored nipple as erect as a pencil eraser. I thought she was being modest for a few seconds, then changed my mind as her hand moved.

I got out of my jeans. Fast. My underwear dropped to join them. Shoes. Socks. Meg was still wearing the above-the-knee skirt and hose underneath. I slid my hands up a sizzle of nylon to the waistband of the pantyhose and rolled them off, smoothing her skin with touches on the way down. Damp panties followed.

I left her skirt on.

"Dan?" she asked. It was Meg's voice, and yet it wasn't; I'd never heard that particular low-in-the-throat whisper. "Come here."

I did.

Sometimes, it's hard to tell the comforter from the comforted.

We were lying in a tangle on my bed, hours later, when I heard someone pounding on the door. It sounded far away. I was sated and tired and sore in ways I hadn't known it was possible to be sore, and the last thing I wanted was to move my arm away from its position as Meg's pillow. She was asleep, curled against me peach-skin soft. I trailed fingertips over her side, dipping for the inner curve of her waist, the outer curve of her hip. I didn't remember her taking the skirt off, but she must have at some point. Skin to skin, warmth to warmth, it was the most peaceful time I could remember in my life.

And someone was knocking on the door to bring it to an end.

Meg's blue eyes opened. It was twilight-sky blue, Caribbean sea blue, deep enough to dive forever. Her ripe lips parted enough to show me a mouth I wanted to taste again.

"Somebody wants to talk," she said.

"Fuck 'em," I murmured. "Let Gentry come back with a warrant."

But the thought chilled both of us. Dragged naked out of bed, Texas Rangers staring down at the two of us—no. I saw the same thing in her eyes. She raised her head and gave me a long, warm, gentle kiss before she got up and began to dress. Black underwear this time, the contrast of it enough to rivet my attention again. Black pants. A steel-blue shirt that hugged her waist and fit close along her arms.

"Dan?" she asked. I blinked and rolled out of bed, groaning at the state of my ribs. I had bruises over forty percent of my body, and some of them felt like they had slivers of glass embedded in the middle. Sex was a wonderful anesthetic, but it wore off. I found a pair of plain white Joe Boxers and dragged them on, padded back into the living room for my jeans. I was pulling them up when a face peered in the living room window.

Farlene. She made binoculars out of her hands and peered inside, focused on me as I zipped and buttoned. I went to the door and opened it.

"Sorry," she said, but she didn't mean it. Her eyes roamed over my bare chest, down to blue jean level. "My goodness, Dan, look at all the bruises."

"Looks worse than it feels," I said. She reached out before I could stop her and put her hand flat against my stomach, where boot-tips had left black-and-blue memories. I stepped back.

"Came to tell you," she said, as if it had never happened. "Kitty Sparkman's sitting down with Ranger Gentry right now telling him all about your afternooners."

"What?" I hadn't heard her right. I couldn't have heard her right.

"I'm disappointed in you, Dan. I would have thought you could have done better," Farlene said, and stepped closer. "Kitty Sparkman? Kitty Litter, that's what we call her. You're not the only cat that sprays that box."

"I never so much as touched Kitty Sparkman," I said tightly.

"She says different," Farlene said. She was looking me over good now, as if shopping for something good that might be available. "She's got Gene over at the Best Inn

Towne who's willing to swear he saw you there with her any number of times. What's Kitty got against you, Dan?"

"Lots of things," I said shortly. "Thanks for the warning, Farlene. Why don't you get on home?"

"Not until I get a reward," she said, and turned a brilliant smile on me. "Come on, Dan, just a little one. You got no idea what it's like out there in the middle of nowhere with just ol' Lester for company."

I didn't want to know, either.

Meg's cool voice from the bedroom doorway surprised us both. "Kitty's been sleeping with Cal Worthen."

She hadn't bothered to button up her shirt all the way. She wasn't talking to Farlene. I nodded.

"It's just another way to get you in that cell, Dan," she continued. "Now there's motive. You and Jimmy fighting over Kitty."

The idea was ludicrous to me, and would have been to Jimmy, but neither one of us had a say in it now. It was interesting to see the speculation drift across Farlene's face as she looked at Meg, half-undressed, me wearing only blue jeans. She looked at me again, a bleached eyebrow cocked high.

"Here I was coming to offer aid and comfort," she said. "You look like you've been aided and comforted enough for one day."

"Thanks for the warning, Farlene," I said. I meant that much. Even if Meg hadn't been in the picture, I wouldn't have been tempted to follow Farlene down the path, but she didn't have to know that. "And for the offer."

Both eyebrows this time. "No expiration date."

She sashayed out, holding her coat against the blast of winter wind. Snow swirled around her like fog, and I lost sight of her in ten steps. I shut the door against winter and looked back at Meg, who had her eyebrow up just like Farlene.

"Lady killer," she said.

"Once I get my hands on Kitty Sparkman, I'll prove it."

Chapter Fifteen

"We're going to get our heads blown off," Meg said flatly, over a late lunch of Chico's tacos. We were nearly the only ones in the restaurant, most casual diners being knocked back by the size of the snowstorm descending outside. Whiteout beyond the cracked plate-glass window. I could barely see Meg's new SUV gleaming in the parking lot ten feet away. The glass radiated chill like light waves. I bit into a jalapeño pepper to counteract it.

"Maybe," I agreed.

"Bank on it. Cal Worthen's a cold-blooded snake, he'd put a clip into either one of us without blinking an eye. Javier's no different. They've got staffs, Dan. We, on the other hand, don't even have two guns between us."

I opened my coat mutely to show her that in addition to my usual hardware I had another Colt Python in a belt holster. "Call it a birthday present."

Her smile threatened to melt my spine. "Does it come with batteries?"

"Three speedloaders," I said. "Not enough to take the Alamo, but it should do the job for tonight."

Meg took her last bite of grease and cheese, washed it down with a sip of Coke, and watched me bite into another pepper with a fascination that sparked more heat than the jalapeño. Mind on your business, Dan. But like most men my mind was not completely mine to control. I had a kinetic flash of the two of us moving together, skin sealing together damply, the uneven fast rhythm of her breath in my ear. I blinked, and she was back to Business Meg, sitting composed and armored across the table.

But she knew what I'd been thinking.

"You know how to show a girl a good time," she said. "Presents and everything. But even two guns isn't enough, Dan, you know that as well as I do. Three would be barely possible."

"I'm not calling Gentry."

"We know Gentry's not part of this, he's not part of the town. Why not bring him in? It's another gun, maybe two more if he brings his Rangers—"

"No," I said. "I don't want to put him in the middle of this. We'll call him when we have Hector safe and some evidence collected, leave it nice and simple for him. I don't want him deciding to slap the iron on me while we're under fire. Besides, I have help on the way."

I'd been watching for the car to arrive in the storm, and it finally had, sliding up in the empty space next to Meg's SUV. An expensive, new luxury rental. Three people got out and hurried through the bite of winter into the front door.

Meg turned to look.

René shook snow from her coat and stamped her expensively-shoed feet. A tall blond Adonis I didn't know was with her, and he took her coat and hung it on the rack along with his own. All that saved his face from being angelic was a slight bent to his nose; he had big blue eyes, golden California skin, and a general air of fragile innocence I supposed was irresistible to women. It certainly seemed to be to René. She gave him a melting smile before she looked at me, challenge in her eyes.

The third member of their party unzipped his brown Sheriff's Office jacket but left it on. He was no longer wearing khaki, but Lew Peyser was still ugly and imposing. His bruises had receded to dark shadows. In the faded rings his piggish eyes were still mean and angry. René, Adonis, and Peyser walked over to our table.

Meg looked at me. I looked back and shrugged.

"He's out on $25,000 bail," René said. "I hinted you might be withdrawing your evidence against him, and even so I had to practically blow Ted Hepplewhite under the bench to get this ungrateful bastard here. Somebody's putting the pressure on."

I nodded. She leaned closer.

"I got the feeling somebody's trying to prove you were involved," she said. "Heads up, Dan. Not that I care, but somebody else might."

"Thanks," I said. I stood up and offered her my hand. She looked down at it, surprised, then met it with her own. We shook like friends. I leaned forward and kissed her cheek. "You've got a bank with me."

"Don't think I won't write checks," she said, and stepped away. She must have been slightly flustered because she collided with surfer-boy Adonis, who was smiling vaguely at all of us. She glanced over her shoulder at him and then at me. Her self-confidence visibly returned. "Oh, Dan, by the way, I don't think you had a chance to meet Leslie. Leslie McCall, my clerk."

Clerk, my ass. Leslie smiled, and I smiled back, and both of us knew damn well his position was something entirely different. I felt a second's flash of anger and regret, but I was enough of a realist to know why things were the way they were, and which of us had chosen to make them that way.

No wonder she'd found it funny when I'd offered to pay her female research assistant for the extra time. Leslie had probably found it hilarious, too.

"Well," René said, and took Leslie's arm. "Gosh, Dan, it's been just like old times. Try not to get arrested, because believe me, I'm not coming back to bail your ass out of jail. If I need to come back for my legitimate clients, I'll be on call. They have my cards." She smiled sweetly. "If you have one, tear it up, would you, Dan?"

"Consider it torn," I said. "Safe trip."

Leslie smiled and waved. I watched the two of them don coats and venture back out into the storm. Leslie smiled and waved again as they got in the car. Big smiler and waver, that Leslie.

I wished René the best of him, but then she'd probably already had it.

"Move over," Peyser said to Meg. I snapped my attention back to the problem as René's car pulled out of the lot, because I knew Meg wasn't going to play nice. Not yet.

Except she did, without comment, slide over. Not even a token "bite me." Her look to me said, clearly, that I had a limited time to explain myself. The truce wasn't permanent.

Peyser sank down on the seat with a creak of plastic. Meg edged as far away from him as possible. Peyser, the man who'd kicked me half dead, stared at me for a few seconds, then said, "I figured maybe you were just getting me out of there so you could kill me."

"It's a thought," I said. "I'd rather go after the man who killed Jimmy, though. I don't figure that's you."

Peyser shrugged. "Folks seem to be leaning toward the theory it was you."

"You think so?" I asked. Peyser's eyes narrowed. "If I had, I would've blown your head off and the whole thing would have been wrapped into a neat little package. By leaving you alive in that cell I put myself in the soup."

"Yeah," he admitted. "Thought you might be having second thoughts when you stuck me with the fat girl for a lawyer. She's okay, though."

I let that pass. René was no longer my problem or in need of my protection.

"Time to pay the bill," I said. "I need you to back us up tonight."

"Where?"

"Need to know. When I need you to know, I'll tell you. Meanwhile, get your hands on firepower and be ready. We'll be leaving as soon as it gets dark."

He cocked his head to the side, the way bulldogs do when they're puzzled.

"Who?" he asked. "Don't give me need-to-know shit."

"The people who killed Jimmy," I said. "And Joe Hillyard."

He chewed his lip for just about ten seconds before he said, "Where do you want me?"

"Meet me at my apartment at dusk." I remembered the snowstorm. "Better make it six, it's dusk now. Don't bring any buddies, and don't tell anybody else, either. Our lives are going to depend on it."

The idea of entrusting my life to Lew Peyser gave me cold sweats. Meg had been eerily silent through all of this, her eyes down, her face a white mask.

"Fuck," Peyser said contemplatively. "You been watching too many James Bond movies, Fox. Ain't like I got a million people to tell around here anyway. Not anymore. You seen to that."

"Six o'clock," I said. He nodded. "We're done."

He seemed relieved. He walked to the door, zipped up his jacket, jammed his hat on his head, and opened up to the snow. Hesitated. As I watched, he shut the door and turned and came back to the table. He leaned on it with both hands, staring down at me and Meg.

"Two things," he said. "First, this don't make us friends. I'll watch your back tonight, and tomorrow you're on your own, and I'll piss on your grave the way I pissed in your car."

"Second?" I asked. He leaned harder on the table, hard enough to make the plastic creak and moan. His pig-eyes shifted from me to Meg.

"Second," he said, "I'm going to prove she lied. My daddy was not a fucking rapist, and I'm not letting her get away with saying he was."

Meg raised her eyes. I hoped never to see a look like that again, and I was glad it wasn't leveled at me.

"Your father," she said, "was a drunk wife beater who lost control. I've hated him all my life, Lew. It's all right for you to hate him, too. I remember when he broke your collarbone when you were in third grade. The best day your family ever had was the day your father put the shotgun in his mouth."

Lew went dirty-white and made a sound as if she'd jammed a fork into his guts. I didn't need him to say it was true. He couldn't think of anything else to come back with. He stalked out into the snow and was lost from sight. I looked at Meg. She looked back.

"He's on foot," I said.

"Let him walk," she said. "Believe me, he'll need it."

I was right about dusk. It was dark in Exile by four o'clock. When the streetlights flickered on, they were hidden by a horizontal blast of wind-driven snow. It was the kind of blizzard that made life on the Texas plains such a treat every ten or fifteen years; by morning we'd have drifts

275

up to our eyes and a sunny cloudless day to melt them off. Tonight we were in the throat of black winter.

Meg was wearing my thick winter jacket, her head covered by the hood but her dark hair whipping around her face like shadows. Under the bulk of the coat she had the Colt Python and speedloaders ready. I was freezing in my Sheriff's Office jacket, which was made for a brisk fall day but not the Antarctic. The chill factor was below zero, the wind blasting at better than thirty miles an hour. It drove tears from the corners of my eyes and froze them on my face. I held my gloved hands up and breathed on them as Peyser's battered black pickup pulled to a rattling stop in the apartment parking lot. He climbed out and waited as we sprinted across to him.

"It's time I needed to know!" he yelled over the wind. "Where and who, Dan?"

"In the truck," I said, and opened up the passenger side of the Explorer. He swung into the back seat. Meg and I took the front. She was driving. I wanted my hands free to draw on Peyser if the issue came up.

The Explorer was a haven of quiet and relative warmth after the refrigerator blast outside. Meg started it up and cranked the heat. They both looked at me.

"Cal Worthen's car lot," I said. "We're following the money."

"Shit," Peyser said. "I knew this was a bad decision. You realize he's the mayor?"

"I never figured you for a political animal, Lew."

He actually smiled. Meg put the Explorer in gear and glided it out to the deserted street. It was like traveling through a plague town, like Chernobyl after the evacuation. Nobody on the streets, not even a car inching along. Only the wind and the snow, and the oppressive weight of the night outside the glass.

"I told you," Peyser said. "I told you it was something to do with Worthen and some big score."

"It was a kidnapping," I said, and turned my head back to face Lew. "About the same time as Doris Leary's murder. Ten million dollars went missing. The little girl died."

He didn't look surprised. He nodded, as if that made some sense to him. "There was some big wreck out on 140, I remember. We were coming back from a football game in the school bus, and we passed the car. It was just a hunk of twisted metal, right there around the John Birch billboard. Wet night, guess he lost control and rolled the car. Poor bastard was thrown out of the car. He was right there on the road, half his head painting the center stripe. I asked Joe Hillyard about it later, he told me it wasn't any big deal, some salesman from out of state. Just another road fatality. But the way he said it—"

"I think it was the kidnapper," I said. "Running for his life with ten million in cash in the trunk. Who was at the crash? Do you remember?"

"Sam," Peyser said, and screwed his face up in a knot as he tried to remember. "Doris Leary and Sam Larkin—they were the other car involved, lucky to be alive by the look of it. Old Lester Gibbs, since it was out near his property. And Cal Worthen. Don't know what he was doing there, but he was there, I remember that much."

All of them, together. The car wreck had been cleaned up, the dead man quietly buried somewhere in the Exile cemetery, the money buried in the treasury. A conspiracy of silence between the two people who'd been in the accident, the sheriff who'd found them, the two onlookers who'd seen them discover the money.

Five people. Doris and Joe were dead. Cal and Lester were rich, and Lester had become a hermit hiding out on his dilapidated ranch.

Sam Larkin was crazy. Crazy enough to talk? He'd been trying to talk, I thought, for days now, but nobody had paid any attention. Except maybe Jimmy, who had died for it.

Peyser had given me the first concrete clue, last night in the cell, when he'd told me Jimmy had been researching some major crime or disaster from the early eighties. Jimmy had been on the trail of the kidnappers, too. And maybe he'd begun worrying about the color of the money he was being paid as Sheriff—a better salary, he'd told me, than most lawmen made in big cities. Better than a hundred thousand dollars.

Oil boom money, he'd said, but he'd known better. Or he'd been finding out.

Peyser had also told me whatever the thing was, Jimmy and Cal had made some arrangement. That was why it was in Jimmy's interest to burn Meg's house, make sure she got quietly out of town before any silences were broken.

I mourned the death of Jimmy all over again, in my heart. A good man had been dying here for a long time, one dollar at a time.

Meg drove in silence, taking us through ghostly streets, until we turned on the country road that led to Cal Worthen's car palace. The car lot was dark, too, a deserted circus with tattered flags flapping in the wind. The giant battered statue of Cal had stopped booming its message, and now it looked macabre and weirdly threatening in the wash of Meg's headlights. She killed the lights and we coasted to a stop, a Ford Explorer with dealer's tags just like all the others.

"What now?" Peyser asked.

"We wait," I said.

Much to my surprise, Peyser and Meg were both good at liar's poker.

I was right that the snow had moved up the timetable. Cal Worthen's big rig loaded with cars ghosted out of the lot at just after nine p.m.

We pulled in behind.

"No lights," I said.

"No shit," Meg shot back. "I've been at this a while, you know. But it isn't safe."

It was more dangerous than it would have been under normal circumstances—no moonlight, only the dimmest suggestion of lights ahead to follow. The only thing good about it was that the road we were on was a straight one, ruler-straight, heading out to the town of Killing Rock. We wouldn't run off the road and collide with a tree, at least not without warning.

Meg stayed right on their tail, risking exposure for safety, but they didn't seem to pay any attention. I was calculating how many men the rig could be carrying—not more than five, probably—and liking the odds. Hector wasn't on their side, so that left it almost even.

"They're turning," Meg said after about twenty minutes of silence. In the flicker of blown snow, I saw the glow of the truck's running lights flare brighter. Meg braked, too. The rig's side lights appeared. He was making a ninety-degree left-hand turn. Meg turned the wheel, but we hit a patch of ice and skidded; she controlled the skid and wrestled the wheel, and managed to slide us into a snow drift with a pillow-soft impact.

"Fuck," she breathed, and put the truck back in gear. Tires spun.

We'd found a patch of black ice.

Peyser and I bailed out and almost slid under the tires. The road was an ice ribbon, gleaming damp but slick as oil. I half-skated to the side of the road, stepped down into the ditch, and dug around with the toe of my boot until I excavated sand. Peyser and I dragged handfuls back to pile around the tires. It took five minutes, maybe, but it felt like hours. The truck was long out of sight by the time we got back in the Explorer and Meg gently coaxed us back onto less hazardous blacktop.

We left the road with a bump.

"Gravel," she said unnecessarily. The pings and pops on the undercarriage were message enough. "Looks like a private road of some kind."

"Haul ass," I said. "We'll look for the truck."

We did, without any luck, for about another five minutes. Meg turned on the lights. Good thing she did, or we would have missed a sudden sharp left-hand turn that ended in a twelve-foot-high upthrust of orange rock. When we'd made the turn, she shut them off again, counting seconds. When she thought she was about at the right spot for the next turn, she flicked them on for two seconds, then off again.

"There," Peyser said finally, and pointed off to my right. Orange and yellow glimmered like Christmas lights through the snow, red taillights flaring as the rig came to a stop. "You got it?"

"Got it," Meg said, and made the turn. We were running blind again, this time off the gravel road. She went as far as she dared, then stopped the truck. "I think we'd better walk it from here."

Stepping out of the cab was like stepping onto another planet, an angry white one. I stayed with Peyser, and we caught up with Meg at the hood of the truck. Nothing now to be seen in the dark, the rig's lights had been doused. Just a vast blackness out here, like an empty snow globe shaken by a fitful baby.

I got my gun out. Meg and Peyser, I noticed, already had theirs. I pointed to my eyes, to them, back to me. They nodded. I set off in the direction of the last lights we'd seen.

By the time I was halfway there, my exposed skin felt dead and rubbery, and my lungs crystallized from the chill. I couldn't feel the gun in my hand, but I supposed that was all right. Cal Worthen and his boys wouldn't be in any better shape.

I heard shouted voices ahead, and went down on one knee on cold snow. Everything was featureless here, a blank snow canvas with occasional random strokes of dark. An exposed piece of wood. A leaning tree.

The bristle of the big rig, only lightly dusted with snow.

Sudden color washed over the snow, heading for my feet. I dodged sideways, ran into Meg and pushed her down on the other side of a snow drift. Peyser was already there, hugging ground.

"Car," Meg said. The headlights had nearly pinned us in place as it turned and rattled up the gravel drive toward the rig. "It's Javier's."

I remembered the car too well to doubt her identification. It pulled to a stop behind the rig and all four doors opened. Four figures got out. Two went to the trunk and opened it; they staggered away bearing a load.

"Shit," Peyser said. "That's a body."

They dumped it over to the side and went back to the trunk. This time the load was not as heavy, but it was still ungainly. Carpet, I thought. I remembered Hector telling me about the trunk carpet from the Lincoln they'd stripped.

There was some shouting going on up ahead, but it was

impossible to hear what was being said. We were in some kind of natural bluff canyon, sheer orange walls rising up about fifteen feet on either side. The gravel road was built over a dry streambed. Inside the walls of the canyon, the wind wasn't as fierce but swirled in circles, whipping up snow like fog.

The shouting stopped. Two of Javier's boys dragged the carpet over to the side of the canyon wall and poured gas out of a can on it. As an afterthought, they came back and got the body they'd dropped and added it to the carpet. More gas. I could smell the sweet stink of it blasted by on the wind.

"They're destroying evidence," Meg said in my ear. "Dan?"

We didn't know how many there were, or where Hector was, but she was right, we couldn't wait any longer. I stood up and gestured Meg and Peyser over to a covering position. I didn't run on my way over to the two kids pouring gas. I was likely to get closer with a gentle stroll.

In fact, I got shoulder-to-shoulder to them just as one succeeded in coaxing a spark out of his Zippo to light a rag-wrapped torch. They were too smart to stand too close to the gas with a lighter, they planned to toss the ignition in from a distance.

The flickering torch revealed the face of the body lying on top of the carpet. Kitty Sparkman wasn't going to be leaving town with her rich lover after all.

I put my gun to the head of the one holding the torch and said, "Police. Down on your knees."

The second one instantly turned to run. Meg intercepted him, her gun steady and her eyes promising no quarter. He went face down in the snow and crossed his ankles and wrists without being told.

My prisoner let go of the torch and dropped, too. I had come with a supply of plastic handcuffs and zipped a set around his wrists and ankles. Meg did the same for her boy—neither of them could have been more than fifteen, at the most. We left them there next to the wet pool of gasoline and Kitty Sparkman's corpse, and moved like a pair of hunting wolves over to the truck where the rest of them were gathered.

Javier and his lieutenant were passing a bottle back and forth while Cal and another guy I'd never seen looked over a list on a clipboard. No sign of Hector anywhere. We hadn't heard a shot, but then it wouldn't be easy to hear it over the wind.

I wondered where Peyser had gotten himself off to. He should have been with Meg. I didn't like him running loose, although I didn't think he was part of the Cal Worthen operation if he'd been set up so effectively. He hadn't traded Cal, after all. And he would've. He would've traded his virgin sister to Visigoths for a key to his cell. After all, he was honoring a temporary truce with me and Meg.

The key word being temporary.

I saw a movement in the swirling snow, the pale shadow of a face. Meg. She had circled around on the other side of Cal Worthen and was waiting.

This was going to work. We could drop in on them just like we had with Javier's boys, end it quick . . .

And then Javier, in the act of handing the bottle to his friend, dropped it. They both cursed good-naturedly and bent over to get it.

And they both saw me at the same second.

I had time for a single, amazed thought of shit, that kid's fast before I realized that I was a sitting duck of a target. Javier and his friend were already drawing their guns. I could shoot one, not both. Not both.

Or I could get the hell out of the way.

Discretion saved my ass. I jumped, rolled, made it behind the skeletal shadows of the truck rig. Something popped hotly in my knee, but I ignored it—sex was a great anesthetic, but fear was an even better one. On the other side Cal Worthen shouted, "What the hell is going on?" but no one bothered to answer him. I rolled up to my feet, shook off a coating of snow, and tried to peer through the latticework of bars and angled cars to see where Javier and his friend had gotten off to.

Not to mention Peyser. Where the hell was Peyser?

A bullet spanged off of metal above my head. I flinched and turned and fired, all in one motion, and missed. Either Javier or his homeboy jerked back around the corner of the rig behind the trunk of a gleaming Taurus.

More gunshots, not aimed at me. On the other side of the rig. Meg. Javier cursed viciously in Spanish and called her a puta, but he seemed to be keeping his head down. The engine on the big rig suddenly caught, and the whole rig shuddered. Either Cal or his accomplice had decided to save their stock from the rustlers. Coincidentally, it was going to remove what little cover Meg and I had to work with.

I abandoned my hiding place and ran to the front of the rig, climbed up on the passenger side step, and yanked open the door. I leveled my gun at the truck driver.

On the other side of the truck, the other door opened. Meg had the same idea. We both covered the driver for a second, staring at each other, and then she reached up and grabbed his shoulder.

"Out, Hector," she snapped. "Stay with me."

He fumbled his way out behind her. I reached over and

yanked the keys from the ignition, then stuck them in a zippered pocket.

I heard a creak behind me as somebody eased the passenger door open for a look inside. I was stretched out on the seat to reach the keys, and I twisted in ways that made my ribs shriek in fear and got my gun in play just a second before Javier's friend would have blown my brains out.

I put two bullets in the most exposed part of him—his shoulder. He shrieked like a grade-school girl and fell backward; I squirmed around and half-dove after him. He wasn't going anywhere, but I picked up his gun and zipped plastic restraints on him just in case.

The glass windows above me shattered in a net of safety glass as somebody on the other side of the truck peppered the cab with bullets. I rolled Javier's homeboy out of the way and up against the canyon wall, leaving a dark trail of blood in the snow, and limped/sprinted for the other end of the truck.

Where the fuck was Lew Peyser?

More gunshots at the other end of the rig. The sound of a big gun, probably Meg's Python. I reached the end of the metal framework, whipped around the back, took two deep breaths, and came around the other side with my gun ready.

Javier was ready for me. We were standing with less than a foot between the barrels of our guns, aiming for each other's heads. I had Kevlar under my coat, but like Jimmy it wouldn't save me. Like Sean. I blinked away an image of my son, because I could not think about Sean now. Javier was a child, too, but he was a child willing to kill, and that made him a man while he held the gun in his hand.

"Where's Cal?" I asked. My voice wasn't quite steady. My hands were. "Run off and leave you, Javier? Leave the Mexicans to clean up the mess?"

"Shut up," he said.

"You pull the trigger on a cop and you know they're going to give you the needle, Javier. Aurelia could have been an accident, I know that. Kitty over there—hell, maybe Cal did her in, you were just doing him another favor. But you pull the trigger now and you pull the trigger on both of us."

We stood there forever, the cold wind whipping at us, snow stinging our eyes, and then finally Javier gave me a brilliant smile, the kind a little boy would give caught in the middle of mischief. The kind Sean used to give me.

"Shit," Javier said, "I ain't so stupid. You got me, man. I give up."

That was when I knew he was going to shoot me. It was in that smile, in the liquid shine of his eyes.

Sean.

I fired first, by a fraction of a second. Javier jerked and staggered back. He looked down at his chest. Another bullet wound opened up, silent as a magic show. He spread his arms, reaching out for something, the gun forgotten in his hand.

Face down in the snow.

I'd been hoping, stupidly, that he was wearing body armor, but as I watched the blood seep out into the snow, as my knee finally gave out and I had to kneel down on my good one, it occurred to me that I'd only put the first bullet in him.

Lew Peyser stepped out of shadows where he'd been standing. Something passed between us, something complicated and angry and covered with spikes.

"Should've let him shoot you," he said, looking down at the boy. He hooked a pointed-toe boot under him and flipped the body face up. Bent down to check his pulse.

When he stood up and locked eyes with me again, he

spat in the snow next to the body and said, "Truce's over. Partner."

Over his shoulder I saw Meg standing, face as pale as the snow swirling around it, her gun still ready. She was watching Peyser with hunted, half-dead eyes.

"Worthen's gone," she said. "I've got the other one. I thought you were taking care of Cal, Buford."

He rounded on her, and I thought for a second the two of them were going to reenact the blood moment I'd just shared with Javier, but then he shrugged and holstered his gun and walked away.

Meg came and helped me to my feet. I had no feeling at all in my knee now, and burning metal shoved between my ribs. I couldn't decide which was worse. I barely felt the pressure of her lips on my frozen cheek.

"Still alive," she murmured.

"Damn sure not kicking," I said. "We'd better call Gentry before these bastards freeze to death."

If Gentry had looked tired before, he looked embalmed now, the grooves in his face like raw wounds. He didn't like the cold much, that was obvious. He didn't much care for me at the moment, either.

"Jeeee-sus," he said in utter disgust. A sigh tattered white from his lips on the wind. "What a mess."

"Kitty Sparkman's over here," I said, and pointed to where coroner Slaughter was working over his third corpse in two days. "Best I can tell, she took three bullets in the chest. Javier's over there. Two in the chest, the second one right through the heart."

"Lew Peyser's work," Gentry said.

I didn't like the taste of what I had to say. "He saved my life." It was a lie, probably; I'd gotten in the first shot, but

Peyser had been willing. I had to give him the credit.

Gentry sighed again and jammed his hands deep in his jacket pockets. "So where the hell's our fine upstanding mayor?"

"In the wind. Literally. Peyser let him go."

Gentry turned and looked out at the wind-scoured snow, the uneven bluffs and plains. "He say why?"

"You know why."

"Money," Gentry sighed. "Well, done is done, and you didn't see him do it, did you? So we'll put out an all-points on Mayor Cal, and he shouldn't be too damn hard to find. Let us handle that. You know what's in the cars yet?"

"According to Cal's little playmate John Colibri, it's Mexican Brown heroin. Bags and bricks, pure and uncut. Cal brings it in from across the border built into special orders of cars, segregates the cars in a special lot, then sends them out here once a month. They have a special holding pen up ahead. They unload the cars and give them special dealer transfer passes, put drivers in them, and send them off. They get passed through a whole network of car dealers until they get to their destination."

"Which is?"

"Any city that has a substantial distribution network operated by El Ojos, Javier's gang. He takes a cut of the drugs that come in for local distribution, but the bulk of it goes on to the gang headquarters. Cal gets paid for muling it in."

"How much heroin?" Gentry asked.

"God knows. Enough to make Cal a rich man every year. By the way, the carpet they were trying to burn has blood and tissue on it. Aurelia's, we think. That'll put him in the fry basket whether we ever connect him to anything else or not."

"I want him crispy," Gentry said. "Tender and juicy on

the inside, crunchy outside."

"Consider him well done."

Gentry gave me a wintery smile that faded too quickly. "Before she died, Kitty Sparkman put in a statement against you. She says the two of you were burning up the sheets behind Jimmy's back, and when he found out he swore he'd kill you."

I tensed up with anger and forced myself to relax. I was exhausted, too, racked with pain and grief. "You were in the squad room with us that night," I said. "Did we act like two men looking to kill each other?"

Gentry shook his head. "If that's how it happened, if he lured you out to that house and tried to kill you, it's self-defense."

"Gentry," I said. "Kitty was a lying bitch, and somebody wanted her to say that. The frame on Lew didn't fit, so they tried to rehang it on me. But it's bullshit, and you know it."

He was looking at me with an unnerving amount of compassion. He leaned close, face intent, and whispered, "I saw you kneeling over his body, Dan. Couldn't have been a minute after the shot, he was still breathing. I saw you. You know how that's going to look to a jury."

"And I saw Peyser going over the fence, that doesn't mean anything either."

"I wish that were true," he said. "We'll find Mayor Cal and see justice done. Now, my folks will finish here and voucher everything. Get back home and warm yourself up."

"You filing charges against me for Jimmy?" I demanded. He looked away.

"Peyser's going to come out of this the conquering hero, and you're going to come out smelling like Jimmy Sparkman's murderer. They may never be able to prove it, but then they don't have to. There's enough shit lying around for everybody to get smeared. You're finished in this town. I wouldn't count on your job, either, because Peyser's going to be Sheriff Pro Tem by end of day to-morrow. If I were you, I'd clean out your desk tonight."

I'd done what I said I'd do. I'd found Aurelia Galvan's killer. I'd cleared Meg of the charges against her. But I still didn't have Jimmy's killer, and I still didn't know enough about Doris Leary's murder, the one that set off the chain of violence. I hated loose ends.

"Time's up," Gentry said. "Know when to quit, son."

Meg and I headed back for Exile.

"We can't prove it," she said once we were back on the main road. "About my mother's murder. No confession, no murderer. We can say it was Worthen, and Larkin, and Hillyard, and even Farlene's husband Lester, but we can't prove it. So it's just as useless as not knowing at all."

Farlene's husband Lester. Lester Gibbs. I blinked as things tried to come together in my head, but my head was as exhausted as the rest of me. Dear God, I wanted to lay down with Meg and sleep forever.

"Whose land was that?" I asked. She paused in the act of rubbing her eyes to frown at me. "Who owned the land where we just were?"

"I don't know," she said. "Cal?"

"He'd never conduct that kind of business on his own land. He's not a man to leave evidence lying around to im-plicate himself, so it'll be somebody's else's land, somebody he can trust."

Meg shrugged. She had no idea. I did.

"Turn left at the next road," I said. "There."

It was another gravel drive, popping and pinging on the undercarriage. At least this time we had headlights to guide

290

us. Nothing to be seen up ahead except more straight road hidden under a cloak of snow.

"Where are we going?" she asked. I rubbed my knee— not so numb, now, which wasn't necessarily a good thing— and stared off into the distance.

"Paying a friend a visit," I said. "Farlene did say there was no expiration date on the offer."

Meg sent me a look that would have boiled lead, but she didn't respond. We bounced down the road in silence toward a glow on the horizon that had to be a house.

It wasn't a house in any conventional sense of the word—it was a dome, smooth concrete arching up at its midpoint to almost thirty feet. Smooth gray stucco exterior, broken by a few windows that glowed lemon-yellow in the night.

It was also a compound, in the FBI sense of the word, a bare stretch of sand and patchy buffalo grass marked off at the edges with a ten-foot fence topped with razor wire and huge proximity lights.

"They've got company," Meg said.

"I never heard of Lester and Farlene entertaining," I said, but she was right. There was a beat-up old gray car, one I'd seen before but couldn't recall where. "Well, we're not getting in there without the ATF and assault rifles."

"Maybe we don't have to," Meg said, and braked the Explorer to a position beyond the range of the proximity lights. She shut off the headlights and the engine. "Maybe we just have to wait."

Waiting was something I'd never been particularly good at, but in Meg's company it didn't seem so bad. We didn't talk about the boy I'd shot to death. We talked about Jimmy Sparkman for a while, until neither of us could go on, and then we held hands for a while and pretended that was to keep our fingers warm.

I must have closed my eyes for a second, because I woke up with sudden pressure of Meg's fingers on mine and one whispered word: "Dan."

I blinked away sleep and wondered how long I'd drifted off, but that was no longer important. What was important was that we'd found Cal Worthen. He was coming out of the front door of the house carrying two bulky leather satchels. Like a good host, Lester Gibbs saw him out into the night. Lester was a big man, I was surprised to see—I'd always pictured him a dried-up old man counting his money by the light of flickering candles. This Lester was at least six feet tall, broad and muscular, with a face shaped more by fists than nature. Beside him Farlene looked tiny and fragile.

"It was Lester's land," I said. "Bank on it. Cal wouldn't depend on anybody else."

Lester, the hermit, had been the keeper of emergency getaway cash. Cal had just tapped the bank. He'd known it was safe here, because nobody thought much about old Lester except as an eccentric, and nobody was going to storm a compound like this without the Army behind them.

Another man came out with Cal, carrying more satchels, and I suddenly knew where I'd seen the gray car before. It had been at Sam Larkin's marble forest, the place where all our gravestones lived.

Sam was carrying money for Cal, too.

Lester and Farlene waved and made pleasant y'all come back now motions—amazing how people kept to habit in the face of murder and extortion—and Lester left Farlene to go to the gate.

"We're too close," I said. "He's going to see us."

"He won't," Meg murmured.

"Meg—"

"He won't. Trust me. Surveillance is my business."

He didn't. He swung the gate open wide and Sam and Cal drove the gray car out onto the gravel road. Lester fastened up his compound again and went inside.

"Stay or follow?" Meg asked.

"Follow. Let the FBI take that one on, if they're still in the suicide business."

She started the engine and we glided after the clunky gray car. We were back to no headlights again, but to my surprise it didn't matter as much. The cloud cover overhead was starting to break up, allowing some starlight through. The wind was beginning to lapse. In an hour, I thought, it was going to be a diamond-chip sky with a big yellow moon, and unmoving fields of snow.

And tomorrow, it would melt like a bad dream.

Up ahead, the gray car came to a sudden stop.

"Shit," Meg spat, and slammed on the brakes. "I think they saw us."

"No, they're not running."

"Then what the hell—"

The passenger side of the car opened. As it did, we saw a sudden flash of light in the darkness, and we both knew what that was.

Muzzle flash. We looked at each other wordlessly. Meg nodded and opened her door. I limped down from the passenger side and tried to keep up with her as she moved to the gray car.

Cal Worthen had the door half-open on the passenger side. I reached it and eased the door open. Cal slumped out, his eyes half-closed, a small black hole in his temple. No exit wound. He was still moving a little, but it was random jerks. I grabbed him as he fell and eased him down to the ground.

There was enough starlight for me to see one of his pupils blow wide open as he died.

"Sam—" Meg's voice. I heard the crunch of snow and looked up to see her stepping backwards as Sam got out of the driver's side of the car. He was holding a gun, and I knew she didn't want to shoot him. I tried to get up, but my knee was well and truly gone now, no strength left in it at all. I grabbed the doorframe and hauled myself up by arm strength, hopped on my left leg and braced my gun hand against the top of the car.

"Sam, stop," I said. "Police. I'm asking you to stop."

He kept coming toward Meg. He had a gun in his hand, a small caliber thing that would nevertheless reduce Meg to what Cal Worthen had become if he got it close enough to her head.

"Sam!" I snapped. He didn't seem to hear me at all. Meg finally stopped backing up, realizing that if she kept going I couldn't cover her without moving.

She let him approach. Closer. Closer.

Sam put his arms around her and started to cry. She stared at me, frozen in equal parts disgust and amazement, then carefully patted his shoulder with the hand that wasn't holding her gun. He sat down in the snow as if his legs had given out. That hid him behind the quarter panel of the car, and I hopped around the back to get a better shot.

"Give me the gun, Sam," Meg said gently. She leaned down for it, but Sam pointed it right at her. She froze.

"Mine," he said. Doc Larkin, burly and white-haired and with eyes like a confused child, had suffered some kind of breakdown, that much was clear. He also knew which end of a gun to hold. It was not a comforting combination.

"Okay, Doc, you keep it," Meg said. I made a gesture at her to tell her to get out of there, but she shook her head. "Doc? It's really cold out here. Why don't we talk in the car?"

"Mine," he said again. "Those bastards just kept hurting you."

That shocked her into silence. Me, too. Larkin's eyes were bright and confused, on the edge of panic. How long had he been slipping in and out of this? Months? Years? But in a town like Exile, the eccentric old man who owned the tombstone factory could be expected to be strange. Nobody noticed.

Until he'd put guns to their heads.

"Me?" Meg finally managed. "Save me?"

"Couldn't save your momma," he said, and the blue eyes filled up with tears. He cried like a child, without any thought for where the tears fell. "She just didn't want to listen! Joe said we had to."

"Joe Hillyard killed my mother?" Meg whispered. Tears were catching, they were glittering in her eyes, too.

"She was going to tell."

"About the money," I said quietly. "She found out the little girl died because they didn't turn the money in when they found it. If they had, the search would have narrowed and she might have been found."

"If Joe killed her, then he knew—he knew I didn't—" Meg said.

She stopped, not wanting to finish. Joe had known she was innocent when she was arrested. He'd known she was innocent while his deputies abused her. And he hadn't lifted a hand to stop it.

She'd been betrayed on so many levels by the men who were supposed to protect her.

"Mine," Doc said softly. He reached out and touched her face, patted her cheek. "Couldn't let them do it to you again, little girl."

Hillyard, Worthen, Gibbs—they'd meant to kill Meg. Kill her and dump her body out there in the desert, maybe, where they'd disposed of Kitty Sparkman. Sam Larkin had stopped them with a bullet to Hillyard's temple.

"Jimmy?" I asked. Larkin's vague eyes shifted in my direction.

"He was the Sheriff," he said. "He put her in jail, don't you see? Couldn't let them do that to her. Not again. Not my girl."

Meg finally understood. I saw it snap through her like a strike of lightning, something that burned her heart into a cinder.

"No," she said, and scrambled backwards from him. "Not Jimmy. Not for me."

"Little girl—"

"No, not for me. You're not my father!"

Sam reached out to her again, a trembling old man.

He reached out with the gun. Maybe he didn't know he was doing it. Maybe he did. Maybe Jimmy had stood puzzled and embarrassed and unmoving, just like Meg, until the bullet slammed into his brain.

Nobody took Sam Larkin seriously.

"Sam!" I screamed, and forced my knee to hold me as I came upright, focused on him. I could have shot him. Should have.

Instead I tackled him sideways into the snow, wrestled the gun away from his hand—he had a lot of strength left in his wiry body, for his age—and rolled him face down to put the restraints on. I looked up at Meg as I dragged him up to a kneeling position. She was still on her knees, frozen in place as if the tears on her face had turned her to ice.

"You didn't have to kill for me. You're not my father," she whispered. "You're not."

But I think she knew, even then, that he was.

Chapter Sixteen

There was money in the satchels Cal Worthen had been carrying away—his getaway stash, I supposed. He had no further use for it. Neither did Sam Larkin. Gentry and a small army of Texas Rangers faced down Lester Gibbs and found another two or three million lying around the place, most of it buried in big glass jars under the ground. The miser's version of a retirement account, I supposed, safe from agents with metal detectors.

Sam Larkin wasn't competent to stand trial. He was guilty of Hillyard's murder, and Jimmy Sparkman's, but he hadn't been capable of anything more complicated than firing a gun and running away.

Somebody had used him. Somebody with authority.

I limped into the squad room three days after it was all over to pick up my paycheck. I didn't expect Gentry to be there, but he was, standing in the doorway of Jimmy's office.

"Dan," he said. I nodded. I'd known we were going to have this talk, sooner or later.

I sat down across from the empty desk. It was stripped of Jimmy now, just another wooden cubicle with a desk and a couple of battered chairs. I had saved his beloved baseball, at least. I'd saved that much of the man I knew.

"What're you going to do?" Gentry asked me. It might have been a question about my future in the Exile Sheriff's Office. It wasn't. He didn't look as tired as he had that night in the snow, but he was still ten miles of hard road.

His black eyes didn't give anything back to me except glimmers from the bottom of a very deep well.

"Not a lot I can do," I said. "I know you were in town long before anybody suspected. Lew Peyser gave you a ticket outside of town five days ago. I saw your truck twice around town before Joe Hillyard's body was found."

He cocked his head. No surprise in his face, or eyes. "Sam Larkin killed Joe Hillyard."

"But you'd already talked to Sam," I said. "You knew everything. You also knew there was no way to prove any of it, not on Sam's say-so. He was crazy as a shithouse rat."

No answer this time.

"You went to talk to Hillyard and found him dead. It was an ideal chance for you to put it all in motion. All the justice you thought they deserved."

No answer. Outside the bullpen was very quiet. Lew Peyser was out there, and Joetta—Farlene had moved out of town, quickly, but no amount of moving was going to save her from the IRS. Lester was back in the cells. Sam Larkin was in a hospital, strapped to a bed and raving.

"You put it on Meg because you knew it wouldn't hold up, but it would get her off the streets and out of danger while you put Jimmy onto Cal Worthen. You and Jimmy already knew, didn't you? That's why Jimmy wanted Meg out of town so bad. To keep her from ending up like her mother."

"If everything's the way you seem to think it was, jail was the safest place for her," he said.

"You knew a good coroner would find out her bullet was fired post-mortem. No second trial for Meg. And it gave you all the time in the world to get Cal Worthen scared enough to run. But you never counted on Larkin, did you? He didn't see it as protection. He remembered what happened to Meg the last time."

Gentry's eyes flickered.

"Darrin Peyser didn't kill himself, did he? Did Larkin kill him, too, or did he have help? Either way, you knew. Your own brand of frontier justice."

"I'd like to listen to some proof in all this speculation," he said mildly.

"You played God, Gentry. You played God and Jimmy's dead, and that's on your hands. You never planned on Larkin killing him, but even then you had the presence of mind to plant Peyser's gun. One more bad guy down."

Silence again. I'd surprised all the comments out of him I could. Cal Worthen was dead, and Hillyard. Gibbs and Larkin were behind bars. There was one last criminal conspirator in Exile, and even though he'd been pulling the strings of everyone in the puppet show, he wasn't going to be touched. He was going to retire quietly, with a gold watch and a pension, to live out his life fishing on a lake somewhere.

"Goddamn you," I said quietly. I got up from the chair and turned to go.

"Dan," he said. He had one last parting shot, though. As always, with Gentry, it was straight to the heart. "Lew Peyser's been confirmed as Sheriff Pro Tem. I expect you'll be looking for another job soon. If you need help, let me know."

I turned back, unpinned my badge and laid it on his desk.

"Give Lew my regards," I said. "You two deserve each other."

"You need to hand over your gun," he reminded me. I leaned across the desk and faced him, eye to eye, for a very long moment.

"It's my gun," I said at last. "You want it, you come on

and get it some night, Ranger Gentry. Make sure you leave your badge at home when you do."

I shut the door behind me with a feeling of loss and relief and rage. Joetta looked at me mutely, her eyes wide. Lew Peyser opened his mouth, but the look on my face must have warned him.

I limped down the narrow winding steps to the main floor, then out the courthouse doors into a cold, clear, razor-sharp day. Blue sky overhead, falling up into infinity. Texas blue, cobalt and silver. Not a cloud to be seen from flat horizon to flat horizon. There was still some snow patched on the ground in the shadows, but the dark winter night was gone like the nightmare it had been.

Meg was illegally parked at the bottom of the steps. She was sitting on the hood of her Lexus, wearing a skirt too short to be legal and hose too sheer to be decent. She was staring off into the distance, her eyes hidden by blue Oakley shades, and the wind feathered her black hair back from her face like silk.

I stopped for a while to catch my breath before I started hobbling down.

"Well, if it isn't Deputy Chester," she said, and smiled. It was a cool, neutral greeting, but the pose on the hood was entirely for my benefit. She slid down lazily, stretched, and yawned. All armor, this morning. All self-possession and attitude like Kevlar. "Took you long enough."

Her eyes flicked down to the blank space on my khaki shirt where my badge had been.

"So," she said. "You quit."

"Sort of."

She leaned elbows on the gleaming silver finish. The Oakleys reflected my face in turquoise. "And?"

"And what?"

"It isn't like Exile has lots of job opportunities for gimpy former deputies."

To be honest, I hadn't thought that far ahead. Jimmy's funeral had hit me hard, but what had been harder had been the visit out to Sam Larkin's monument factory. He'd put the date of death on Jimmy's headstone, I'd found. All ready to go.

There had been a date of death on mine, too. It had only been a matter of time. He'd been intending to punish all of us for Meg's pain.

"You're not staying here," Meg said. I managed a smile.

"Nothing to stay for," I said. "Just not sure how far I can stand to get in the Vega. It still stinks like Buford's piss."

She wasn't smiling now. After a long moment, she dug in her pocket and took out something that she jingled in her closed fist, then tossed across the car to me. Silver gleamed in sunlight.

It was a set of car keys.

"The Explorer's yours," she said. "I'm not an off-road girl."

"Meg—"

"Don't," she interrupted. "Just listen. I'm going back to Dallas now. What you do is up to you. If you get in the truck, you can follow me. I have an office and cases piling up, I could use the help. First month's salary in advance so you can get a place. No promises, no charity, no guilt."

I didn't say anything. The keys felt very heavy in my hand. I couldn't see Meg's eyes, but I felt her waver just for a second. The armor went back in place, along with a smile that could slice bone.

"Or you can just give it a wash and take it back to Cal Worthen's lot," she said. "Your choice."

She got in the Lexus and started the engine. I listened to

the rough purr for a few seconds, closed my eyes, and heard the gears engage as she prepared for the road.

She drove out of the lot while I was still standing on the last courthouse step, weighing the keys in one hand and my future in the other. As far as I could tell, she didn't look back.

I limped across to the Ford Explorer, popped the door, and swung up into the driver's seat. She'd left me a present—a sealed envelope. I ripped it open.

The papers to the car, paper-clipped to the card of the saleswoman from the car lot. In case I had to take it back.

A map of Dallas, with directions written along the side in bright red marker.

A single slip of paper, in Meg's sprawling handwriting, that read, *Your choice.*

In five minutes, Exile was in my rear view mirror. I set about catching a silver Lexus that flickered like a mirage in the distance.

My choice.

About the Author

Roxanne Longstreet Conrad is the author of seven previous novels: *Stormriders*, *The Undead*, *Red Angel*, *Cold Kiss*, *Slow Burn* (as Roxanne Longstreet), *Copper Moon* and *Bridge of Shadows* (as Roxanne Conrad). She is currently working on three new novels to be published in 2003 and 2004.

Her somewhat eclectic career choices include web designer, communications specialist, professional musician, insurance investigator, and CPA, to name a few. She and her husband, artist R. Cat Conrad, live in Arlington, Texas with two giant economy-sized iguanas and a *mali uromastyx* named—of course—O'Malley. Visit her Web site at www.artistsinresidence.com/rlc.